The Waltons

To my family
Nothing is more important than family

The Waltons

Robert Ettinger

With Janet and Graham Walton

Weidenfeld and Nicolson
London

Copyright © Robert Ettinger, 1989

Published in Great Britain by
George Weidenfeld & Nicolson Limited
91 Clapham High Street
London SW4 7TA

ISBN 0 297 79681 X

Printed in Great Britain by
Butler & Tanner Ltd
Frome and London

Contents

Acknowledgements   vii
Preface   ix

 1 Odd One Out   4
 2 Wedding Bells   9
 3 The Treatment Begins   15
 4 Malta and the Fertility Stone   24
 5 More Than One   28
 6 Thirty-Two Long Weeks   39
 7 Miracles Can Happen   46
 8 The Homecoming   56
 9 A Full House   66
10 The Christening   77
11 'Jim'll Fix It'   86
12 An Ill Wind   98
13 Return to Wallasey   110
14 Growing Pains   121
15 The Eye of the Public   129
16 Fame in the Far East   144
17 Schooldays and Holidays   164
18 Reflections   176

Acknowledgements

Whilst work in earnest on this book began in the early summer of 1988, I suppose, subconsciously, I began research five years ago when I first met the Waltons. I am grateful to Janet and Graham for all the extra effort they have made to organise their already hectic schedules to allow time for me to build as much background material for this book as possible and for taking such great care in reading through the manuscript.

I am equally grateful to the various members of their family and friends who readily volunteered for babysitting duty at the times we have been working on the book and who have contributed by way of conversation and observation.

Over the years since the birth, my brother Philip and I have, along with Janet and Graham, sifted through and dealt with all sorts of commercial approaches and opportunities which, as a natural occurrence, have arisen from such an unprecedented event that captured the imagination of the world. From my own point of view it has brought about a close and valued friendship which I hope is reflected in the very personal way Janet and Graham have helped me to tell their story.

If life is the greatest gift we have then surely the creation of life must be positioned alongside. Advances have been made in the field of infertility which have given so much joy and happiness to so many who believed that they would never be able to have children of their own. Sam Abdulla, the consultant gynaecologist who dealt with Janet's case and headed the delivery team, is one of many dedicated professionals in this area of medicine, and, knowing of the long and devoted hours he gives to his work, I am especially indebted to him for the time he has given to looking over the manuscript and checking the medical facts.

Nothing is more important than family. I am and always will be deeply grateful to my parents, Leila and Malcolm, my brothers Philip, Graham and David and my sister Joanne for all their support and encouragement while I was concentrating on the book.

I would especially like to thank David Roberts, my Publisher at Weidenfeld and Nicolson, who immediately lost his heart to Hannah, Lucy, Ruth, Sarah, Kate and Jenny when I first took him to meet the family in Wallasey, and my editor Jane Blackett whose experienced hand passed over the manuscript so professionally.

There are no doubt a number of good people who have in one way or another at some time touched the lives of Janet and Graham before and after the remarkable birth of their children. In the words that follow they may not have been mentioned but the part they have played, no matter how small, in making life a little easier and helping to cope with such exceptional circumstances is, I know, gratefully acknowledged by Janet and Graham.

ROBERT ETTINGER

Liverpool, 1989

Illustration Acknowledgements

The photographs are reproduced by kind permission of the following:

Camera Press/Richard Open 5, 6, 8, 9–14, 15 above, 16; *Robert Ettinger* 7; *Patrick Lichfield* 1 below, 2; *Alistair Morrison* 3, 4 above; *Chris Sowe* 4 below; *Syndication International* 1 above, 15 below.

Preface

We believe we are blessed to be the proud parents of six very happy, very healthy girls who are full of fun and mischief.

Our way of coping since Hannah, Lucy, Ruth, Sarah, Kate and Jenny were born has been to take one day at a time – indeed sometimes one hour at a time.

One thing is for certain and that is without the great support and help of our parents John and Betty and Peter and Nancy and all our family and friends things would have been a lot tougher, and we would like to take another opportunity of thanking them now.

We would also like to thank the many hundreds of people who have taken so much time and trouble in writing to us over the years.

The girls have known our close friend Robert, or Bobby as they call him, since their earliest days and there is no one, we feel, who could have told our story in such an intimate way.

We hope you enjoy reading it.

JANET and GRAHAM WALTON
Wallasey 1989

'Mummy!'

Janet had her back to the breakfast table. She had heard her daughter's voice immediately but her mind was, as usual, concentrating on getting things organised and as quickly as possible.

'Just a minute, Lucy!' At only four years old, a minute does not mean very much. All Lucy knew was that she was not going to get her mum's full attention straight away. The little girl was aware that eventually her calls would capture the curiosity that she was seeking but she didn't see the harm in trying again.

'Mu ... u ... m ... my!' She practically sang it this time.

Janet took the coffee, tea, milk and orange juice off the tray she had just carried into the breakfast room and lined up an assortment of mugs on the worktop. She turned and glanced at each of the plates on the table. Most of them were reasonably clear of the lunch she had served. The light-brown wooden surface of the large table, however, was speckled with colour having been well and truly pebbledashed with peas, potato crisps, and patches of mayonnaise and tomato sauce.

A different child's voice rang out. 'Look what Ruthie's done!' Jenny was not making trouble, merely an observation. In an effort to show her independence, Ruth had attempted to pour a drop of ketchup on to her plate, misjudging the speed with which it flowed from the bottle. A large red pool had appeared on the table. Janet at once plopped a damp cloth on top of it, and the mess, along with all the other splotches, was swept away before it came into contact with any sleeves or elbows.

'But Mummy!' Lucy had not given up but there was a little wisp of frustration straining through her vocal chords.

1

'Right!' Janet said, looking straight across at Lucy and successfully diverting her attention. 'First of all, what do you want to drink, tea, milk or orange juice?'

'Ehh . . . orange juice!' It was not the subject Lucy wanted to discuss but her eyes were sparkling at being the focus of attention; she knew all her sisters were watching closely and that her choice of drink might well influence one or two of the others. Just as Janet's arm moved towards the jug of juice, Lucy changed her mind. There was mischief written all over her face, endorsed by a rascally smile. 'No, tea please'

'Are you sure, Locket?' Janet began to pour from the pot. 'It's too late if you change your mind now anyway.' Her voice took on a slightly sharper tone that was not going to stand any further messing about, and she passed the cup to Lucy.

Blending harmoniously with the others, Hannah's voice happily rang out. 'Please to pass the one-hole?' She was referring to the saltcellar. Ruth picked it up at an angle and pointed it precariously in her sister's direction. Silently bisecting the table, a neat and narrow white line began to form, coming to an abrupt end as Janet's hand turned it the right way up and completed the manoeuvre on Ruth's behalf. As she cheerfully shook the salt over the remnants of her sausages, Hannah asked for some tea.

'Right, who else wants tea?' asked Janet. Kate and Sarah, sitting side by side, shot their hands in the air like a couple of synchronised swimmers, and chorused, 'Me please!' Janet obliged her daughters. 'Jenny, what do you want? Jenny curled some strands of her straight brown hair around her fingers and her eyes scanned the table examining the contents of her sisters' cups as she hesitated in her reply. She giggled. 'Come on, quickly Jen. Tea, juice or milk'

Jenny thought about it a little longer. 'Juice!'

'Are you forgetting something Madam?' Janet put on her very best mock school-ma'am accent.

Jenny looked up and saw the smile on her mother's face. 'Please?' she called out, receiving a satisfied glance from her mum.

'That's better. Right,' Janet looked at Ruth out of the corner of her eye, 'is that everybody? Everyone had drinks now?' There were squeals of delight as the sisters swooped and seized the opportunity to catch their mum out.

'You did forgot me, Mummy!' said Ruth indignantly.

'Oh Ruth, I'm sorry; I didn't see you there. I thought you'd gone to

2

bed!' Janet's voice was full of fun and the girls loved it.

Every mealtime was a major event around this remarkably unique family table. Now that the girls were discovering new words every day, the breakfast room was filled with a mixture of excited chatter, giggles and short-lived heartbroken howls as the momentary moans of one were quashed by the kindness of another. At times it was like a nursery boardroom with Janet and husband Graham, the joint managing directors, endlessly trying to keep a semblance of order during the proceedings.

The walls of the room were just as colourful as the table, with an array of art begging for interpretation proudly positioned and pinned to the cupboards. A range of matchstick men and women were surrounded by everything from pink apples and purple aeroplanes to yellow horses and green houses that sprouted wispy spirals of scarlet smoke, and each piece of paper had either and 'H', 'S', 'L', 'R', 'K', or 'J' scrawled for a signature in the corner.

Lucy, like all her sisters, had learnt to accept patience as part of her life. The girls were beginning to understand that their parents each had only one pair of ears and that if they wanted to be heard they had to wait until either their mum or dad was ready to listen. However, there were times when it seemed that the only way to gain attention was for one of the six pairs of lively lungs to bellow and battle above the rest. Lucy, with her mind now firmly on the query she needed to discuss with her mum, decided it was time to blow the roof off; she was bursting to speak, and besides, she knew she had the loudest voice of them all.

'Mu ... u ... u ... mmy!'

Kate and Hannah, who were sitting on either side of this siren, quickly plugged their ears with fingers and palms. It was not the first time they had had to take this course of action for protection.

'O.K. Lucy,' Janet said. 'Everyone's got their drink now and everyone's listening. What is it you wanted to say, luv?'

'But Mummy? . . .' Ten twinkling bright eyes put Lucy in the spotlight once again, and this time brought about a bashfulness that made her hesitate for a moment. A simple but simmering question, innocently stirred by the smiles of strangers, could rest no longer in her mind.

'Are we the Waltons?'

One

Odd One Out

♡ ♡ ♡
♡ ♡
♡

Janet Leadbetter was aware from the age of twelve or thirteen that something was wrong. But even when she suspected that everyone else in her year at Wirral Grammar School for girls had started having periods she still hoped that something would happen very soon. The days, though, passed and the weeks came and went quickly, and an uncomfortable feeling of being different began to eat away at her. It soon became a matter of when would she say something to her mum rather than when would she have her first period. Night after night when she was alone in her room she would stare at the reflection of her face in the mirror expecting to detect an obvious sign that she was different from all her friends. Why should this happen to her? Why should she be the odd one out? It was not the fact that she had not begun to have periods that made her feel bad, it was the fact that she was so certain that she was the only one with the problem.

For some teenagers the waiting for nature to take its course can turn excited anticipation of womanhood into a private nightmare, and the mental stress and fear of never being able to have children can be too much to bear. At first, however, Janet tried not to let the absence worry her too much. A march to the doctor with her mum gave a reassurance that there was nothing to be concerned about. It was not unusual for girls to start their periods later than others, everyone developed at different times, and he was sure that it was only a matter of time. Janet was, after all, in excellent medical condition otherwise.

As month after month passed by without event, however, Janet stayed in the silent group of late starters but eventually after one year moved on to the next and Janet left behind her fourteenth, fifteenth and sixteenth birthdays, her faith fragmented into splinters of suspicion that she was in the very lonely position of being the only girl at school who was still to start her periods. She was the odd one out.

During a second consultation with the doctor, it was decided that another opinion would do no harm. Janet overheard the doctor telling her mum that although she was too young yet for him to be certain it was possible that she was suffering from amenorrhoea. It was not a disease or an illness as such, he explained, more a name that labelled the condition of an absence of periods. 'Mum,' Janet whispered not wanting to make a fool of herself in the surgery, 'ask him to write it down.' 'What down?' Nancy was puzzled but not surprised at her daughter's curiosity. 'That 'eah thing the doctor says I've got!' If there was something the matter with her then she at least wanted to know what it was called.

The doctor made arrangements for Janet to have an appointment for further tests at the Southern Hospital in Liverpool. The idea of going to Liverpool was on the one hand exciting but on the other slightly forbidding because of the reason that lay behind her journey. The big city was a far cry from the quiet and peaceful country life of Neston where she lived but the lure of the shops and department stores, which Nancy promised they could visit after they had been to the hospital, made the prospect much more attractive.

The resplendent Victorian architecture of the Southern Hospital had, though, long since lost its glory, and the shadows of the decaying docklands nearby did little to enhance the building. The tainted red brickwork had lost its shine, and appeared cold and unwelcoming to the staunchest of out-patients and visitors, let alone a nervous young country girl who had been up most of the previous night wondering what the doctor had meant by 'tests'.

It seemed to Janet that there was a doctor at the hospital for every test and there was an endless stream of stethoscopes as she underwent examination after examination. One after another each doctor mimicked the mannerism of the one before and they collectively commented on how healthy she looked. That was all very well, she knew she looked fine, but it was not necessarily what she wanted to hear. The doctors assured her that no doubt by the time she came to see them all again the following year, her periods would be well under way.

But they were not, and the panel of doctors became a part of Janet's life as each year she and Nancy made a pilgrimage to Liverpool, sometimes to the Southern Hospital and sometimes to Walton Hospital further north. Throughout all the questions, examinations and long words the doctors were using, the one thing that did become clear to Janet was that it was unlikely, if the condition remained, that she would be able to have children of her own.

Janet never confided in any of her friends at school. Whilst everything else in life for her was as normal as for the next girl, the isolation of this confined and closed corridor was not an easy thing to bear. Abandoned and deserted by nature in that one critical area of her young life, it was something she had to deal with on her own.

A few weeks after her seventeenth birthday, Janet went on holiday with a friend, Eileen Jellicoe, to the Isle of Man. The sea-side boarding-house where they were to stay had been highly recommended, and as they stepped from the Liverpool steamer with a suitcase each in hand and made their way along the streets of Douglas, they happily chattered about the good times ahead.

They immediately warmed to the landlady who was waiting for them at the makeshift reception desk in the hallway. Mrs Jackson welcomed them with smiling painted lips, rouge-rubbed cheeks and bright sparkling eyes. A short-term surrogate mother to many a young holiday maker, Mrs Jackson was proprietress, waitress, head chef, chamber maid and tour guide all wrapped up in one.

One hot afternoon while walking along the promenade sporting their new summer outfits the girls noticed a couple of lads sitting on the railings with their backs to the sea. They had given each other a gentle dig in the ribs as soon as they had seen the girls approaching and, as the young ladies came closer, they flexed their muscles, breathed in and expanded their bare chests like a pair of prize pigeons.

Graham Walton and his closest mate Kenny Philips were on their annual camping holiday to the island and, like any other couple of holidaying lads of twenty years old, they knew that the stories they would be required to tell in the pubs back home would not be complete unless they had found themselves some female company.

It was the familiar tones of the scouse accent that gave good enough reason for the four to find conversation, and it was not long before Graham was entertaining Janet with stories of his many visits to Neston where his elder and married sister Nina lived, just around the corner from Janet.

The couples double-dated during the holiday but as each day drew them closer to the boat trip home there was no sign from Graham for any future plans. Despite reassurances from her friend as they whispered to each other in their bedroom at night Janet began to believe that it was just a brief holiday romance and she would not be seeing Graham again.

The lads could have continued camping on the island longer than they did but with Janet and Eileen going home there seemed little point, so they rolled up their sleeping bags, packed away their tents and used their tickets to travel on the same boat home as the girls. Janet couldn't understand it. Why hadn't Graham asked her for a further date? They had got on so well and after all, she thought, even though it was quite a long way from Wallasey to Neston, if he was already in the area on his visits to his sister surely he could come and call. With their cases and bags arranged between their feet, and the spray from the Irish Sea on their faces, the young couple sat awkwardly on the wet wooden benches holding hands until the boat docked in front of the two famous Liver Bird statues that held court high above the Liverpool waterfront.

Graham carried Janet's case off the boat, and at the very last possible opportunity, just as Janet was kissing goodbye to any hope of a date, Graham asked if he could see her again. The holiday was complete. Janet went home with a smile that lasted for days and Graham went back to Wallasey wondering where he was going to find the money to pay for their first date.

Graham found the answer by selling off his favourite asset. It was a long time before he told Janet of how he packed away the pieces and parted with his train set, but the sacrifice was the most worthwhile he ever made. A year later he was back in the Isle of Man with Kenny, this time, though, enjoying the luxury of a solid roof over his head and appreciating the home cooking of Mrs Jackson.

Time moved on, and as they became closer their conversations became more intimate and, eventually, when Janet's instincts told her that the time was right, she summoned up the courage and unfolded her story of that secret part of her life. She was frightened, scared of losing him, and as she spoke softly into the early hours of the morning, her voice quivered with apprehension at the bleak prospect of being alone again. Graham was the first person whom Janet had talked to about it other than her mum. It would have been difficult to live with but she would have understood had Graham walked away from the relationship. Graham, though, needed no time at all to think about it; it was Janet he wanted, and he told her that it did not make any difference whatsoever to him if they were never able to have children. As long as they had each other, that was all that mattered.

The hospital appointments, however, continued. On the next visit Janet and Nancy were told that the time had come for Janet to go through a series of more extensive tests, and that the only way of monitoring the procedure properly was for Janet to stay at Walton Hospital for a full week. The doctors had suspected that, as in the majority of cases, Janet's problem could well be hormone related but they had to be sure and it was important to discover whether or not there was any other underlying cause that may need treatment.

Janet was a long way from home, it was the first time she had been subjected to such embarrassing examinations and she naturally felt miserable all week. When Graham came to visit her with Nancy, he too felt the misery as she cried when the bell went and the ward sisters asked all the visitors to leave. The week passed slowly and the results seemed even slower in coming, but when they did finally arrive they only served to confirm what she already believed, that having a baby was out of the question. At that stage the details and explanations did not seem relevant.

From then on whenever the conversation got around to children, Janet and Graham would discuss the prospects of adopting after they were married, and whether or not they would be acceptable for it. Adopting a baby was something Janet had thought about since her early teens when she first realised there was a problem. She had become accustomed to the idea and had grown up believing that adoption was perfectly acceptable; the one thing she had always worried about was whether or not she would find someone who would understand. Now she had Graham to share her faith and all the feelings of emptiness that had shadowed her life at long last disappeared.

· Two ·

Wedding Bells

Not long before their wedding, Janet found herself alone one November morning in the house. She had been given the day off from her work at the bank, and with her sister Alison at school and both parents at work, Janet had spent an extra peaceful hour in bed wallowing in wonderful thoughts of marriage. As she lay there she checked off the important things that had been attended to: all the invitations had been sent out; all the arrangements for the reception had been made; the wedding cake had been ordered. Her thoughts hiccupped for a moment as she considered the cake. Had they definitely confirmed the order? She went over the day she and Nancy had spent the afternoon choosing the design of the cake, and then she relaxed when she remembered her mum handing over the money.

Janet had never been an early riser and she would probably have remained in bed a lot longer that morning had she not happened to glance towards the wardrobe which housed the most important thing of all – the wedding dress. The bells pealed a little louder in her mind as she whipped away the bedclothes and scrambled out of bed having decided secretly to try the dress on while everyone was out.

Janet quickly washed and breakfasted and ran back up the stairs to her room. She hesitated as her hand grasped the wardrobe handle. She had not tried on the dress since August when, under a cloud of sadness, she and Graham had reluctantly agreed to postpone the wedding because they simply did not have enough money to pay for it. They had done their best to save as much as possible but Graham was then made redundant, and so for three months the dress had hung patiently on the rail. Janet cast aside the other hangers, carefully took out the dress and slowly removed the outer coverings. It had lost none of its beauty. She glanced in the mirror as she cradled the dress against her body. There wasn't enough money for the real thing but it was white, silk-like and simple, flowing without frills, and it was the style she had always wanted for her wedding.

Janet knew that it would probably fit alright but it was important to double check that no alterations were necessary. She put it on and looked at herself again. It looked magnificent as it flourished to the floor. She paraded from one end of the room to the other practising the ceremonious slow steps of the Wedding March. Satisfied everything was fine, her right hand reached around her back and her fingers scaled the smoothness of the material as she reached for the zip. It was an awkward operation and as she gently tugged at the small piece of metal it slipped from between her fingers. She tried again and the same thing happened. Taking extra care not to cause any rips she wriggled her elbows and redoubled her efforts. Nothing was happening. Which ever way she tried the zip stubbornly stood its ground and stuck at the top.

Like a straitjacket, her wedding dress had trapped her and no matter how Houdini-like she contorted her arms she could find no means of escape. She was in the house on her own and simply could not get the dress off. Janet waited and waited in the upstairs bedroom anxiously looking through the window to see if anyone she knew walked past. Living in a quiet cul-de-sac, however, the chances of a rescuer seemed remote but waiting was a slightly less embarrassing proposition than marching down the road in all her white glory. After an hour had passed and nobody was in sight, she could stand the encumbrance no longer. Her dad, mum and Alison would not be back until at least late afternoon so she decided to take action. Hitching the folds of material up and securing it around her with one of her father's best brown leather belts, Janet put on her old mack and scurried to her friend's mum who lived next-door-but-one where thankfully she found relief and release.

On the day of the wedding, the small town was hustling and bustling with shoppers and there were lots of onlookers. The church was situated directly opposite the Neston branch of the bank where Janet worked, which meant that Janet's colleagues who had to miss the service were at least able to catch a glimpse of her. They formed a rota and half came over to the church to watch her going in while the other half came to see her coming out.

Apart from Janet and Nancy, everyone else was a bag of nerves at the house as the limousine pulled up ready to take Janet and her dad to the church. The bridesmaids fluttered about fidgeting with pins trying to secure her veil and flowers but the bride remained calm and quiescent throughout, not allowing anything to ruffle her composure. She was determined to enjoy every second of the occasion. Nancy and all the bridesmaids went off to the church and the only thing left for Janet to do was to fasten the cuffs of her dress. As she struggled with the buttons she thought of how ridiculous she had felt when she had tried the outfit on a few weeks earlier. This time there was help at hand. She looked up at Peter, 'Dad can you just fasten this for me before we go?' she asked as she stretched out her right arm. His fingers were quivering like feathers in the wind. He never normally showed any signs of being nervous but his hands were shaking so much that no matter how he tried there was no way he could fasten the buttons. So, to save any embarrassment at the church, the simple task was quickly taken care of by the limousine chauffeur as they stood in the doorway of the house.

Meanwhile in Wallasey, Graham's family had gathered at his mum's house where a bottle of champagne was opened. It was not exactly the ideal remedy to help redress the balance in the bloodstream from the night before, but it seemed a fitting way to start the day. With the ring safely tucked away in his waistcoat pocket, Dave Walton performed his first job of the day as best man by getting his brother to the church on time.

The wedding service had gone perfectly, and Janet and Graham stepped from the church into a shower of confetti. They climbed into the limousine and waved goodbye, and as the car pulled away they shut the window and settled back into the sumptuous upholstery to enjoy the drive to the reception. Janet brushed off the last of the confetti from Graham's suit. 'Thanks,' he said, rewarding her with a kiss. 'For that you can have an extra special present.' His hand disappeared into his pocket, brought out a piece of chewing gum and, as it if were a ritual to seal the marriage, he carefully split the gum in two and offered the better half, of course, to his wife.

The reception was limited mainly to members of the family and it was to be followed by a party for a much larger number of guests in the evening. Although they had arranged for a change of clothes for when the reception was over, Janet decided to keep her wedding dress on throughout the rest of the day and into the evening so that her friends who could not make it to the service and who obviously wanted to see her in the special outfit would not be disappointed.

In between the reception and the party in the evening, most of the guests went home to change. Only a couple of Janet and Graham's friends stayed behind and together they all sat in the bar of the hotel. Bemused regulars looked on as the bride in the corner happily giggled her way through a game of Put and Take. It was a game Janet and Graham often played in their local pub. The rules were simple; an octagonal spinner was used with each of the eight sides clearly marked 'put', 'take one', 'take two' or 'take all'. Everyone had to place ten pence on the table, each took a turn to spin and consequently followed the instruction. Spirits were far higher than stakes in this particular game of chance but, even so, fortune firmly fell on the fluttering lady in white as time after time Janet won the kitty.

Had the betting been a little more serious, the arrangements for the evening may have been a little different. Unlike many, Janet and Graham were not planning on leaving half way through the party to find romance in the form of a honeymoon. They simply could not afford it after paying towards the wedding and their new home, and they were quite content to do without. They both enjoyed the day so much they wouldn't have changed a minute. Besides, the party was for them and it would have been a shame to leave half way through the proceedings.

While Janet had decided to keep her wedding dress on, Graham had used a hotel room to change out of his groom's suit. It was still in good shape and since it was brand new and going to be his best suit for a while to come, there was no point in taking any undue risk at the party, and he gave it to his brother to take care of.

A mini-bus had been ordered to take Janet and Graham back to their new home in Browning Road and to drop other guests off on the way. The house was a small three-bedroom semi that was perfect to start off married life, and while not big enough for a large family it was ideal for their first child if they were ever accepted for adoption. However, thoughts of children were far from their minds as the car pulled up outside the house.

It was pouring with rain as Graham hurriedly paid off the driver who wished them all the best and skidded off along the road. Graham's hand automatically slipped quickly into the right-hand side pocket of his jacket. He felt only the smoothness of a couple of cards, and his fingers dived in and out between them. He was sure that was the pocket in which he had put the house key. He tried the pocket on his left side, but still there was no sign of any key. He felt like Charlie Chaplin as he stood with the knuckles of both hands bulging from either side of his trousers, which now looked more like a pair of untidy jodhpurs. The performance ended with his right palm slapped against his damp but empty breast pocket.

'I don't believe this!' The horror on his face spelled out the fear of letting his bride down on their wedding night. They suddenly realised that the front-door key was in the pocket of Graham's wedding suit snugly packed away in the boot of the best man's car. So they were stuck soaking outside their house in the driving rain with no coats and, more importantly, no key. At a loss about what to do, Graham looked up to the heavens for help from a higher source. As his eyelids blinked away the drops of water from the rain he noticed the small window in the main bedroom was open. He immediately went down the alley at the side of the house and climbed over the back to fetch a ladder.

By the time he returned he was feeling the effects of the drink which had merrily flowed ever since that first bottle of champagne. He was putting up a good fight but the ladder was winning the battle as he grappled with it against the house. Then, with perfect timing, a vehicle pulled alongside them, and the familiar head of Jimmy McKinnon, a friend who lived around the corner, leaned out of the window.

Seeing Graham struggling with the ladder, he got out of the car and offered his help. Weighing up the situation, Janet sensibly regarded it as silly for all three of them to get wet so she slipped into the back of the car while Jimmy and Graham figured out the best way of breaking in to the newlyweds' house. Jimmy steadied the steps with his foot firmly placed on the bottom rung, and as Graham wobbled his way up to the window the neighbour's curtains began to twitch. Convinced there was a break-in going on she was about to ring the police but as the figure moved closer and closer to the level of her bedroom she recognised who it was and what was happening.

First his head, then his backside and finally after flapping about for a few moments, his feet fell through the small opening and finished on the floor of the bedroom. The groom, unbruised and in one piece, charged down stairs looking for his bride. He opened the front door and found himself face to face with his friend. Janet, for better or for worse, was still sitting in the back of the car keeping dry.

Graham looked at Jimmy. 'Eh ... would you like a cup of coffee?' he asked hesitantly. Having been a guest at the wedding Jimmy told him not to be so daft and left the couple together standing on their door step in the rain.

It was three o'clock in the morning, they were soaking wet but Janet would not budge until finally the groom carried his bride in the true and proper fashion over the threshold.

· Three ·

The Treatment Begins

♡ ♡ ♡
♡ ♡
♡

Proudly positioned at the centre of the teak shelf that was fixed above the fireplace in the lounge at Browning road, sat the cherished Gherkin Plate. Named after the small cucumbers it had once served, the plate had been Janet and Graham's reward for their victory late on a wind-swept Monday afternoon in May in the grand final of a mixed-doubles pitch-and-put challenge.

Every Monday Janet and Graham would rush to finish work and make their way down to the edge of Liverpool Bay where they, along with their friends, played the pint-sized game of golf on a pint-sized course. Weather never posed a problem to the group; rain or hail they could still be seen swinging away. Not even locked gates and closed signs on the ticket shed formed a barrier for them as they used to scurry over the fence on days when the course was closed. The challenges were taken seriously and after a while competitions were organised with home-made trophies serving as awards for the winners, and the prize givings were celebrated at the local pub.

The real importance represented by the Gherkin Plate lay in the memories it gave of the good times they had shared and the close friendships that had formed. But no matter how intimate and personal the conversations became as they chatted late into the night at one home or another after the pubs had closed, none of Janet and Graham's friends ever knew about the problems they faced about having children. Whenever the conversation had come around to children, Janet and Graham became quite adept at neatly side-stepping the issue with knowing nods and smiles but without revealing that they could not have children of their own. At work, Janet found it even more difficult to avoid the topic, with the girls constantly comparing notes while she constantly ducked the conversations. Even though she was normally a very open person, for reasons she could not explain, it was the one subject she would not discuss with or confide in anybody.

The one problem Janet and Graham did not need to face after they got married was when to start a family in the normal way. As far as they were concerned they simply could not have one of their own. As difficult as it might have been, it was accepted. They had a good crowd of friends and a busy social life that kept them well occupied, and, although they had little money, they had lots of fun.

Like so many couples when they first get married, Janet and Graham could not afford to think in terms of an extra mouth to feed, and although adoption was, as far as they were concerned, the only way forward for a family, they still wanted to wait for a while. This, though, had to be balanced with the consideration that the adoption process can take a long period of time and that it could be a number of years before they were accepted as suitable parents for an adopted child. So even though they did not want an early addition to the household, it was not too long after they got married that they contacted the Department of Social Services that dealt with adoption and put their names down on the list.

Then something happened that brought a shock to both their systems. Every year since they had met, Janet had continued to go along to the hospital for a check-up. Every year it was the same – no results and no progress. Now that they were married Janet could face the panel of doctors at least with the support of her husband.

'How are you, how have you been?' one doctor asked as Janet and Graham listened to the same old questions. 'Has anything changed?' he continued. It was as if there was a possibility that magically everything all of a sudden might go right. Graham moved about uncomfortably on the hospital chair, thinking the questions ridiculous. Of course Janet's fit and well, he thought; she's always healthy, and anyway they should be telling her how she is, not the other way round. The questions, though, were not so silly. Previous tests had established that Janet had something wrong with her pituitary gland that did not affect anything else other than ovulation, but stranger things have happened and it could just have been that periods and cycles may have begun even at that late stage.

The doctor's eyes rose above the rim of his reading spectacles. He looked at Graham, then across at Janet. 'Now that you're married,' he went on in a very matter of fact and casual manner, 'as soon as you want to start a family, come along and we will start you on fertility treatment.'

Graham nearly fell off his chair. This was something they were totally unprepared for; they had never ever considered having their own children as even the remotest possibility and now this doctor had begun talking about it as if it were the most natural thing in the world. After years of going to hospitals for check-ups, examinations and tests, all of a sudden this bolt from the blue had ignited a tiny flame of hope deep inside. Janet had no idea at that stage what all the treatment would entail but that did not matter. Whatever it was she had to go through she would do it without question.

Until now Janet had felt the cold isolation brought about by the feeling of being alone with a problem. It was quickly becoming clear that far from being alone there were thousands of other people suffering similar fertility problems. As with many other women, the signals in the form of hormones that were being sent down from her pituitary gland, positioned just below the centre of the brain, were not causing the right reaction in her ovaries. It was a bit like having a car with a flat battery. Even if it does send these hormonal charges down to the ovaries they are sometimes not powerful enough to cause the release of eggs. In Janet's case, no eggs at all were being released and so one of the problems was clearly the lack of stimulation received to aid the formation of the follicles in the ovary.

Janet was to be treated with a course of injections of a powerful and expensive but effective drug called Perganol. It was a drug that was only used in special cases where there was a definite hormone problem. Either substituting or enhancing the hormone flow Perganol helps the ovaries to create several egg-carrying follicles thereby increasing the chances of pregnancy. When Janet and Graham discovered the method of manufacturing the drug, they were, to say the least, a little bit surprised. It is made from subjecting the pituitary hormone-rich urine of menopausal nuns to purification and chemical process. At that stage in life the ovaries begin to fail causing the pituitary to send even more hormones down thus creating an excess that is rejected and passed out of the body in the most natural way.

Towards the end of 1979, however, before the treatment was to begin, Janet was put on the pill for about three months. Seemingly contradictory in the pursuit of pregnancy, it was, in fact, merely a final check to see if her body would react and create a cycle. At the same time, Graham willingly went through a series of tests to make sure he was clear from any fertility problems himself. It was obviously no good starting any treatment for Janet if there was any question as to Graham's fitness in that area.

With Graham having been given a clean bill of health, and the experiment with the pill proving fruitless, Janet finally started her first course of Perganol injections nearly a year later in November 1980. It was the beginning of the most traumatic years of their lives where the suffering was not only in the physical pain Janet had to endure but also in the mental anguish that afflicted them both causing an enormous strain on their marriage.

For some, who are more fortunate than others, success may come from just one course of the drug. Janet was not so lucky. With six attempts and another year gone by, ward 3B of the gynaecological department at the Royal Liverpool Hospital became as familiar as her own front parlour, and Joan Warburton, the nurse that was dealing with Janet each time she came for her injections and tests, had become more of a friend than anything else. Each course lasted for about ten days and involved a series of injections, blood tests, and urine samples. The disappointment grew with every phone call that Janet made to Joan who told her not to bother coming in for a follow-up injection of another drug called Pregnyl that served to release the egg from the follicle and was only given if the Perganol had proved effective.

The fire of hope that had burnt within them as they had passed through the early treatment had become a feeble scattering of smouldering embers. Two years was a long time. Long enough perhaps. All Graham could think of was the never ending needles tearing away at Janet as she suffered a seemingly incessant series of jabs and heartbreaking failure after failure. But Janet's determination kept the embers alight and hope alive. She would never give in, not until the doctors told her that there was no further path to travel.

There was another route to take. It was a relatively new idea that had been showing some success in other countries but it was still regarded at that time as experimental. In March 1982 Janet and Graham were sent to the university department of the hospital where a special clinic had been set up to deal with hormone deficiency. As they sat listening to the doctor explaining the principles of the method, an oblong black box sat ominously in the middle of the desk.

The hormones released by the pituitary gland for reproduction are dependent on other hormones being released at regular intervals from another part of the brain called the hypothalamus. In Janet's case, it could have been that this was not happening but the idea was that with the box strapped to her side and a tube going from it into a small vein, a mechanical pump hidden away in the box would imitate the action of the hypothalamus thereby fooling the pituitary into sending the required signals to the ovaries. The therapy has since been refined to give greater comfort to the patient but for Janet the box was irritating, cumbersome and awkward.

Between March and July of that year the pump literally never left her side. It made its presence most felt when Janet and Graham lay in bed at night. Their quiet conversations were punctuated with a calm 'click' closely followed by a muffled 'woosh' as the fluid was injected through the tube. As the position of the box was changed to ease soreness, the bruised area on Janet's skin seemed to get bigger and bigger. She kept telling herself that it was all worth it, but with every 'click' and 'woosh' her powers of perseverance were being tested to the full.

With the pump having failed and still no sign of the doctors giving in, Janet went back to the Perganol course in October. She was working 'relief' duty for the bank which meant that most days she was working in a different branch and was able to continue her out-patient visits to the hospital without causing too much attention and having to surrender any secrets. Every other day for a fortnight Joan Warburton made sure Janet had her injection of Perganol in roughly the same area at the top of her leg. In the meantime, on the days she did not have the jabs, she was closely monitored with blood tests, urine tests and scans to see if it was taking effect. They were, in essence, creating a cycle within her body. There was no myth about it; it was purely a case of the very best of modern medicine at work. In the same way that medical technology of today can help to sustain life, here it was working in an effort to create life.

The night after the final scan, not long after they had both got in from work, Janet sat at the bottom of the stairs in the hall at Browning Road and prepared to make the call to Joan Warburton to find out whether or not she could go on to have the final injection. Graham stood behind the bannister watching Janet's fingers slowly and nervously depress the buttons on the phone.

This was always the worst moment. Worse than the interviews, worse than the tests, worse than even the pump. There was no easy way of passing on the news and on each of the previous occasions when Joan had had to tell Janet 'No', and not to bother coming in, she had done so in the gentlest possible way. But however delicately the message was relayed, it felt like a well-sharpened sabre slicing across her last sinew. After she replaced the receiver, Janet would sit sobbing all the tension of the ten days' treatment out of her body and Graham would do his best to console her desolation, each time secretly wishing that the whole thing would come to an end.

As he heard the ringing tone, he quietly stepped out of the hall and into the lounge. He knew he should be close to Janet but at the same time he could bear no longer to watch on helplessly. It was that night that they first started talking about ending the treatment.

There was doubt as to whether or not Janet could have the final injection of Pregnyl and it was perhaps because of that uncertainty that on this occasion they decided to give her two chances with it instead of the usual one. A day had to be allowed for in between each of the injections which meant that, in all, this time the course had lasted nearly three working weeks. By then Janet's right leg was so stiff it felt like it was permanently two paces behind her left. At the same time, with all the psychological pressure it was difficult following the doctor's orders of going to bed and completing the therapy!

Even though, once again, there was disappointment, Janet still insisted on carrying on until the doctors told her there was nothing left they could do for them. As the courses continued into 1983 comfort was found in the progress they were making for acceptance as being suitable for adoption. While the initial enquiries they had made at the Department of Social Services, not long after they were married, had gone by the wayside, since February 1981 they had been writing regularly to the Catholic Adoption Society. Although they could not be certain until they got a final letter of acceptance, it seemed as though their patience and persistence had finally paid off when, in March 1983, they were first interviewed together and then separately, and told to go to their doctors to each have a medical.

Janet and Graham had made sure that the hospital was aware that they had been trying for adoption and the adoption society that Janet was going through fertility treatment. On her next visit to the hospital, Janet was finally told by Adrian Murray, one of the doctors who had been working under Sam Abdulla, the consultant gynaecologist in charge of Janet's case, the news she least wanted to hear. They were reluctantly coming to the conclusion that the treatment simply was not going to work. For three and a half years they had tried everything to no effect. It was time to rest. He suggested, however, perhaps out of compassion, perhaps from a hope that a miracle might yet happen, that she might as well continue with the treatment until they had news of the adoption.

It seems that when an important letter is expected, the noise the postman makes as he goes about his delivery is far more acute. Graham was making coffee in the kitchen when he heard the postman turn on his heels and move on to the next house.

Invariably it is the less important items that plunge to the ground first; unsolicited advertising blurb, or details of a major new prize-winning draw, treating you as a long-standing friend and claiming you have been specially selected. However, the more important mail on this occasion was sitting smugly on top of all the other letters. As Graham walked through the narrow hall towards the front door, his eye focussed on a small white envelope. He grabbed it quickly, instinctively knowing that this was the news they had been waiting for, confirmed by the familiar embossed emblem of the Catholic diocese of Chester. The result of all those months and years of hoping and coming to terms with adoption, all the interviews and all the emotion was now here nestling in the paper between his fingers.

He couldn't bring himself to open it. This was something that had to be shared. Lunch and his coffee had been forgotten, and all he wanted to do was get into his van and drive straight to the bank in Moreton where Janet was now working full time. He decided to telephone instead. Nervously, he held the phone in two hands against his ear, and paced the hall floor as he waited to be put through to Janet. Graham described the envelope to her and she consciously began to control her emotions. The last thing Janet wanted was to make a fool of herself in front of the people she worked with every day and she knew that whether the answer was yes or no she wouldn't be able to control herself either way. It was sensible to wait until they had both finished work and could share the moment in the privacy of their own home.

Curiosity, however, is a powerful animal and once it gets its teeth into you, it will prove a formidable opponent for any emotion. It didn't take long, therefore, after they had finished their call and had agreed to wait until later, that Janet, with her close friends and work-mates Tony Lee and Barbara Kendrick at her side, dialled her home number.

Graham hadn't moved from the hall. He was still pacing up and down, thinking this must be no different than if he were in a waiting room at a maternity hospital, with Janet in the delivery room. He wanted a doctor to walk in, take the letter, open it, and tell him that he was the proud father of a healthy little boy or girl and that mother and child were both fine. He told himself to stop being silly. But what if the answer was no? It wouldn't be fair. They had gone through too much. What would there be left? He thought of their last visit to the fertility clinic where the doctors had all but given up hope, and Janet had as good as been given her final chance with the treatment. And what if it was yes? A bead of sweat ran along his forehead. The same thought that crosses most men's minds when their wives present them with the good news now flashed through Graham's; he was not sure he was ready for the responsibility of fatherhood. He was working himself up and he needed to calm down again, to have a second chat with Janet, and just as he determined to call her, the phone rang.

Janet was doodling with a Biro in her right hand as she listened to the dull ringing tone. The phone clicked and without waiting for the familiar voice she simply said, 'Open it!' Graham told Janet his hand was on the receiver as she rang and he was about to call her. The doodling continued across the pad on the desk, and without realising it Janet had drawn a line straight across Tony's hand as it lay flat next to the pad. Being careful not to rip the paper on the inside of the envelope, Graham opened it and took out the letter. Purposely he avoided glancing through it so that as he read each word it would be as new to him as it would be for Janet.

As he read through each paragraph, Janet's doodling got more and more frantic, changing from harmless little circles to wild aimless lines. Her pen had become a danger and while Barbara laughed with Janet as she shared with Graham the joyful news of the adoption acceptance, poor Tony's arm had become a sea of blue ink as the doodling pen had developed a mind of its own.

Four

Malta and the Fertility Stone

♡ ♡ ♡
♡ ♡
♡

Not long after having been accepted for adoption, Janet and Graham decided that they would take a break before the arrival of the new baby, and Malta was the obvious choice as they spent an early spring evening sifting through pages and pages of holiday brochures. There was no question of going anywhere else; they had both fallen in love with the tiny cluster of islands on their first visit a year earlier. It was not just because of the sun, which was guaranteed to shine every day, or the ease of access to the sea at any one of the many natural harbours for which the islands are famous.

What perhaps attracted Janet and Graham most of all to Malta was the fact that the local people were so easy to get along with. Throughout history, the islands have played a central and strategic role in countless struggles and battles between powerful nations. Great courage has been called for on many occasions and this has given rise to a singular kind of pride in their homeland, and the Maltese are famous for their hospitality.

It seems that Britain has always had a special relationship with Malta. During the Second World War when the islanders were totally behind the Allied cause, they showed tremendous strength and resilience defending with all their might what was then a colony. The war gave rise to the de-colonisation of the islands and finally the people were able to enjoy what they really wanted which was independence and control of their own future. Malta became a Republic in 1974, and in the Grand Harbour at Valletta stands a monument as a reminder of the final departure of the British military presence in 1979.

The rewarding thing about their first visit to Malta was that they were there as a result of a lot of hard overtime work by them both. On this occasion the reason for being there was different. It was to be their last holiday together as a couple before they took on the responsibility of a child when the adoption came through.

The day before they were due to travel, Janet began to feel unwell. She thought nothing of it and took a couple of paracetamol tablets, which had always seemed to settle her down before. She was determined that nothing was going to spoil this holiday; they had both been working hard recently and had saved up as much money as possible for spending at all the places they had enjoyed the year before.

Graham was looking forward to climbing the fifty-nine steps up to the bar and restaurant that took its name from that ascent. Graham remembered vividly the last occasion they were there. They were celebrating their last night on the island and each time Graham had a drink he asked a new person to join him. By the time they had got to the tenth round, he was, of course, the most popular man there, making friends as fast as a winner on the pools. When the bill arrived, that was exactly what he wished he had been. Not carrying sufficient Maltese pounds, the bill was settled with a piece of plastic. As is always the case when you pay by card when travelling abroad, the bill does not surface and rear its head until long after the party's over. In this instance it didn't arrive until October, three months after the last sip of Maltese malt. The damage was over £100, and the hangover lasted until December!

Rather than feeling better, sprightly and ready to go, Janet felt worse, lethargic and ready for bed. The nausea she had felt at first had turned to sickness and she began to feel that she wasn't going to be well enough to travel. All the usual routine things that needed to be done before going away, including packing, which was something that Janet always attended to when they travelled, were simply not being done. This was totally out of character, for however under the weather she used to feel, she would normally still carry on and somehow get through. With only an hour to go before they were due to leave the house, Janet was sitting on the edge of her bed, feeling awful and surrounded by clothing and empty cases. Graham suggested they cancel there and then but Janet wouldn't let him. She was sure it was only a bug, and even if she did have an uncomfortable journey she would probably only have to spend the first day in bed at the hotel and would be fine after that and fit enough to enjoy the rest of the fortnight's holiday.

Janet gritted her teeth and somehow summoned up the strength to get sorted. With Graham's help she finished packing, and while he attended to securing and checking the house she waited for him curled up on the lounge settee until the taxi arrived. It was not the best of moods in which to start a holiday, especially such an important one. Obviously, had they known what the nausea and sickness was all about, there would have been no way that they would have travelled, but for Janet, so conditioned to thinking she was unlikely to conceive, the thought of relating nausea to the symptoms of morning sickness, was very far away.

Religion plays an enormously important role on the islands, and to the local community nothing takes precedence over prayer. Many people come to the islands specifically because of the feeling of fulfilment they experience visiting the multitude of holy shrines. In the capital city of Valletta it is difficult to walk a hundred yards without stumbling on the steps of a sanctum of one denomination or the other, and from the main street the sounds of a mass can be heard in many different languages at any time of day

It was on their first visit in 1982 that they decided to go on a guided tour and take a boat ride to Gozo, the second largest of the three inhabited islands. As part of their itinerary, Janet and Graham chose to visit, not surprisingly, the sanctuary of a famous fertility stone that had stood there for centuries. It took the form of a seat, and their guide, with a 'nudge nudge' and a 'wink wink', delighted in teasing the girls with legends of fruitfulness and multiplication. It was all taken as a bit of a joke, and most of the young couples were talking more about being fruitful back in the hotel bedroom rather than multiplying!

Graham insisted on a photograph, and as Janet dutifully sat and smiled she reflected on the absurdity of the situation. For so long now she had been battling away, alone at first, then with Graham, through the forest of infertility, hopelessly trying to comprehend all the different and most up-to-date medical techniques and here she was 3,000 miles from her clinic sitting on a piece of primeval sandstone seeking an alternative solution. In many ways it had been a little depressing, laughing and joking about such a serious problem. The best that could come out of this, Janet thought, would be a good story to tell those she confided in back home.

It is, though, slightly unnerving to consider that on their second trip to Malta, less than twelve months later, Janet was so seriously afflicted with morning sickness she was hardly well enough to leave the hotel bedroom for the whole of the fortnight's holiday, let alone make a pilgrimage back to the fertility stone. Even the most sceptical of non-believers may have raised an agnostic eyebrow at what was to come.

· Five ·

More Than One

♡ ♡ ♡
♡ ♡
♡

Janet and Graham made the return journey from Malta on a Saturday evening. Feeling no better, and relieved to be on her way home, Janet couldn't take her mind off the thought that she might be pregnant. There was no other sensible explanation. Another voice inside her kept saying that it was impossible, and they had gone too long with too many disappointments and that the chances were so remote. But she was; she just knew it. Why else was she so sick during the second week in Malta? It *had* to be morning sickness.

Although the possibility of pregnancy had entered Graham's mind, as their conversation naturally got round to the subject during the second week, he dismissed it right away. Again and again Janet had said, 'I must be . . . I must be!' But as far as Graham was concerned, he believed that Janet's illness in Malta was totally due to the drugs that she had been taking. It had hurt him seeing Janet suffer so much over the years of treatment and tests, and he had been thinking for many months that it would be best for her to come off the treatment. He thought that she had had enough and he didn't think it was fair to subject her body to any more. But it wasn't his body and he was trapped in an impossible dilemma. Like the wife of a boxer he felt every punch but knew that the decision to retire finally from the frontline either lay in the hands of the one who was out there physically taking the punishment or in those of the doctors.

Of course it would have been marvellous for them to have their own children but it was not the be-all and end-all of life. Besides, with the adoption acceptance received they were going to be the proudest parents in any event. Graham knew that he and Janet would give just as much love to their adopted child or children as they would to any of their own. The more he thought about it, the more he felt that that last course of treatment Janet took should be her final one.

However, they had readily agreed that the first item on the agenda when they got back to Wallasey was to make arrangements for a check-up at the hospital where Janet had been receiving the treatment and to ask them for a pregnancy test.

With the next day being Sunday they decided, even though Janet was still feeling quite rough, not to disturb their local doctor and to wait until the clinic was open the following morning. Having had so much treatment at the fertility unit, they felt that, under the circumstances, they would have to be referred there anyway. It was a very bright, sunny and hot day, hardly different from the temperatures they had become used to over the past couple of weeks, although there was a slight breeze in the air that always seems to bring a welcome relief on an English summer day.

Amongst everything else on her mind there was all the holiday washing to be done, and Janet wanted to make a start to try and at least get things ready to be hung out on the line in order to make the best use of the weather. The way she was feeling, though, she didn't hold out much hope of getting the ironing done as well that day. During the day Janet gathered up the strength to go along with Graham to see his parents, and tell them all about the trip and how ill Janet had been, but they decided it was best not to mention the possibility of pregnancy.

As Janet and Graham passed by the parked ambulances and made their way through the entrance into the large reception hall of the Royal Liverpool Hospital, the whole place felt busier than ever on that Monday morning. Way above their heads bright sunlight filtered through a glass ceiling, and it felt like being in a warm greenhouse. It seemed as though the place was awash with white as the uniforms of the nurses mingled with the overalls of the orderlies and the familiar starched coats of the doctors. In the centre of the hall a glass show case housed a wooden model of the whole hospital complex, and beyond that there were rows of seats and wheelchairs where some older people sat waiting patiently.

Even though the route they had to take through the hospital corridors was by now a very familiar one, once they had passed through the reception area they still halted to look up at the green-and-blue signs directing them to 'Ward 3B'. As they looked up at the information board their hands met and clasped and they turned and followed the passage through to the lifts and up to the third floor. Janet suddenly felt haunted by all the disappointments of the past and began to wonder whether she was right about the pregnancy. 'Well,' she thought, 'I'll soon find out.'

The ward was very busy that morning but Janet spotted a couple of young nurses she knew, and she and Graham went over to have a word with them. They related the story of how ill Janet had been while on holiday, and Janet could hear herself telling them that she thought she was pregnant. It was so strange to be actually saying it to these nurses, especially after all the times she had been back to this ward. It was almost as if she expected them to say, 'Oh don't be silly now, you're getting far too emotional about the whole thing.' But, of course, they didn't. The nurses looked around, and seeing that there were no doctors to ask to do the test, and realising how much it meant to Janet to know as quickly as possible, they took the specimen and did the test themselves.

This was it now; they were going to find out one way or another. For them, all of a sudden the test meant everything. It was the difference between being like most other average couples, or not; between being able to create life, or not; between seeing themselves as normal, or having to compromise.

The test was positive. Their world was shaking and they held on tightly to each other. In their daze they heard the nurse having to say, as a formality, 'You can't take it as read, though, because we shouldn't really have done it, so we'll have to get someone else to test the specimen before it is definitely confirmed.' But Janet and Graham knew that it was definite.

Incredibly there was no-one else available at that time to confirm the test. So, even though Janet and Graham were convinced it was a certain pregnancy, they still could not celebrate because the girls were not supposed to have done it in the first place. It would be a while before Janet would be able to have a further test so they went out for a walk to get some fresh air. As they walked and walked three inevitable words kept repeating in Janet's head, 'I am pregnant ... I am pregnant ... I am pregnant.'

Once the second test was completed later in the day the news was finally confirmed. The registrar said, 'Yes, you are definitely pregnant. Under the circumstances, though, we had better book you in for a scan.' This was a perfectly normal procedure for any patient who has been undergoing fertility treatment.

So that was it then. They knew, they absolutely knew. There was to be no more hoping and praying, no more testing and treatment, no more tears of frustration, but there was to be plenty of excitement to come, and Janet could feel it shooting through every vein in her body. Never before had she felt so fulfilled, and the feeling was wonderful.

Graham could see the exhilaration in Janet's tanned but drawn face. Her happy smile and sparkling eyes said it all. He shared the excitement; it was the first time that he really believed that Janet was pregnant – but his own excitement was subdued. He could not accept that Janet's dreadful illness was all to do with her being pregnant. It was not like the feeling he had when they had been accepted for adoption. Then, there had been no doubts involved. They had been accepted, had been through all the processes, and the final confirmation meant that they were going to get a child. But here his wife's health was at stake, and something was niggling him. He just could not help worrying that it was not all cut and dried.

It was about eleven thirty in the morning, and the earliest that they could book in for an appointment to have the scan was two o'clock. For those two and a half to three hours Janet felt just like any other normal woman who had just been told that she was definitely pregnant. She was on cloud nine and thinking, 'That's it! We've done it! Bingo! Brilliant! I'm just the same as everyone else!' and, 'I'm pregnant!' She also kept thinking of the adoption clinic and how she was going to tell them the news.

Janet was looking forward to seeing Ila, the young girl who had been so kind each time she had previously been down to the scanning department, and about an hour before the scan Janet began what was already a familiar process of drinking loads and loads of water in advance. This was to ensure that the uterus was in the best possible position for a clear and successful scan. The highly sophisticated technique of ultrasound means that X-rays are not necessary and is thus a safer method for analysis, and it is through the reflection of soundwaves that a picture can be created on a nearby screen. At first the screen appears to be a blotchy haze of smears and smudges and it takes a trained eye to point out the various important outlines.

Janet lay back on the bed and felt Ila apply the jelly-like substance to her stomach. Although she knew that she wouldn't be able to interpret what came up on the scan, despite having had scans before, she turned her head and kept her eyes firmly focused on the screen. Ila gently and evenly rubbed the transducer against Janet's stomach, while Janet strained her eyes trying desperately to make out a head or a spine or something, but it was useless. Then her eyes moved from the screen to the face of the young nurse, and as Janet watched Ila's expression she didn't need any expertise to interpret that Ila had seen something she clearly was having difficulty understanding; her eyes were popping out of her head, and Janet wanted to know what was the matter. Ila tried to remain calm and said, 'Oh, I think maybe I should get a second opinion.' Janet asked 'Why?' Ila looked at her, 'Well, I think it may be more than one,' she answered truthfully, but afraid to go any further. Janet pushed her though, 'Do you mean it's twins?' she asked, getting more excited than she had before, if that was at all possible. Having a baby was brilliant, but twins, that was unbelievable. It was something that Janet had dreamed of ever since they had met; she had even told the adoption clinic she would love to have twins if the possibility ever arose. So this latest turn of events was too good to be true. Ila, by this time, was already half way out of the room. 'I'm just going to get the doctor to check.'

Meanwhile, Graham was waiting outside. Janet went out to join him. 'It's more than one,' she said excitedly, 'I think it's twins!' It all became clear now to Graham. Now he realised why she had been so ill. They were going to have twins. It was the answer to all their prayers. This was it! A whole family in one go! Within seconds Graham had become as excited about the whole thing as Janet. The doubts and the worries he had felt earlier had disappeared and he held Janet as she cried, totally overcome with joy. So the two of them sat clutching each other and holding hands in a waiting room not far from the scanning department, happier than they had ever been in their lives and waiting for the doctor to check and confirm the good news.

It was not long before Janet was called back into the room but as she approached the door she immediately sensed something was causing a stir. All sorts of people were gathering together, rushing to the scanning room from all angles, clearly attracted by some unusual event. As two more carelessly brushed passed her as she was led through she wondered what all the fuss was about. Had somebody collapsed? Maybe there had been an accident. You can always rely on a good accident in a public place to create a good crowd, she thought. It was as if the department had become one gigantic honey-pot.

On the other side of the busy doors she straight away saw that the source of this goldrush was the screen on which she had so recently been scanned. Janet was puzzled. Surely, she thought, twins couldn't cause this much interest. But then she was excited about it, so there was no reason why everyone else shouldn't be; and, having been on fertility drugs, it was a miracle to conceive at all, let alone have twins, so perhaps all this fascination was justified. She was beginning to feel a little uncomfortable; she knew she was being treated on the National Health but surely everyone was entitled to some privacy. It was as though tickets were being sold to come and see the show, and all Janet wanted to do was go to the toilet. She was absolutely bursting. Under normal circumstances everything would have been over by now and she would have been able to make her visit ages ago but she had had to wait and now Adrian Murray, Sam Abdulla's right-hand man, was in the room and wanted to take further scans.

Janet climbed back on to the bed, and Ila assisted Adrian Murray in giving her the second scan while all around her the sound of murmuring voices was swelling in her ears. She glanced in the direction of the screen but saw nothing but the cold impassive backs of this uninvited group of medical people who were prying into her private picture. As they shuffled about she saw their expressions. They were like over-excited children in Disneyland seeing Mickey Mouse for the first time, bustling and shoving each other to get a better view. Janet could not work out what was going on; all she knew was that the joy she had felt with Graham moments earlier was rapidly fading, and an unknown fear was filling the gap. She was confused. Each time the transducer swept across her body there was a sound of, 'My, god!' or 'Look at this!' and everyone seemed to be chattering away to each other as if she was not there or did not matter.

She refused to tolerate the ignorance any longer and she raised her voice above everyone else's in the room. 'For goodness sake! Will you tell me what's happened?'

There was a deathly silence. It was as if, all of a sudden, everyone apart from Adrian Murray and Ila, realised that there was a human life behind the picture on the screen. This was not just a medical example from the archives, and expressions of excitement turned to concern and worry. Adrian Murray looked at one of the other doctors in the room, then turned to Janet.

'Mrs Walton . . .' He glanced back to the screen as he spoke, as if to double check once more and, doing his professional best to hide his disbelief, said, 'It is more than one but it is not twins. It's a multiple birth and we are as sure as we can be that six babies are showing up on the screen.'

For a few moments it was as if Janet had been enveloped in a large transparent sound-proofed tube. She was aware of everything going on around her and could see everyone clearly; Adrian Murray was gesticulating in front of the scanner and his mouth was opening and closing rapidly, like a goldfish gasping for air; but she could hear nothing but the number six being repeated time and time again. Seconds went by, and all of a sudden Janet felt quite alone in that crowded room. She wanted Graham. She needed him. Where was he? As each moment passed she was getting more uncomfortable, bewildered and more upset. With all the excitement earlier of being told she was pregnant, she had forgotten how unwell she had been and now that, too, was beginning to take a new grip.

In that astonishing brief period of less than five minutes, Janet had stepped on every possible stone crossing the river of emotions. Moments earlier she had been splashing about in the joy and happiness of being pregnant and the euphoria of fulfilment of a woman who had virtually given up all hope of being a mother. Now she was drowning in emptiness and was being swept away from reality in a tempest, struggling to return to her sensible and logical world. And as the storm became too much to cope with, the river burst its banks, and as Graham walked into the room Janet could not contain herself any longer, and she cried and cried.

The torrent of tears was an accumulation of many things. It was the combination of the illness, the result of the first test, the long wait for the scan, the tremendous high feeling they had shared when they thought it might be twins, and now the thunderbolt of something that seemed so impossible.

The atmosphere in the room remained claustrophobic with no-one clearing the scanning department to give Janet breathing space. On top of everything else her physical discomfort was steadily on the increase as she was by now absolutely desperate to get rid of all that water she had had to drink an hour before the scan. She was grateful, therefore, when Adrian Murray suggested that she should go off and get dressed.

The doctors began to discuss what had been revealed and what their immediate course of action should be; Adrian Murray was aware that with Sam Abdulla not available for consultation until the next day, he was responsible for the final decisions at that moment. The critical question was whether or not Janet should be allowed to go home that night.

After the doctors had talked among themselves, Adrian Murray came out to the waiting room where Janet was being comforted by her rather stunned husband. She took a fresh tissue from her handbag and wiped her tears away. 'Is it definite doctor?' Graham asked, thinking that maybe on perhaps their third, fourth or fifth examination of the screen the doctors might have altered their opinions. Maybe there was something wrong with the machine, he thought; machines are always going wrong. It was only a piece of metal, surely it was possible that it could become faulty now and again. But he stopped himself making these points knowing that there was no way the hospital would risk being uncertain about such a serious matter.

'Obviously it is always difficult to get an absolutely accurate picture with a scanner,' replied Adrian Murray with a little more confidence in his voice than earlier. 'It isn't, of course, easy to pin-point the precise positions of each baby, with some overlapping others, but as far as we can tell, the answer to your question is yes, it is definite.'

'Clearly,' he continued, 'this is not a straightforward pregnancy as I'm sure you've already realised, but I have to tell you that there are probably going to be problems. You'll have to come into hospital,' he went on, looking at Janet, 'you'll have to be admitted.'

This was something they had not yet considered. They were hearing all these words but nothing was really registering properly. All they knew was that things seemed to be getting grimmer and more serious by the minute. The thought of Janet being admitted to hospital, though, brought home the reality that this was no ordinary pregnancy.

'Do you mean now?' Janet asked, intending her reply as a kind of joke thinking that the doctor was going to suggest that she should be admitted perhaps a couple of months before the expected date of the birth. By thinking this she was also subconsciously taking the first steps of convincing herself that there was actually going to be a birth.

'No,' he said. 'You can go home tonight but you have got to be back here at eight o'clock in the morning.' He had considered the situation deeply and was acutely aware of the danger in letting his patient out of medical custody even for the shortest period of time. The pregnancy, however, was at such an early stage that the probability of anything happening to Janet that night was extremely remote. She had as much chance as falling down the stairs, being knocked over or slipping on a banana skin as the next person, but the problem was that if the unlikely did occur and an accident of any sort did happen then the responsibility would doubtless be on his shoulders and he would probably be shot by Sam! He balanced all this against his instinct that it was best for Janet to go back to familiar surroundings, calm down and spend the night at home, rather than to be put unprepared into a hospital bed.

Both feeling equally upset, they left the hospital and began the difficult task of preparing themselves to spread the word among the family. They felt as queasy as if they had just stepped off the 'big-dipper', and with all the ups and downs of the day they had not thought of ringing either set of parents, all of whom were by this time getting slightly puzzled as to why they had not heard anything.

They went straight to Wallasey and to Folly Lane where Graham's parents, Betty and John, lived. Janet had started to get a grip of herself, but she felt if she tried to speak she would probably begin to break down. Graham did his best, but how can you explain the impossible? There was nervous laughter and joking as he broke the news. As soon as his parents began to ask questions, however, he struggled to fight off a lump in his throat and to avoid any eye contact. He searched for the answers until he finally broke down and had to leave the room.

There was no joy at this time for Janet and Graham. The wall of happiness that had been built earlier in the day had now been totally demolished, and, as easy as a candle flame is blown out, their dreams were extinguished. All that remained was a tiny spark of hope for a miracle. As far as the hospital staff were concerned, the whole reason for Janet's admission the next day was so that she would be on the spot if she had a miscarriage. They were going to care for her and comfort her but none of them at that time really believed that there would be total success. Far from Janet and Graham's minds were thoughts of the joy of six babies at the end of all the years of pain and anguish; much closer was the fear that having been through all this Janet was now going to go through hell.

By the time they left Betty and John it was approaching five o'clock, which meant the staff at the bank where Janet worked would soon be going home. She had had a two-week break from her job to go on holiday and was now worried about not turning up for work the next day. It never occurred to Janet that the bank would immediately and totally accept the situation. Before they made the journey across the Wirral peninsula from Wallasey to Janet's parents' house in Neston, they decided to stop off at Browning Road to make a call to the bank. With Janet still unable to speak properly, knowing that if she started talking she would begin to cry, it was left to Graham to telephone.

He asked to speak to the accountant at the bank, Peter Challinor. The easiest way to handle this Graham thought, was to get straight to the point. 'We've just come back from holiday,' he said, 'and I'm afraid Janet won't be coming into work tomorrow because she has to go into hospital. She is having six children.' There. That sounded perfectly O.K., Graham thought, asserting himself. But then came the response, which left him holding the phone in disbelief long after the call ended. 'Thank you very much for letting me know,' Challinor said, and hung up! It was exactly that. No reaction at all, as if it were a perfectly normal everyday occurrence. Perhaps it was because of the matter-of-fact manner in which Graham informed him, but it was more likely that what he had heard was so preposterous it just did not register immediately.

Peter Challinor's desk was situated on an upper level looking down upon the other desks in the open-plan room. He replaced the receiver, stood up and made his way down to where Tony Lee and Barbara Kendrick were sitting. Quite suddenly, the number six became the most important figure he had ever dealt with in his whole career as an accountant. As he held on to the edge of a desk to stop shaking, all he could say was, 'I don't believe it! I simply just don't believe it!' before he eventually stunned Janet's workmates with the news.

The journey to Nancy and Peter's house settled Janet down considerably and by the time they arrived she was composed and able to speak. 'We've got something to tell you,' Janet said as soon as her mum opened the door. Nancy had been keeping busy doing the Monday washing. Since lunchtime, each time the phone had rung she was convinced that it would be Janet with some news, and having heard nothing she was by now getting worried. Her daughter had a strange glazed look in her eye and Nancy was concerned. 'You needn't cry,' Janet began, 'because Graham's mum's been crying and everybody has been crying and there's been enough tears for today.' Janet then told her everything that had happened during the day. Somehow, Nancy managed to hold back the weeping and show her daughter a brave face but as soon as Janet and Graham had left and were out of sight, Nancy could control her emotions no longer and the tears caressed her cheeks for three full days.

That night when they arrived back at Browning Road from Neston Janet began packing a case full of things she thought she might need in the hospital. They were both lost in a sea of their own thoughts and conversation between them was sparse. As the night progressed Janet felt the same determination that had lived with her through all the treatment seeping slowly back into every part of her body. It was a feeling telling her secretly she was going to be all right. 'Well we have no choice,' she thought. 'We have to follow exactly what the doctors say ... I've got to go into hospital tomorrow and whatever happens, we have to accept it. But it won't be my fault if anything does go wrong. I am going to be the best patient they have ever had!'

· Six ·

Thirty-Two Long Weeks

♡ ♡ ♡
♡ ♡
♡

Anyone who has ever spent any considerable time in hospital will appreciate the difficulty Janet faced in keeping her spirits up. There is nothing entertaining about the drabness of a hospital bed and Janet found herself constantly having to fight off the weariness and tedium.

At first there was no point in Janet being admitted to the maternity hospital; it was planned that she would be transferred only if she managed to reach the twenty-fourth week of her pregnancy. So in the meantime she was given a bed in the familiar surroundings of the gynaecological ward of the Royal Liverpool Hospital where she had made so many visits for treatment in the past.

After a couple of weeks, and more than a couple more scans, the doctors decided that their initial reading of six babies had in fact been incorrect, and from then on Janet and Graham both thought in terms of the possibility of having quins whenever they dared think that things might go well.

Apart from family visits, which were so vital throughout the whole of the five months, there were also times when Janet really appreciated her friends. Barbara Kendrick not only visited Janet as regularly as possible but also wrote a constant stream of letters, which helped Janet stay in touch with everything that was going on in the bank. After all, one thing that was for sure was that if things did not go well Janet could find herself back at work a lot sooner than she hoped.

Much was confided in Barbara; she was one of the very few people outside the family who had been aware of Graham and Janet's adoption applications. Her letters were a great source of amusement and also gave Janet the opportunity to write back with all the latest information of her progress and to detail the various tests that the doctors were performing on her and how they were monitoring everything with such care and attention.

There was however another reason why Janet looked forward so much to Barbara's visits. On one occasion Janet noticed her chatting to the nurse on duty and could see that Barbara was pointing to a flask in her carrier bag, and the nurse was giving her a reassuring friendly nod and a pat on her arm.

'What was all that about?' Janet asked, straining to peer into Barbara's bag.

'Oh, nothing. I was just telling her that I'd made you a nice cup of home brew and she was agreeing that it would probably do you the world of good.' A mischievous smile came over Barbara's face. 'Mind you,' she continued, 'I didn't let on what kind of a brew it was!'

It was only a drop, but that Blue Lagoon cocktail tasted sensational to Janet, and all of a sudden the ward took on a whole new appearance. The gloom lifted, and those short visits did Janet the world of good.

Little Neston is tucked so far away in the countryside that visiting was never easy for Nancy. It meant a bus trip then a train journey to Birkenhead followed by a second train journey into Liverpool, and then another bus ride to the hospital. And apart from transport difficulties, Nancy worked full time which meant that it was absolutely impossible for her to make the trip every day. She is, though, a very determined lady and one way or another she ensured that she got as much time off work so that she could visit her daughter as often as possible. She was a cook at Yeoman House, a home for physically and mentally handicapped children, and fortunately had a very understanding group of workmates who went out of their way to make the most of the flexible working hours to help with the visiting situation.

The visits Nancy made regularly on a Saturday were the ones that Janet most looked forward to. That was when Nancy would produce a delicious, freshly baked granary loaf and some butter. It was a treat which Janet kept only for herself. She would plan her week-ends around the loaf, carefully slicing it, spreading her ration of butter, and making it last as far into the Sunday as her tempted taste buds would allow.

On 3 July, only a couple of weeks after Janet had been admitted to the Royal, Nancy's mother died having been taken ill a week earlier suffering from a cerebral haemorrhage. Up until then, she had enjoyed relatively good health, so it had come as more than a little shock to Nancy when her father had come to the house in a state of panic with the news that she had been admitted to Clatterbridge, the local hospital. The first thing that crossed Nancy's mind was how she was going to tell Janet. The last thing she wanted was to upset her, especially considering the seriousness of her daughter's condition.

For two weeks Nancy somehow managed to visit Janet in the afternoons and her mother in the evenings. Even though there was always a little bit of hope, Nancy was virtually resigned to the fact that it was unlikely that her mother was going to survive, although that fact did nothing to stem the pain. Her mother was deteriorating rapidly, and Nancy still had not told Janet how bad she was. She had all the worry, sadness and fear of losing her mother, while at the same time she could not bring herself to tell her eldest daughter about her grandmother's condition for fear the shock might affect the pregnancy. Even if it had been a normal pregnancy Nancy would have hesitated to tell her, but this was different. Not only was there the likelihood that all the babies would not survive, but also Nancy knew that for as long as her daughter was pregnant in this way her own life was in danger.

On the evening of the third, however, when Janet rang her mum to see how her nan was, Nancy could only tell her daughter the terrible truth. Janet cried for days after the news but her health remained stable and although she desperately wanted to go to the funeral it was, as far as the doctors were concerned, out of the question.

On occasion the atmosphere within the ward would become forlorn as emotions of some of the patients ebbed and flowed. It was inevitable that now and again within the close quarters of a busy gynaecological ward women who had been admitted for infertility treatment, going through the same pain, anguish and heartache as Janet had done would hear of others who had considered terminating their pregnancy. Tears triggered by despair would reflect the desperation for children that was made worse by the feeling that perhaps they were lying so close to the creation of a life that might not be given the opportunity to breathe in this world. All Janet could do was quietly pray for the others that the

41

treatment they were being given would be successful.

When she was admitted to the Royal, Janet was given a choice of being on her own in a side ward or with others in a main ward. The decision was not a difficult one to make; on no account, realising how long she may be in hospital, did she want to feel cut off. It would have been dreary, boring, and, worst of all, it would have been dreadfully lonely.

Janet quickly became accustomed to life in ward 3B. Even though the sickness remained with her for the first few weeks, two months in all, her still golden brown tan and thin figure gave the impression that she was a picture of health. At times it really did not look as if there was a thing wrong with her. Patients in the ward seemed to come and go as often as the visitors, and as each new one arrived there would be the usual question of, 'Oh well, what's wrong with you then?' and the usual response of, 'Oh my goodness! You're not, are you?' whenever Janet told her story. The reaction was always the same. Then the new patients would conjure up a never ending stream of relatives and friends to whom they would whisper about the lady 'over there', followed closely by a much louder unrestrained whisper of, 'Oh crikey, she's not, is she?' There were six beds in the ward altogether, and Janet was invariably one of the main topics of conversation at visiting times.

During her time at the Royal an old lady was admitted to Janet's ward to have a kidney stone removed. She was given the bed opposite Janet's and it was not long before she was slowly coming round after the successful operation. The end result was clearly placed for all to see floating in a glass of what appeared to be, but obviously was not, water. The nurse had decided after a suitable time to give the old lady something to eat, and, having padded her pillows, the old lady was sat up and positioned before her dinner. She was still far too groggy to keep anything down, and unfortunately her food made a return journey. After that, all the poor dear wanted and needed was a simple refreshing glass of water ...

Slumping back against her pillows, and flagging from the effects of her forced efforts, she reached out her right hand towards the tempting and thirst quenching drink she had noticed on her vanity unit next to her glasses. Janet's eyes opened wider and wider as she realised what was about to happen. She began to get out of bed with the intention of ensuring that the old lady survived at least till she was discharged, when, at the same moment, the sister flew through the swing doors of the ward and, immediately anticipating the old lady's next trick, swooped the floating kidney stone out of reach and switched it for a safer solution. The lady thankfully gulped down the water, the sister thankfully took the display glass away, the surgeon thankfully did not have to do a repeat operation, and Janet thankfully and quietly got back into bed.

It did not take long for Janet to become institutionalised. She developed a specific routine within which she would read, sleep, eat and become an expert at flower arranging and at giving recommendations to new patients about the menu. She became friendly with all the nurses but quickly noticed that although they would talk to her about everything and anything the one subject they avoided was her condition. The future was taboo. Not one of the nurses ever talked about the day when Janet would have the babies; for most of them it was a case of when was Janet going to have a miscarriage. The first question that was always asked by nurses coming on duty was, 'Is Janet Walton all right?' but no-one really believed there was to be happy ending.

But like a prisoner making chalk marks on a cell wall, Janet faithfully marked her diary, and as each day and each week went past, a tiny pocket of hope grew as slowly and as cautiously as a new-born crocus in spring. And then after over a hundred days in the Royal, on 26 September, Janet was moved to the Oxford Street Maternity Hospital. It was a major hurdle to cross. Janet and Graham both knew then that the doctors must have thought there was a chance. Why else would they have made the transfer?

A private room was agreed upon at the Maternity Hospital. This time there was no choice. If the monitoring process was to be given the best possible chance, absolute peace from the everyday hustle and bustle of the wards was essential. By this time also Janet was beginning to feel the real effects of the abundance of life growing within her body, and the enormous overbearing strain left her now not feeling very well. Besides, it would have been distressing to watch the constant flow of women that were being admitted, having their babies and happily trotting off home with their new additions, all within the space of a few days.

As more weeks passed, Sam Adbulla began to feel that there may be a possibility that Janet would make it as far as the thirty-second week of the pregnancy, after which there would be a greater chance of success. It was he who would make the final decision of when to deliver the babies by Caesarean section. And when Janet had an uncomfortable venture into labour on 31 October, which had fortunately been controlled, Sam decided on 4 November to carry out the critical X-ray to establish as precisely as possible the babies' positions.

Janet realised that the uncontrollable butterflies and tummy rumbles she had felt while at the Royal had in fact been the first signs of the babies moving. At first there had been no visible indication. Later on, though, after she had been moved to the Maternity Hospital, Janet spent hours just staring at her stomach being entertained by little legs, knees, elbows, arms and heads pushing, shoving and stretching her skin, like a baker's fingers forever forming new shapes by kneading away at a soft and supple puffed expanse of dough. At times things would get out of hand and her tummy resembled a Tom and Jerry cartoon as it struggled relentlessly against an onslaught of belly bullying.

The X-ray was no easy affair. Janet had put on over forty pounds in weight during the pregnancy and by now was not even able to stretch her arms to meet around her stomach. It was virtually impossible for her to stand up. She was so 'top heavy' that she had to lean as far back as possible to avoid falling over. As well as her own, Janet was carrying five sets of extra bones in her body and felt as if every one of them ached. Every move she made was difficult, but somehow, as she lay awkwardly on the table, Sam managed to get a clear picture of her backbone and the multitude of tiny bones that lay above.

Later on that day Sam came to see Janet with the results. As he came into the room he was practically bursting with excitement. Janet had never seen him in this way; he was normally so cool and calm. Not knowing what to expect, Janet asked, 'What's happened now?' Before he answered, Sam asked one of the nurses to bring a screen into the room so that he could show Janet the X-ray. He told her that he had spent the past two hours with another expert carefully examining the pictures, tracing all the backbones and limbs and working out which head belonged to which legs.

When the machine arrived he placed the X-ray up against it and switched it on. Shades of black and white suddenly appeared in front of her as hundreds of little haloes glimmered against the borders of darkness. Then her attention focused on Sam's forefinger as it began following the snake-like lines of the babies' backbones. He christened each one with a number. 'One ... Two ... Three ... Four ... Five ...' He hesitated for a moment like a magician about to astound his audience at the end of a mind-boggling trick. As if they knew their secret was about to be exposed, the babies struggled uncomfortably in the confines of their cocoon, and Janet's stomach began slowly to turn. Her ears confirmed what her eyes told her as she followed the finger along another broken stream of shimmering light. '... and ... six!' Sam turned to Janet, and, anticipating any uncertainty, said, 'There's no doubt about it. We've checked and double checked. It's definitely six babies!'

That day Graham's dad, who worked at the Citizens Advice Bureau, had given his son five maternity forms that the hospital had advised Janet to fill in before the birth took place. Janet had got over the excitement and was quite relaxed by the time Graham popped his head around the door for his afternoon visit. As soon as she saw him, though, her eyes lit up. 'I've got something to tell you,' she said as calmly as possible, and without giving Graham a chance to ask what it was, she continued, 'Did your dad get the forms?' His hand was already clutching them in his pocket and he quickly produced them and waved them in the air. 'Well,' she said, unable to stop a smile breaking across her face. 'I think you'd better tell him to get another one!'

· Seven ·

Miracles Can Happen

♡ ♡ ♡
♡ ♡
♡

By the morning of 18 November the patient patient was becoming very restless. She was approaching her thirty-second week. She thought of Sam. He would be in to see her later today. So many people had been in to see her; she had had enough of all the voyeurs. The problem was that Janet had become not only a curiosity but also a personality within the hospital domain. She was always happy to see Phil Tromans and Helen Tebbutt, the registrars working with Sam, and John Beddard the consultant anaesthetist who would have seven lives in his hands as Janet was prepared for the Caesarean. But the only one she really wanted to see now was Sam. He was going to deliver her babies, and it would be he who would bring her relief from the fears and frustration.

Unfortunately she was not going to be that lucky, and ahead of Sam that morning came a stream of people. She could not get the thirty two weeks out of her mind. The following Monday, the 21st, was Sam's birthday. It would coincide with the end of the thirty-second week and Janet suspected it would be then that Sam would operate.

Two more doctors arrived. Their faces were not familiar and the last thing Janet wanted was to be examined by them. They did not stay long, though, and with sympathetic smiles, as if to say there still was not much chance of success, they turned away to discuss the case.

46

Her mind went back to that magical figure of thirty two. 'Well,' she thought, 'as nice as it might be for the birth to be on Sam's birthday, now that I've got this far I don't care when it is although the sooner the better.' The more she thought about it the more Janet just wanted to get on with it; she began to believe she could not carry on another day.

Right at the end of the bed the two doctors continued to discuss the case and then Janet overheard one say to the other something about thirty-four or thirty-six weeks. She nearly passed out! Here she was, bursting at the seams with a waistline that was well over sixty inches, and strangers were casually talking about an extra fortnight! At that moment it would have been no wonder had she fainted and had kittens!

Janet turned her thoughts to the scan she was due to have that day. Sam would be looking after her then, and, as always, she would totally accept anything he said.

As soon as Graham arrived, the room was buzzing with people popping in and out all the time, just to see if Janet was all right, and everyone seemed to be aware that Sam was about to make his decision based on his examination of the scan.

This particular scan was possibly one of the worst moments for Janet. All forms of concern for propriety went straight out of the window as an absurd scene took place in which Janet, aided by a number of nurses, attempted to find a position suitable for the scan. Embarrassment was gradually replaced by indifference as Janet allowed herself to be manoeuvred. Like Gulliver, she lay there helpless as everyone else scurried around her enormous body going about their business.

Even with everyone's efforts they could only manage to get Janet half on the bed. Beyond the point of caring, and in a wash of jokes to hide everyone's embarrassment, Janet lay spread with arms and legs akimbo, supported from behind by a nurse who had to push and struggle to keep her in a scannable position. One small point of relief for her was that there was no need whatsoever on this occasion for Janet to drink plenty of water in advance of having the scan. Her uterus was at this stage very low, and the babies could not have been in a better position for a successful scan.

Anxious to get on with things in order to minimise Janet's discomfort, Sam took hold of the transducer and began to scan the surface of Janet's well-oiled stomach. Graham, who had been given permission to attend the scanning, looked on in amazement with everyone else in the room as Sam outlined each baby's position on the screen.

Janet and Graham had become adept at interpreting the scan and they were able to spot immediately the six outlines that appeared to lie crumpled and squashed up. This seemed to underline one of the concerns Janet had been keeping to herself over the past few days. She had become accustomed to the absurd sight of her stomach bubbling away in front of her like a simmering soup. It was as if the babies were desperate to escape the confines of her body but Janet could do nothing to help. Recently, though, she had noticed that the lumps and the movements had become less frequent, as if they were tired of banging and kicking on the door and had given up from exhaustion. The stillness worried her and it was only Sam's reassurances that helped release this extra mental pressure.

Janet was at the limit and Sam knew it. It was vital to scan as near to the operation as possible to determine exactly where the babies were lying, and, therefore, if he did not go ahead today there would only be more movement and more discomfort for Janet. He was now thinking of Janet's safety above all else. This had always been of paramount importance to him, but now that Janet had come this far and there was a genuine chance that all the babies may survive, to go any further, with the babies growing healthily inside her, might well endanger Janet's life. The decision was made in Sam's mind. It was time to go.

As Sam methodically swept the transducer in his hand across her skin, he looked over to Janet and, in an almost nonchalant manner, asked, 'Have you had any lunch –?' Everyone in the room then knew that today was the day. When Janet confirmed with a very dry and nervous whisper that she had had a couple of pieces of bread, Sam, taking into consideration how long he would have to wait before he could operate, proclaimed, 'Seven o'clock!' We'll do it at seven!'

Janet felt herself enveloped in a great cloud of relief. She was not a bit upset or worried.

Graham was petrified.

His heart pounded away against his ribs and he could feel echoes of his pulse all over his body. His brave face became pale and it was all he could do to stop himself saying, 'Perhaps we could leave it a week ...' He steadied himself, however, with the thought of what they had been through, and whatever happened it was coming to an end that day.

When Janet and Graham arrived back at her room, it was already visiting time and Janet's dad, Peter, was there to see her. Totally unaware of all that had just happened, he sat looking at this strange figureless shape whose face, so gaunt and thin, he hardly recognised. Whose body, so bulbously misshapen seemed to laugh at the helplessness of her arms and legs. His daughter's condition was impossible to comprehend and Peter's way of combating it was to make light of the situation. He immediately asked how she was and joked that she looked fantastic. 'Don't worry. I'm fine!' Janet reassured him. 'And by the way, ... I'm having the operation at seven o'clock tonight!'

Throughout the whole ordeal Peter had been marvellous, always joking and pretending he was not worried. He used to say things to Janet like, 'Oh well, you'll just have to hang them on the line when they are born and hose them all down because you won't have time to wash them!' But now he completely dried up. There were no jokes, no well-timed one-liners. He just went grey. Janet had never seen him look so ill. Peter sat next to Graham and the pair of them looked like the living dead. For a short while hardly a word passed anyone's lips, but the same thing was on both men's minds, and they had begun to pray for Janet.

Graham took comfort from Sam Abdulla's words when a few weeks earlier they had discussed the matter. Sam had said that the thing that was uppermost in everybody's mind was Janet's health. While Janet would have without doubt willingly sacrificed her own life for those of her babies, it was she who came first as far as the doctors were concerned and Graham believed that that was the way it should be.

Janet was not concerned in the slightest for her own safety. Something had kept telling her all the way through that everything was going to be all right. Besides the support of her family, the only thing that had kept her going was that determination and faith, and she was not about to let it go now.

She looked at the two most important men in her life and decided that they needed some fresh air. Janet suggested that they both go for something to eat and that they should knock on the priest's door at the nearby cathedral. The priest had an important role to play. Due to the likelihood that some of the babies might not survive more than a few hours after the birth, the priest was to be on the spot for an immediate baptism. Graham had taken the hospital's advice and had been to see the priest a few weeks earlier.

As they left the maternity hospital through the front door, Graham and his father-in-law were far too wrapped up in their own thoughts to notice a small group of people walking out of the gate at the far end of the hospital car park. A few members of the press had presented themselves two days earlier at the hospital's reception, and were now joined by fresh troops of front-line journalists sporting raincoats, note-pads and anxious expressions. And each of these soldiers of fortune had been commanded to be first with the story.

The reporters warily walked together, familiar with their company, careful not to let slip any tiny morsel of leading information they may have thought was worth holding and building on, while every so often dropping the odd crumb into the conversation hoping it may result in their being able to fit another piece into their own jigsaw. And they made their way through the gate and across the road to the Cambridge for yet another pub lunch, totally oblivious to the fact that the face of the man walking away from them at the other end of the building would be the one that would find its way to the front page of nearly every newspaper in the world over the next twenty-four hours.

The priest Graham and Peter were looking for was resident at the magnificent Catholic Metropolitan Cathedral that stands in true biblical fashion at the top of a mountain. Well, Mount Pleasant was at least the name of the road that led up to it. Many a pilgrimage had been made from the city to the top of this hill over the centuries, and the journey that Graham and Peter made on this day was filled with as much hope and prayer as any before. The Cathedral is suitably situated at the end of Hope Street, a mile away from the equally impressive Anglican Cathedral that stands in full glory at the other end of the road.

Together, when viewed from nearby or afar, they form one of the most impressive and awe inspiring sights of any city in the world. The Anglican Cathedral was built of sandstone, and construction had begun in 1902. It had taken nearly eighty years to complete the traditional styled building, with each stone carved by the hands of craftsmen; some of whom had spent their whole working life on the one project. In contrast the futuristic design of the Metropolitan Cathedral is a controversial piece of architecture that rises from the earth like a great spaceship, ordained with an enormous circular stained-glass crown, and it was towards here that the two men walked.

The housekeeper answered the door and, having explained the priest's absence, promised faithfully to give the message of the time of the birth to the priest the moment he returned from his business.

Graham then remembered the list that Janet had prepared over the weeks she had been at the maternity hospital; the one that had all the key names and numbers he should call immediately after the birth. He searched all the pockets of his trousers and jacket before realising that it was in the drawer of his bedside table for safekeeping. He understandably never imagined it would be like this; he thought that he would at least be told that the operation was going to be tomorrow or in two days' time, but never on the same day. He considered making the journey back across the Mersey to Wallasey but his instinct was to remain near Janet. He was aware of his fears and nervousness and knew that this short break was necessary for him to calm down but these feelings also fired up a courage and strength he had not felt before, and it made him want to return to Janet as soon as possible. He remembered how he had felt so helpless in the lounge of Browning Road when time and time again Janet had been given the negative results over the phone as they foraged through the fertility programme. Now he was determined to give Janet every ounce of support he could in these last few hours.

The two men agreed that they would make their lunch a quick one. As they approached the pub doors they decided that one pint each would be enough to settle their nerves, and that they would take Janet's advice and have something to eat. Then it would be straight back to the ward.

Among the first calls Graham made late that afternoon was one to his brother Dave, and within an hour he was parking his car in the hospital grounds. As Dave and Graham's sister, Sue, got out of the vehicle, Dave noticed another car pull up at the same time, and that the driver was Sam Abdulla. Dave had seen Sam once or twice while visiting but had never actually been introduced. Nevertheless Dave found himself staring like a schoolboy supporter at a football hero, and as he watched Sam calmly and confidently stride towards the back entrance of the hospital, he realised that this was the man who was about to take charge of one of the rarest and most difficult of births. Dave was going to be nowhere near the operating theatre and he was already wiping the beads of sweat from his brow.

With the other important calls having been made, a peacefulness filtered into the room as Janet relaxed before the operation. She thought about when, as a teenager, she first knew there were going to be problems about having children, and how she sensibly resigned herself to the only option of adoption. She thought of how she had explained to Graham before they got married what her problems were, and how he had reacted without hesitation saying that it made no difference whatsoever to him. She thought about how together they had gone through the stages of adoption and about the traumas of the fertility programmes, the pain and the heartaches, the disappointments and the torment. Then about the wonderful joys and thrills of being accepted for adoption, and then finally becoming pregnant. She thought also about the last five months; the time she had spent in hospital, the endurance and the determination, the discomfort and the suffering and of how Graham had always been there, never missing a day of visiting, ever reliable and a constant source of love. She held his hand.

It was as if a hurricane was about to strike. All the warnings were there of what was about to happen and what time it was likely to strike; yet, for the time being, there was nothing, just a mild and harmless breeze that was even quite pleasant.

The only interruption came late in the afternoon when the sister entered to give Janet her pre-med. And as the atmosphere around her grew more tense Janet was feeling more and more relaxed. She had remained so remarkably calm throughout the whole afternoon that the drug seemed hardly necessary, but, obedient as always, she made no fuss. Graham and Peter would probably have benefited more from the pre-med as they struggled, restless and fidgety with agitation, to show as much confidence as possible.

As the clock in Nancy's house approached seven o'clock, a key scraped against the metal of the lock of the front door before sliding snuggly into place. Nancy was sitting in darkness by the phone at the bottom of the stairs, and the noise made her jump and look up. From the light given out by a street lamp, she could clearly make out the familiar outline of her younger daughter through the frosted glass. Nancy had phoned Alison at work with the news that the operation was about to go ahead, and Alison had stopped off on her way home to alter her evening's arrangements. They both knew it would be at least an hour before there was a call from the hospital, so to give herself something to do Nancy made them a cup of tea and they waited together in the silence of the front room.

In Wallasey Graham's parents were keeping a close eye on the time, and as they sat together on the settee, mesmerised by the minute hand as it edged towards seven, they began to pray.

The journey to the operating theatre from Janet's room was not a long one. Janet did not have to change beds, she was to go to the theatre on her own bed. As they moved off, one of the wheels let out a little squeak. With the sister in attendance, Peter alongside and Graham pushing, the bed was slowly manoeuvred through the door of the room and positioned in the centre of the passage. The wheel continued to make a noise and the gentle squeak became drawn out and regular as the procession moved sedately towards the operating theatre. Janet looked over to her left as she lay on the bed and smiled as she passed Dave and Sue who were sitting in the open waiting area that was annexed off the corridor.

Graham grimaced as he grappled with the problem of trying to make the ride as smooth as possible for Janet. This was not as easy as it should have been. There was a powerful resistance as he pushed and pushed as if something was telling Graham to hold back. He stopped and looked over his shoulder to see how far he had gone. Behind him lay a large black track of rubber from the wheel that was tightly clamped by the brake. Among all the excitement, the sister had not taken the brake off the bed. However, the problem served well to break the tension in the air, and the wheel was as relieved as Graham. As they reached the theatre doors, he gave Janet a quick kiss and took a step back.

'Don't worry,' Janet said. 'Everything will be all right.'

The trolley was locked into position inside the room full of green gowns. There were fifteen medical staff members in all who had prepared and practised for what was to be one of the rarest Caesarean section operations ever performed, but there was only one face that Janet now wanted to see. As she lay on the table she looked up and was comforted by the reassuring eyes of Sam Abdulla. His head was positioned directly in line with the powerful spotlight that hung from above and for one precious moment an aura of light surrounded his capped and masked head. He gently placed his hands on either side of Janet's face and she could feel his smile of confidence as it beamed down from his eyes.

'Everything is going to be just fine ...' The words were spoken in a familiar warm and soothing tone, and Janet relaxed and was happy to allow the darkness of unconsciousness take control of her body. She totally trusted that voice, and as his words faded into the oblivion induced by anaesthetic, Janet had a deep feeling of contentment supported by an unquestioned inner knowledge that Sam had always told her the truth.

At 7.56 precisely the first baby emerged. It was a girl. Then came another girl. Then another ... and another. The excitement in the theatre grew as the possibility of them all being one sex was suddenly realised. The fifth was yet another girl, and then as the doctors, the nurses, and the midwives performed their individual specialist skills, there was almost a moment's silence as Sam delivered the sixth. The atmosphere was filled with as much euphoria as professional prudence would permit when Sam announced the final baby was also a girl. It was eight o'clock. All the babies were alive and as healthy as their tender prematurity would allow, and the whole delivery had been completed in just four miraculous minutes.

Oxford Street Maternity hospital had one of the best equipped intensive care units for babies, and all the technology and necessary machinery was at the ready; ventilators, incubators and monitors, all there to help with the ensuing fight for life. Consultant paediatrician Richard Cooke now took over the reins from Sam. His first responsibility was to steer the babies delicately through their first critical hours of life, and then until they were strong enough to go home. His task was helped by a mixture of medicine and luck that had seen the pregnancy through to thirty-two weeks. He knew, though, that there was another ingredient. The extraordinary calmness, determination and patience that Janet had shown throughout the whole time she had been in hospital must have contributed much to the success. Even at the most critical times when she had gone into labour she had not shown any signs of panic.

The only identical things about the girls, as one by one they came out of the operating theatre, were the little pink labels on their arms. They had different facial features; their hair ranged from a light blond to dark brown; they were different sizes and they had different blood groups. The labels were numbered one to six and the numbers were to correspond in order with the six names Janet and Graham had decided upon. First was Hannah Jane, the lightest at 2lb 1oz. Second was Lucy Anne, 2lb 15oz. Third was Ruth Michelle, 2lb 11oz. Fourth was Sarah Louise, 2lb 5oz. Fifth was Kate Elizabeth, 2lb 13oz. Sixth was Jennifer Rose, 3lb 8oz. Baby Jennifer had been the cause of the turning in Janet's tummy. She had been lying across the base of the womb which had given her the best position and a little extra freedom for development. But she was supporting all the others, and so when she moved, Janet really knew about it.

Graham's fingers felt like jelly as he tapped out the numbers on the phone. Only the hugs of joy from Peter, Dave and Sue in the waiting room, where the four of them had been incessantly sipping tea and pacing the floor in formation, had temporarily halted the trembling that possessed Graham when the news had come through that he was now the proud father of six baby daughters. He called his mum and dad, and then Nancy and Alison, turning both houses from silent sanctuaries of peaceful personal prayer into palaces of joy and jubilation. He then was taken to see his new-born flock and, finally, after a further hour he found himself sitting next to Janet who, feeling glorious even in her grogginess, kept repeating the same thing again and again. 'Six girls ... six girls ... six girls ...'

Later that night, as news of the extraordinary birth flashed across the globe, and as editors altered their front pages for the following morning, Graham lay in bed at his sister's house. He thought about how he had quietly left the hospital by the back door, avoiding the assembling members of the press. His van would not start in the car park, and he had found himself absurdly fiddling with the engine while journalists, desperate to interview him, were at the front entrance, pleading and begging the faithfully stubborn receptionists to tell them where he was. He thought about how he had driven past them thinking he had escaped their clutches, only to discover more of them encamped outside his and his parents' house in Wallasey and how Nancy and Peter were no doubt getting the same treatment. The bedclothes were warm and he tried to sleep, but a gentle trembling that had been with him all evening now turned into uncontrollable shaking as the reality of what had happened began to sink into his mind.

Confidence was high among the senior doctors that all the babies would survive. Four of the babies were breathing normally virtually straight away and only two were being given ventilation support. All of them, though, were going to be closely monitored around the clock and the first forty-eight hours were critical. At the end of that period only Lucy was still giving cause for concern. She was suffering from an illness common to premature babies known as 'respiratory distress syndrome', the result of immature lungs. Her chest needed massaging as regularly as possible to loosen gathering secretions. Normally fingers would be used but Lucy was far too small for this method so Richard Cooke used the unusual services of a simple electric toothbrush, a trick that had worked to great effect in the past. After a few days Lucy had recovered, was out of danger and was fit enough to join her sisters who, with a lot of dedicated nursing help, were concentrating on growing and getting strong enough to be introduced to the world.

Eight

The Homecoming

♡ ♡ ♡
♡ ♡
♡

Fretting was not a favourite pastime for Janet. As she had lain in her hospital bed she had often stared into the eye of anxiety with a steely indifference towards fear of the unknown. She had created for herself a canopy of protection that hung above her bed like a great mosquito net, keeping out the stings and suffering of unnecessary worry, steadfastly refusing entry to any other burden than the physical one she endured. The writhing discomfort of the pregnancy in its fullness was enough torment to bear without carrying the agitation of concern for the details of what may or may not be. How much help were they going to need? Who was going to supply this help? Would they be able to cope with six babies if the birth was successful? And if it was not successful ...? These questions had hovered above Janet and Graham as they talked only of the present, hardly daring to look any further than the next day, and as the time had drawn towards the thirty-second week, the next hour.

Outside this vacuum of Janet and Graham's, in which time had seemingly stood still, these questions had to be answered and it was essential that somebody helped them prepare for all eventualities. About four weeks before the birth Janet had started receiving visits from Gwyn Lautenberg who worked as a welfare officer on behalf of the hospital.

56

It was her job to take the pressure off a patient if it was clear that there was a strong possibility their hospitalisation would produce problems of a social, psychological or economic nature. She seemed to know how Janet and Graham felt, and she understood how they could not bring themselves to consider the future in case they were tempting fate.

In contrast to the doctors and nursing staff, Gwyn wore no uniform nor a white coat, and like a young and sprightly Miss Marple she went about her business without any fuss. Her visits had the comfort of a fireside chat; never overpowering or officious, always like a friend popping around for a cup of tea. There was a relaxed atmosphere and a feeling of confidence engendered by her matter of fact manner as she relayed stories of the latest suggestions of the Wirral Health Authority who had the task of deciding how much assistance the family would require.

But behind the joviality expressed in her regular catchphrase call of, 'Don't say fine if you're not fine!' at the end of each of her cosy visits, there was genuine and serious concern for the couple's well-being. She had to be sure that they could cope, and with almost psychiatric low-key counselling she gradually broke through the barrier and gently led them to talk about everything. It was invaluable therapy that drowned those other worries they did not want to be concerned with before the birth, and left them confident in the knowledge that someone was dealing with matters in their best interest and thus giving them as much peace of mind as was possible under the circumstances.

Gwyn acted as go-between, mediator and negotiator with the various social services that would be able to give help when needed. The greatest problem was that the situation was so unusual that nobody really knew what would be right, and everything, in many respects, had to be guess work. It was clear there was going to have to be a bit of experimenting to see exactly what was required once Janet and Graham finally got home.

The exodus of the Walton girls from the hospital began on 2 January 1984. In order to make things as easy as possible to settle into crowded domesticity, Janet and Graham decided upon an Arkian plan of bringing their offspring out of the hospital two by two by two. It would have been like asking a lame lion tamer to juggle on a tight rope to expect Janet and Graham to adjust and cope with all the girls coming home at once and diving into routines so suddenly. It was far too much too soon to deal with and it was clearly vital for them to be able to take things gradually from the shallow end.

Before the birth neither Janet nor Graham had come into contact with a nappy, and now their lives were going to be insulated with them for the next two years. They knew that the activity in their house was going to have to become fully automated, and like any large piece of machinery there were going to be many parts to consider, some very delicate and the situation needed a running-in period. By the time the nursery revolution had gripped the Walton household, Janet and Graham were determined their machinery would run smoothly. They felt that they had to learn quickly and Browning Road would have to become a kind of preparatory school for parental nursery training whereby they would gradually over the next few weeks become expert at the logical art of bringing up babies.

If things were going to be crowded and busy then it was something to which they were going to have to become accustomed over a period of time and so, even though they had become naturally more and more impatient to bring their daughters home, it was sensible to wait just a little longer before they would all be together at home as a family.

It was not difficult for Janet and Graham to decide which of their six children would be the first to come home. Jenny had always been the biggest and had shown herself to be the most sturdy of the babies, and so there was no doubt that she would be one of the first to leave, and Kate had made such remarkable progress that the doctors were pleased to advise that it would be sensible for her to join Jenny. Lucy, though, had been the one that had given the most worry at the start, so the extra stay in hospital was not going to do her any harm. Hannah, Sarah and Ruth having been so tiny at birth were benefiting from the specialised care and gaining strength each day, so Janet and Graham agreed it would do no harm for them to miss the cold weather of the heart of winter for at least another couple of weeks.

Since the birth had been so close to the new year, more than a few glasses had chinked over the celebrations in Wallasey at the end of 1983 to toast the arrival of the town's most famous babies, and much champagne was enjoyed as everyone tried to remember each of the girls' names. Kate and Jenny would possibly have been ready to come out a little earlier but any extra days that a premature baby gets in a special care unit are a bonus, and, besides, there was a feeling of significance in the family beginning their new life in the freshness of a new year.

The Homecoming

So with celebrations over, resolutions cracking at the seams, the world once again sober, and everyone depressed by the wind, rain and thought of only one more day's holiday before returning to work, the news of Kate and Jennifer's homecoming was one of the few things to smile about on that grey Monday morning. The worst of weather, however, could hold no misery for Janet and Graham as they proudly waved their goodbyes to the nursing staff for the first time and made their way from the special care unit each with a daughter in their arms, well wrapped up for protection against the elements. Like so many successes before them, the great stone pillars of the main entrance of the Maternity Hospital in Liverpool, witnessed yet another happy couple carrying away life's most precious gift; unlike so many before they were carrying one each; and unlike any before they were leaving four behind – to be called for later! The cameras were there, of course, to record the event, and as Janet and Graham left for home with Hannah, Lucy, Ruth and Sarah in mind, they whispered to Kate and Jenny of how they would be bringing their sisters to join them soon.

There was no room for broken resolutions in Browning Road. The gratitude they had for their good fortune had cemented their single mindedness and determination to devote themselves entirely to the girls, and, in the spirit of starting as they meant to go on, they set about taking their two daughters for their first walk. This was not as straight forward as one might first imagine, for the world's most famous babies were as yet without their own transport. The problem was quickly solved with the delivery of one large green pram. The thought, however, of housing six of these traditional-sized modes of transport made Janet and Graham chuckle when they considered how much furniture and how many walls would need to be removed to accommodate them.

Even three twin ones would be out of the question. Sadly, the well-sprung suspension and padded upholstery of this particular perambulator was one of the finer luxuries the girls were going to have to do without. In the meantime, the carriage that was on loan from Graham's sister-in-law, Chris, had passed its MOT, would just about permit people the room to pass it when parked in the narrow hall, and was perfect for at least one of the girls to travel in comfort. And that was enough.

On the second day after the girls had come out of hospital there was snow on the ground. With Janet still feeling quite weak, they protected themselves and their daughters from the freezing cold, and like a scene from *Doctor Zhivago*, they slowly took the walk to visit Graham's parents, with Janet pushing one baby in the pram and Graham carrying the other inside his coat. Jenny had the pleasure of the ride on the way there, and Kate had her turn on the way back. Janet was exhausted when they finally got back home, and they were cold, but it was such a big moment for them to be able to go out for a walk with their own children that it was worth the effort. That first walk was something special. They had both secretly dreamt about it for so long now that it was as fundamentally important to them as the first walk on the moon was to Neil Armstrong. It was the most wonderful feeling in the world.

As each day passed, Janet and Graham knew that their original idea of the girls coming out two at a time was not going to work. They had been a part of Janet for twenty-four hours a day since she went into hospital six months ago, and while she knew they were in the best of care she was desperate to have them all together again. They were also getting more and more adept at handling the babies, carrying out with relative ease all that they had been shown in the hospital, with Graham becoming just as skilled as Janet in nappy changing and feeding. They were aware things would be totally different when all six were at home but the arrangements they had made through Gwyn Lautenberg had now been sorted out and they were now confident that with the extra help of the nursery nurses they would be able to cope with all the babies at home. Visiting also was not as simple as it had been expected. They did not want a day to go by when they were not involved at some stage in the feeding of all their girls. With four of them still in hospital, and with Janet and Graham only able to visit separately because they could not arrange for babysitters for Kate and Jenny, it was impossible to give Hannah, Lucy, Ruth and Sarah their full attention. It was getting harder and the best solution was to get it all done in one go and bring all four out together.

The date was set for 16 January, two weeks after Kate and Jenny had come home. It would be forty-nine days after the girls were born that the family would at last be together at home, if not alone, at least together under their own roof. Sunday the fifteenth was to be the last day that either of them would be visiting alone. That morning, leaving Janet with the girls at home, Graham whistled his way in the van through the Mersey Tunnel across to Liverpool happily looking forward to the next day.

As usual, Graham walked into the small changing room conveniently situated in the foyer area of the special care unit. It was opposite a wall adorned with hundreds of photographs of all the babies that had been under the watchful eyes of the staff. He slipped off his jacket and into the long white gown, impatiently securing it at the back. Then he stepped into the overshoes that were also compulsory attire. Every precaution was taken by the hospital to avoid any possibility of infection being brought into the unit.

Covered from head to foot in white, his disguised ghost-like figure passed through the double swing doors of the department. As he entered, he glanced to the left and he noticed a couple of the nurses tending to some of the babies that were in incubators. Thankful that all his girls had come through that nerve-racking period when their lives were supported by wires, tubes and machinery, he decided not to bother the nurses with small talk and to leave them to more serious matters. Both he and Janet were treated almost like members of staff and had been told that whenever they arrived to just put on the white garments, clean up and get on with tending to the girls. Either the sister or one of the nurses would be along soon and he saw no reason to wait so he briskly walked towards the room at the end of the corridor.

The rooms were set out in a line from left to right; those on the extreme left housed the illest or the smallest babies and, as they got better and bigger, they would gradually move room by room over to the extreme right. It carried much emotional significance for parents and staff alike as each baby eventually made it to a cot in that end room and prepared for departure.

A window alongside the door displayed the four cots, but anxious to have contact with his daughters Graham did not stop to admire the scene. He went in and as usual let his eyes pass from one cot to the next as he said hello to Hannah, Sarah, Lucy, and ... The fourth cot was unoccupied. Where was Ruth? There was no way, he told himself, that she should or could be anywhere other than in that room.

Looking forlorn and shroud-like, a cream crumpled empty blanket haunted Graham for the next few moments as each of his senses registered shock. The distress was as sharp as a sword as it cut through his confidence persuading him that something was very wrong. He kept swallowing and his temples throbbed as thoughts scrambled about his head like panic stricken people in an air-raid. Where was she?

Peacefully indifferent to the explosion Graham was living through, his three other daughters lay asleep with their sheets unruffled and up to their chins. Seeing them seemed to calm the ripples of turmoil and it did not take him long to gather himself together. He did not want to show any sign of the pandemonium that he had been feeling as he realised that he must find the nurses to see what was going on. He made his way to the other end of the corridor, back down towards the incubators.

The nurses Graham had seen earlier were attending to Ruth. There was no explanation; she had simply blacked out, and had stopped breathing. Graham was devastated. The girls had come so far and done so well since the birth, and now he had to face the fact that one of his daughters had been close to death. Losing one of them now, after all they had been through, would have been so much more painful than had any not made it at birth. The doctors had prepared Janet and Graham for that possibility, and while the loss would have been very great, death at this stage would have been more difficult to accept.

Ruth's crimped countenance seemed to reflect the hard time she had just gone through as Graham looked at the pitiful sight of his puppeted daughter strung up once again with a myriad of wires. Rapid assurances flew at him from the nurses. She had responded immediately to treatment and would only be kept in the incubator as a precautionary measure to monitor her over the next twenty-four hours. The doctors confirmed a little later that she would be absolutely fine, but as Graham relayed the whole story over the phone to Janet it was obvious that Ruth would not be able to leave hospital with her sisters the next day.

A veil of secrecy was placed carefully over why Ruth would not be joining her sisters at home. All the press reports were identical, informing the public that she had developed a slight cold, and, with Janet confirming that she had a bit of a snuffle, it was enough to throw everyone off the trail. With the expected interest in their departure, the hospital felt that it would put unnecessary pressure on Janet and Graham if the real reason for Ruth's prolonged stay in the special care unit was revealed. It may easily have been that Ruth's sudden and mysterious turn would have dominated the news items about the family the day after Hannah, Sarah and Lucy went home, but, as it turned out, it was neither the illness nor the homecoming that was ultimately of interest to the editors of Fleet Street.

With the assistance of Gwyn Lautenberg the amount of help had finally been decided upon, although everyone agreed it was impossible to know precisely what was required. For the first two weeks while

Janet and Graham had only Kate and Jenny at home, the Social Services supplied just one extra pair of helping hands in the capable form of Sue Perry. She was enough at that stage and was just what Janet and Graham needed. The nursing help was to begin in earnest when all or most of the babies had arrived home. The day before the foursome were due to come out, the young women who had been appointed as nursery nurses went along to meet Janet and Graham to get to know them and make things easier for the next day. The next day, though, the Wirral Area Health Authority, who were supplying the extra nurse, buckled to the pressure of the press and distributed information that most might have regarded as personal and private.

On the day Janet and Graham said their goodbyes to the staff at the special care unit for the second time, this time under the cloud of concern that Ruth had created, the headlines on the front page of a local paper unjustifiably shouted out, 'The Free Baby-Sit'. It carried an article querying the generosity of the nursing help, saying that it had already led to controversy. The paper told its readers that the Waltons were 'to have a team of four nurses on duty at night in their Wirral home'. The article went on to say, 'To many, the idea of three nursery nurses with a fourth to be appointed to care for the babies from 10 p.m. to 8 a.m. is excessive, over the top'. Who could disagree with that? Who could sleep with that? So many nurses sitting on the other side of a wafer-thin wall caring for six babies? Even if that many could have been accommodated in the front bedroom at Browning Road they would not have been able to move about without causing problems. It would not have been over generous, it would have been just plain foolhardy, and it certainly was not something that Janet and Graham had asked for. They were grateful for the help that they were offered, and had agreed on only two nurses at first to help through the night.

The next day the national press carried stories of numbers of helpers ranging from eight nannies to thirteen helpers to a team of seventeen! The Authority had revealed that the cost of the help for the first three months stood at £8,000. The team of seventeen, as one paper put it, included the eight nannies, health visitors, home-helps, a nursing officer and a G.P. All of a sudden, it seemed having a G.P. was a privilege to which others are not entitled. In actual fact, during the day there would be one nurse and an assistant from the social services on duty from eight in the morning until five in the afternoon; the night shift of two nurses was to run from ten at night through to eight the next morning.

Brenda Buttle, the Assistant Director of Community Nursing, was bombarded with questions, but she could only reflect the discussions she had had over the past few weeks with Gwyn Lautenberg and Janet and Graham. She confirmed that the family wanted to help themselves and had not been demanding assistance. Along with Gwyn she was aware of how too much help could be just as damaging as not enough, and the last thing that Janet and Graham wanted was to be treated as hired hands in their own house, to be over-run with assistance and to be distanced from their own children.

It was all a bit of an experiment to be reviewed after three months, and there was an understanding that as soon as Janet and Graham felt that they could look after the girls themselves then the help would be reduced. The issue had generated a great deal of public interest, and it was not long before all the newspapers turned the spotlight on to Karen Davies, Debbie Bullen and Christina James, the first of the nurses to dip their elbows in the bath water.

As Graham yawned, feeling the effects of a sleepless night, he tried to concentrate on the next job in hand. He stood in his kitchen and felt like an apprentice as he was shown by one of the nurses how to use the sterilising units that had recently arrived. On the radio he heard the midday news report the story of the nurses and the help that he and Janet were receiving from the Health Authority and Social Services, and once again Graham thought of what had happened to Ruth over the week-end and of what news reports he may have been listening to that morning.

The next programme on the radio was 'Town and Around', a phone-in programme that invited comment on up-to-the-minute news stories. Graham held his breath when he heard the presenter, Roger Phillips, announce that one of the topics under discussion for the next hour was to be the so-called 'Free Baby-sit', and that the telephone lines were open so any one wanting to make any comments should phone now. Graham called Janet and together with the nurses they listened in the bedroom as they fed, as they cleaned, as they changed and as they embarked on a routine that would carry on regardless of all the opinion. They had been upset by the story, but as they listened to call after call all feelings of tiredness disappeared as they were heartened by wonderful words of encouragement from the local people. Nearly all disagreed strongly with the story the paper had run, and most said they felt it was right for the family to receive the help it was offered.

In the middle of all the activity going on in the bedroom they heard Roger Phillips ask, 'Perhaps if Mr and Mrs Walton are listening they would like to phone in and put us right?' Janet looked at Graham through the haze of talcum powder as she splashed water over Jenny in the plastic bath, and she laughed as she watched him pull a face as he changed another of the girls and placed the results in a bin bag. 'Even if I had another pair of hands,' she said, 'I think there are a few other things I'd do first before making any phone calls! Maybe we should give him a ring and ask him to come round and give us a hand?'

Nine

A Full House

♡ ♡ ♡
♡ ♡
♡

Three weeks after Kate and Jenny had left the hospital, and seven days after Hannah, Sarah and Lucy had done the same, Ruth, or Babe Ruth as she was newly christened by the press after the American baseball star, weighing in at a fine and healthy 6 pounds and 15 ounces and sporting a pink and white shawl, finally made her home run to join her sisters. And at last the family was complete.

All of a sudden the little house seemed ridiculously overcrowded. With Graham at home and their mothers ready and willing to help whenever needed, they decided to cope without one of the day nurses. One of the things that Janet and Graham had decided right from the very start, even before the babies were born, was that whatever help was offered they would definitely insist on having some time to themselves. It was a way of retaining their independence and a vital way of proving to themselves that they could cope.

The hours between five and ten in the evening were designated as family-only hours, and do or die they were determined to do without the help of outsiders. With all the press coverage about the amount of help they were receiving it was paradoxical that they had to argue quite strongly to get this period on their own. The Health Authority, perhaps understandably, thought that the five hours was too long for them to be without nurses and suggested that they should have a shorter period alone. They were genuinely and clearly trying to look after Janet and Graham's best interests, but whatever reasoning was put forward the couple politely but firmly refused to budge. It was important for them to find out how they were going to manage on their own. Graham's mother would sometimes pop in to help out, and now and again a friend might come round during those hours, but in the main they were on their own.

One evening, just after the day nurse had left and the girls had settled down to sleep, the phone rang. 'Who was that?' Janet casually asked as Graham walked into the lounge with their coffee. 'Just one of the lads,' replied Graham, referring to his friends from the local five-a-side football team he used to play regularly for. Understandably, though, he had missed quite a few games recently. 'They were a man short for the game tonight and wondered if there was any chance of me playing. I told him to behave himself; there was no chance. Maybe in a few weeks when we are a bit more organised.'

All of a sudden Janet saw an opportunity and decided to go for it. 'Why don't you go?' she asked in a totally nonchalant way that surprised him. She knew that he would love to play and the exercise would do him good but was equally sure he would not dream of leaving her alone with all six girls. But something inside her persisted. 'The girls are all asleep and it's only for an hour, and there's bound to come a time when we are going to have to be on our own with them. So why not now? Go on, give him a ring back and say yes. I'll be all right.' She gave a host of other reasons why it would be perfectly all right, and got so excited about the opportunity that the whole idea began to sound sensible. Graham's resistance collapsed in the face of her confidence, and he made the call.

The moment she closed the door Janet felt a shiver go down her back, and she thought to herself, 'Oh, no! How on earth am I going to manage if they all wake up?' Maybe it was madness or just the instinct of a mother but somehow she knew that if they did all wake up at once one way or another she could cope. Besides, she knew she could always phone Betty.

The babies slept without noticing their dad's absence, and were still fast asleep when he returned exhausted from the strain of exercise and worry. Janet was equally exhausted, but only from worry that the girls might wake. It made them think twice about doing it again for a while, but the exhilaration Janet felt being alone with the girls for the first time gave them both a tremendous boost and encouragement that the future was indeed going to be all right.

At breakfast there was always someone else in the house and at lunchtime it was no different, but now at least they had the chance of having their evening meal on their own. And as each day passed, Janet and Graham came to appreciate more and more the privacy and intimacy of the five hours they had alone as a family. It was not, however, the quietest period of the day, and it certainly was not a time for putting their feet up, but no matter how much they had to do at least they could talk to each other without being overheard in their own house. Now and again when they wanted to chat about something personal, they would often find themselves furtively whispering in the bathroom or in some other quiet corner. And if they wanted to shout or curse they found themselves having to hold their tongues, aware that the extra help about the place came packaged with extra eyes and ears. The nurses were always pleasant, hard working and respectful, but while they were there Janet and Graham's house was not a home.

Once Ruth was home, she moved straight into the principal bedroom with her sisters. No matter which way they had looked at the best way of accommodating their new family, space was at a high premium. The six navy-blue carrycots were easily large enough for the girls to sleep in comfortably but they still took up considerable space when lined up together. Janet and Graham were faced with the fact that there were only two rooms big enough to be the nursery: the lounge on the ground floor, and the principal bedroom. The lounge was the only room suitable for entertaining, eating, and relaxing, and was a key to their sanity. The ultimate sacrifice was therefore made, and the master and mistress of the manor evicted themselves from the main bedroom taking their bed through to the small back room. It was a squeeze, but a far better option than losing the whole of the downstairs to the babies.

The routine charts and timetables covering the wall in the makeshift nursery could now be finalised. There were so many figures to fill in, it was not long before the wall looked as if it would be more at home in an auditor's office. Everything was in columns of six with the girls' names always in the order they had been given at hospital: Hannah, Lucy, Ruth, Sarah, Kate and Jenny. There was a weekly record of their height and weight, and records of feeds, baths and changes were kept on a daily basis, not so much for posterity but for more practical reasons.

With so much activity there was more than one occasion when one of the babies screamed out in protest to make the point that bathing her a second time was not going to make her any cleaner, or a full bottle would be offered to one who had just been fed. The rotas and timetables made sure that these events were few and far between – it was enough work doing it all once in a day.

When all the babies were first at home the routine of changing, bathing and feeding took place every four hours. Six changes and feeds for each baby meant thirty-six nappies per girl per day, and the same quantity of bottles. (Janet and Graham were going to have to buy over 250 nappies per week for the next two years, which would amount to a grand total of more than 13,000!)

When it came to feeding time it was all hands to the pump, and any relative or friend who happened to arrive as the milk began to flow was usually made more than welcome. Even when it was the Lord Mayor of Wallasey or Lynda Chalker, the local MP and Minister of Foreign Affairs, there was no escaping a bottle, a bib and a burp. And it was certainly useful if there happened to be six people in the house available to help feed the babies all at once. Everything was so much more efficient whenever that was the case but the procedure still took ages. It was never just a case of giving them their bottles. Winding the babies could not be rushed and there were always one or two of them who took their time no matter what method of back rubbing was used. They obviously did not like to burp in public and, with a room invariably crowded with people, who could blame them? And as soon as the sixth girl had been changed and finally put to sleep, it was almost time to start the whole process again before Janet and Graham had a chance to take a break and a cup of coffee.

The pressure was slightly eased at home by the generosity of the milk company who provided the family with enough disposable bottle feeds to last for the first six weeks at home. The feeds were very easy to use. The teats were packed and sealed separately, and all that was needed was to remove the top of the bottle and attach the teat. Anything that saved time or helped to make things easier was gratefully received. Always thinking ahead, and being thrifty, Janet and Graham would not throw the bottles or teats away, they were going to need so many in the future that it was worth the effort of sterilising and storing them.

Once the well of disposable feeds ran dry, though, the small kitchen became a small milk factory. On the workbench sat three sterilising units, each cleansing two bottles at a time with as many teats thrown in as possible. Meanwhile, the feeds would be prepared. There would have been a little dissension in the babychair ranks if the girls had to wait long for their milk, so Janet would make sure that there were stocks of at least three feeds always on hand in the fridge, and it wasn't always easy to find room for eighteen bottles!

At three o'clock one morning, battle-weary from lack of sleep in the cramped and claustrophobic back room, Graham turned back the duvet and dragged his legs over the side of the bed. As he opened his mouth to yawn, the only sound he heard was the hungry cry of a baby.

It made no difference that the nurses were there. If either Janet or Graham were woken by the sound of any of the babies crying it was only natural that they should go to them. Graham sat for a few seconds in the dark and strained his ears. He tried to guess which one it was. Night after night as the first distress signals were heard through the wall, he and Janet would whisper the girls' names to each other, trying to recognise who it was. Invariably, though, by the time they arrived in the nursery to help with the feeds and changes the crying of one had blended into a chorus of six.

Graham turned and was not surprised to see Janet awake but was slightly puzzled that she had not yet got out of bed. Normally, he thought, she would have gone straight to the girls. She lay quite still, with her hands behind her head on the pillow. Her eyes glistened and he could see she was clearly upset. She had been so calm and strong since being in hospital and nothing had seemed to worry her, but now Graham knew that she was beginning to hurt.

At first Graham thought that it might have been the lack of privacy. They had talked so much over the past few days about how awkward it was just getting dressed in the morning, with most of their clothes hanging in the wardrobe in what was now the nursery. There was something else as well, he thought. It only happened the day before. One of the nurses had waltzed into the bathroom, while Janet was having a bath, to ask if her boyfriend could come in and wait for her in the lounge. He knew that episode had embarrassed and upset her. Maybe that was it.

Although the sound of crying came from next door Graham did not have to move to see the real tears. Trying to coax Janet into the familiar guessing game, and encourage her into a better mood, Graham said, 'That's Ruth I reckon.' But there was no agreement or contradiction.

Any reaction would have been better than the cold silence that hung over the bed. Whatever was on her mind had to be discussed. They both knew that bottling things up would only affect the way they would tend to the girls.

'It's unfair,' Janet said, composing herself and not waiting for questions. She was bitter with herself for allowing resentment and complaint to fester, and she knew it was best to talk about it. She wiped the corner of her eye and looked at Graham, 'Why can't we cope without all this help and look after our own children? Everyone should be able to ... Why can't we?'

Now Graham understood. 'They are our children Jan and we can cope,' he answered reassuringly. 'We're there all the time, and we're doing all that we can. The work doesn't frighten us does it?'

'It's not the work,' Janet continued in a whisper. 'It's the fact that we just haven't got enough hands to look after our own. It's the impossibility of looking after them without help, just the physical impossibility!' There was an uncomfortable degree of despair in her voice.

'There's nobody here between five and ten Jan – we're on our own then and we cope all right, don't we? The important thing is that the kids know who their parents are, and, besides, the nurses are only going to be here for a few weeks.'

'It's not that I'm not grateful for the help. I am. It's just that I want to do things for myself.'

Coming to terms with the impossibility of being able to give themselves fully to all of the girls all of the time was probably the single most difficult fact for Janet and Graham to face. There was no way that they could have managed without the nurses but the frustration at times was difficult to bear. There always seemed to be someone else in the house and it was as if Janet and Graham were not allowed to be alone with their children. Over the past few days especially, Janet was constantly finding her actions being pre-empted by the nurses. She would go to mix the milk and someone would already have done it; bottles would be in the steriliser ahead of her; and one of her babies would be attended to before she had a chance to turn round.

Just talking about it made Janet feel at least a little better, and as she got up and put her dressing-gown on she said, 'And anyway, I'll bet that wasn't Ruth. I reckon it was Kate.' They were both wrong. The first to wake had been Sarah but it made little difference when they walked into their old bedroom. There were welcoming looks on the nurses' faces as four of the girls were awake and Lucy was showing signs of following suit. Only Jenny looked as if she might make it through the night.

As the weeks moved on, Janet and Graham had an idea that the girls would sleep longer if there was nobody in the room. As it was, when the girls did wake and see the nurses they would cry for attention, whereas if they did not see anyone they may just go back to sleep.

It was decided, and from then on the nurses stayed downstairs in Browning Road until any of the girls cried. The four nurses, Debbie, Tina, Julie and Karen, changed their shifts every three nights, and would arrive at ten o'clock in time for the scheduled feed. At first they would make up the bottles and carry out all the usual preparations as soon as they got there. However, Janet and Graham decided they would do it themselves. They prepared the feeds for the whole night ahead during their five hours alone. For once, they felt they were in control, were taking the initiative and enjoying every minute of it.

Soon it was time to consider reducing the amount of bottles the girls were having during each twenty-four-hour period, and it was only sensible to drop the night feeds as soon as possible. At first the feeds were every four hours, but now the plan was to let nature take its course and 'feed on demand' rather than to wake them. Janet and Graham had become concerned that some of the girls may get too used to having that feed in the middle of the night. If they continued to wake them it was almost like forcing a situation that was unnecessary and they were worried it may become habit forming. Sometimes they tried a last feed at midnight instead of ten and on occasion some of the girls slept right through to seven the next morning. But never all of them. No matter which way the wand was waved at least one was always going to wake! If they had realised at that point that, allowing for a couple of week-end breaks here and there, they were going to have about five nights full and undisturbed sleep over the next five years, they would probably have considered joining the Magic Circle to search for some somnific sorcery or slumber inducing spell!

Given the choice, Janet and Graham would have preferred the nurses not to have worn their official uniforms every night. It was, though, something that Miss Buttle insisted on and she used to remind Janet to make sure it was done. Even though they were coming each night and day to do a job, for the time they were there they became part of the family. Among other things, though, it shot holes in their social life. If they had invited friends to the house Graham would develop a nervous twitch as ten o'clock approached and all the girls were soundly asleep. When the nurses arrived it made no sense to send them straight upstairs, so they asked them to sit in the only suitable room they had downstairs, the lounge. There were times, however, when Janet and Graham felt they could hear their friends thinking, 'What are they sitting here for?' as they ate a Chinese and sipped their wine with two uniformed nurses for an audience.

Hunting that rare breed of animal 'the perfect house' is not easy at the best of times, and for Janet and Graham, who seldom found time to step foot outside their own front door, it involved a series of major explorations. Nevertheless, they knew that they could not carry on much longer within the confines of Browning Road, and wanted to carry out the move as quickly as possible.

The reality was that with all the girls now home from hospital the house felt like a brick-built pressure cooker bubbling over with all the activity going on. There were no arguments or raised voices, just a constant feeling of tension in the air. The little house was often as tightly packed as a tin of sardines and as busy as a rush-hour bus stop. Occasionally bodies in the narrow hallway came to a standstill as people queued to get from the lounge to the kitchen, and at the same time the front door would yawn open as yet another person entered trying not to trip over the three double buggies tucked to the side of the stairs.

Early on in their property search, Janet and Graham soon realised that their ideal home was not going to be a sensible proposition. They had wanted a large old house with high ceilings, plenty of rooms, lots of nooks and crannies, and a large garden for the girls to play in as they grew older. If they had taken on a house fitting that description there would have been far too much work to do to make it habitable in time. With this in mind, and some interesting noises being made by one or two larger housebuilders in terms of a discount, they concentrated on new houses that were being built on estates in the area. Nothing was being built at the time in Wallasey itself, and they did not want to move too far away, which would make it difficult for the grandparents to visit, so finally it came down to a choice of one.

The construction firm Wimpey had completed the first stage of an estate they were developing in an area called Bidston not too far from Wallasey. Eleanor Road was the only access to the site. Darkened by the shade of overhanging trees it was bordered by large and impressive rambling houses on one side and a forest on the other as it wound along the side of Bidston Hill. High above and well camouflaged by the foliage were an observatory and a windmill, both well-known Wirral landmarks that could be seen from both Liverpool and North Wales on clear days. Just before a gate that led to Bidston Hall and a footpath to Bidston Hall Farm, a new road had been created to the left that led to a flock of young York-stone homes.

The first time Janet and Graham drove down Statham Avenue they could not help noticing the gaping emptiness in the distance as only a handful of properties had been finished and a field still dominated the patch. The light-brown buildings, though, had a friendliness about them as they nestled comfortably next to each other in the field. They were all four-bedroomed, all detached, all with fair-sized gardens and all spoken for ... except for the show house. It was not in the same league as the huge stately houses on Eleanor Road and it was not the type of house they would ideally have liked, but it did have the extra space they were so desperate for. More importantly, it was available, and with a few small alterations they would be able to move into it in the first week in March.

The fact that it was a show house made life so much easier. Not only were they able to forget about installing damp courses and central heating, modernising bathrooms and kitchens, repairing roofs and all the other problems associated with buying older properties, they now did not have to worry about carpets, curtains and decorating. There was nothing to do! They would literally be able, in one day, to move everyone and everything from Browning Road into the new house in Bidston and carry on with the routines of living the next day. The double garage that was purpose-built for the property and had been temporarily converted into offices for the show house became, with a little alteration in advance of their arrival, two badly needed extra rooms. One was to be a laundry room, for which they would need to install a second washing machine and drier, the other a play room for the babies.

A couple of weeks before the move the question of the cots came up. Graham was feeding Ruth and, as usual, without hardly realising it they were speaking to each other through the girls. 'Well Kate,' said Graham, repositioning the bottle in his daughter's mouth, 'just think, it won't be long now before you'll be moving into a nice new house.' Kate dribbled her milk in approval. 'And guess what?' he wiped her chin and did not wait for a reply, 'there's going to be no more slumming in tiny carrycots. You and your sisters are going to have nice new big cots as well! Would you like that? You would? Well mummy and daddy better hurry up and buy them then!'

'Judging by your size already, Jen,' quipped Janet, 'I think you'll be made up! Won't you?' And turning to Graham, she continued, 'She's giggling just hearing about it. Look at her smile, Gray. I'm sure she knows what we're talking about.' She straightened Jenny up and began rubbing her back and gently patting it. 'Well we can't bring the cots here, Jen, can we, there's no room, and we can't leave them in the street can we?' Jenny burped and Janet took that to be a mischievous yes. 'I beg your pardon!' Janet said in a mock school-marmish manner, to the delight of her biggest daughter. 'I beg your pardon!' she repeated, and was rewarded by an even bigger giggle. 'We'll just have to buy them as near to the time as possible and store them in the new house till we get there. Won't we Jen?'

The discussion was taking place in the nursery and, as usual, as well as each of them feeding a baby, a third was being fed by the day nurse Sue Perry. Listening to the conversation, Sue offered her help to put up the cots when the time was right. 'I'll see if my boyfriend will give a hand as well,' Sue said, anticipating the task that lay ahead. Cots are notoriously awkward things to assemble. Two people attempting one cot is a job in itself, but putting six together was a task more fitting for an assembly line at Fords. They were grateful for the offer of help.

They decided, in between a few agreeable gurgles, that they would purchase the cots the day before the move and arrange for babysitters the same night so that they could assemble them at the new house. Not surprisingly, it took much longer to finish constructing the wooden frames, and the four weary workers struggled with metal bars, loose screws, and obstinate nuts and bolts into the early hours of the morning.

Finally, with the last mattress in place, and two cots in one room and four in another, Sue and her boyfriend left and Janet and Graham went back upstairs to decide whether to put Lucy with Ruth in the smaller room, or Jenny with Kate, or maybe Sarah with Hannah. It was far too late to think about it, and they knew it would be trial and error in any event, with sleeping arrangements for the girls something that would no doubt be a game of musical beds over the years. Graham's mind wandered into the future imagining the girls in a couple of years' time bouncing on their beds, running from room to room, hiding under duvets. 'Won't always be as quiet as this,' he said, leaning on the doorpost of the larger room and looking at the four empty cots. They were tired but happy with the night's work. 'You're not kidding!' agreed Janet. There was no other furniture in the house so they sat shoulder to shoulder on the floor and sipped coffee from a flask and soaked in the peace before returning for their last night at their first home.

The day of the move was absolute bedlam. Not only were there the removal men, Wimpey people, gasmen, electricians, general helpers and family, but there was also a film crew recording the event as part of a documentary, and the press who were allowed to attend on the understanding that they did not obstruct the job in hand. In fact, the media that day surpassed themselves. Rather than getting in the way they did their best to help, to the extent of carrying cameras and note pads in one hand and a chair, lamp or coffee table in the other!

· Ten ·

The Christening

♡ ♡ ♡
♡ ♡
♡

No matter how much thought and planning was put in to the rapidly approaching christening, Janet and Graham knew that it was going to be a difficult day. It was also, however, a very special day, and once again determination began to play a dominant role to ensure that no matter how many press or television people were there, no matter how much hustle and bustle there was, the day was going to be perfect.

There was much to organise, but plans for the big day began to fall into place. The first and most important thing was to book the church. Sunday would not be the most convenient day to perform the service because with so many people involved the normal services would be affected, so it was agreed that Saturday would be better.

On an early March morning Janet, equipped with Sarah under one arm, a telephone in one hand and Graham's Liverpool Football Club fixture list in the other, made a call to Canon Keogh. Her finger nimbly scanned over the dates, helping her separate the 'Homes' from the 'Aways' as the priest made suggestions for a mutually convenient day.

'How would the fifth of May be suiting you, Mrs Walton?' he asked, with a soft Irish accent.

'Eh ... Janet hesitated, glancing down at the list and seeing the red print of a home fixture. 'A little later may be a bit better. It would give more time to get the invitations out. There's over 200 coming you know.' She waited for the bolt of lightning but all she got was a harmless little burp from Sarah.

'Ah, yes, I see,' he said, slightly puzzled as the date of the fifth was still a long way off. 'Now, what about the nineteenth of May, how will that be suiting you?' Sarah burped again, this time without restraint. 'I'm sorry, I didn't quite catch that, Mrs Walton.'

Seeing that this second suggested date was the hallowed day of the FA Cup Final, Janet, making full use of her daughter's timely interruption, ignored the Canon's offer. Wembley Stadium, where the Final would be held, was the Mecca for all true football supporters and, due to their success of recent years, had become a second home for Liverpool. The chances, Janet thought were extremely high that the team would play there again. 'Really,' she said as sweetly as possible, 'the very best day would be the twelfth of May. Would that be all right with you?'

As he hesitated in his response, suddenly Janet had a vision of Canon Keogh holding on to an Everton Football Club fixture list. Liverpool and Everton were traditionally great rivals with their grounds so close to each other that it was on very rare occasions that they could both play a home match on the same day. He mentioned that he would have to move a couple of things around and she imagined the disappointment of the priest as he made the ultimate sacrifice of missing an Everton home game. It did not really matter if the date was not possible, Graham would never have minded. The important thing was that they were now getting on with the arrangements and this was just adding an extra little bit of icing to the christening cake to make the day even better. She crossed her fingers and patiently awaited the Canon's reply.

'Seeing that it is such a special occasion,' the soft Irish tones showed no signs of an upset, 'I cannot see that there'll be any problems at all in confirming the twelfth with you right now, Mrs Walton.' Janet was delighted. She thanked Canon Keogh and agreed that she and Graham should meet with him at the church nearer the date to finalise all the details for the day.

Once the date was confirmed everything else began to fall into place. The reception was booked to cater for over 200 people at a local hotel; invitations, specially designed by an artist who had delighted Janet and Graham with examples of her work, that portrayed six babies and had the girls' names beneath each one, were sent out; and the couple turned their minds to the problem of deciding who to ask to be godparents to their children.

Choosing the godparents was not going to be an easy task. Graham's Catholic upbringing taught him that the people who are asked to be the godparents of any child are supposed to be chosen on the basis that if anything happened to the parents, then the child would be brought up by people with the same views on Christianity. But they were not looking for just a couple of people, they had to find twelve who were prepared to take on the responsibility. He knew that it was impossible to find that many people who could necessarily fit the bill in a strictly religious sense, and so, like many others today, he and Janet made their choice on the basis that the godparents they chose were responsible caring people whom they trusted.

The choice for Sarah was an obvious one. Janet and Graham had noticed that whenever Aunty 'Ali' came to visit, the first little pair of arms to shoot up in the air in a plea to be picked up belonged to Sarah. Alison, like all the close relatives, did not have a favourite among the girls but on every occasion Alison was at the house to help, it appeared that Sarah was always the one that Alison ended up feeding. There were definitely signs of an extra special relationship between them so it seemed fitting for Janet and Graham to ask Alison to be Sarah's godmother.

Of the rest of the family, Graham's sister Susan and her husband Martin were to be godparents to Ruth, and Graham's brother Dave and his wife Chris were asked to be Hannah's. They asked their close friends Lynn and John Pritchard to be godparents to Lucy, and Graham's best friend Kenny was asked to be Sarah's godfather. Kate's godparents were to be Reg and Kay Feeley. Reg was a workmate of Graham's whom he had known since he was an apprentice, and although Janet did not know them as well she knew that Graham and Reg went back a long way.

That only left Jenny. A while ago Janet and Graham had talked of how happy they would be for Sam Abdulla to be godfather to one of the girls. In a way Janet had thought of Sam as a godfather to all the girls and she would have been bitterly disappointed if he and his wife, Linda, had not been there at the christening and been part of the service. They had so much to thank him for, and what better way to show the man their appreciation than to ask him to be a godparent. And being the largest at birth, Jenny was his biggest success!

Janet then had to decide how she was going to dress the girls for such an important first public outing. The expense of buying six extra long christening gowns, together with shawls and special bonnets, would have been astronomical, and there was no way she could justify or afford the cost of six times over. Using her imagination, she purchased instead six very pretty white dresses with long sleeves and an embroidered design across the front. It was also quite possibly the first time any children had been christened in mobcaps. The outfits were unusual but nobody could have look prettier than the girls did on that day. They looked absolutely gorgeous. And after the big day mobcaps kept turning up at christenings all over the place. It seemed the girls had started a new fashion.

As the day approached, the time came for Janet and Graham to meet with Canon Keogh to talk about the procedures for the day and to have a dress rehearsal without three quarters of the main cast. So while the stars slept in their cots, mum and dad went to make sure they were happy with the arrangements and to listen to the priest.

The christening was to be the final part of an exclusive arrangement that the *Sunday Mirror* had enjoyed with the family, and its reporter and cameraman, together with the television crew, were the only press members to be granted access to the church and immediate surrounding area. Janet and Graham were determined that their babies should not be overwhelmed by crowds of enthusiastic press photographers and onlookers. More importantly, this meant that only familiar faces would surround the family during the day. Howard Walker, the *Sunday Mirror* photographer, had taken the first pictures in the hospital and had got to know Janet and Graham well over the six months, as did Bernard Falk and his television crew. They had all developed a deep respect for the family which always resulted in a relaxed atmosphere when taking photographs or filming.

It was, therefore, understandable that it was the family's wish that there should be no advance notice about when the christening was to take place, and in an effort to do this a veil of secrecy was thrown over all the details and only the invited guests and those that needed to know were informed of the date. Whenever it was mentioned, the family would only say, 'Soon. It's coming soon!' with a smile and a wink.

Unfortunately, an innocuous little notice in the parish newsletter served to ignite major news stories. And it was not long before it was announced that at twelve o'clock on the twelfth of May 1984 (or this coming Saturday – as most of the nationals put it), Janet and Graham

Walton, the proud parents of the world-famous Walton sextuplets, would reach a landmark when the christening would take place of their six beautiful daughters, Hannah, Sarah, Lucy, Ruth, Kate and Jenny.

However, by the time the word had got out and it became obvious that the Saturday was not going to be quite so smooth as had been hoped, it was too late to worry about it. In any case, there were others that would look after the media and crowds. Janet and Graham were only interested in the christening itself and were still determined to enjoy and appreciate the service as much as any parent would do on such a special occasion.

All the national newspapers were by this time aware of which one of them had the exclusive and therefore the privileged access to the family. The privileged access makes all the difference to a news story and all the tabloid editors know the benefits of paying to have that edge over his or her competitor. On this occasion the picture that counted was the incredible line-up of godparents, two to a baby, with Janet and Graham in the middle. It was a picture the whole country was waiting to see.

With the service still four hours away, the press reared its head outside the church as early as eight o'clock that morning. The principal competitors of the *Sunday Mirror*, the *News of the World* and the *People* were determined to get inside the church. Poor old Canon Keogh did not stand a chance! They knocked on the door and as he let down the draw-bridge to heaven he was offered the same password from all of them. 'Press!' They greeted him with choral harmony and, without giving him the opportunity to reply, said they were there to cover the story of the christening and that one of the most important things they wanted was a quote from him.

As more and more gentlemen of the press turned up, the same question was asked, 'Where can we sit and set up our equipment?' He remembered Janet and Graham's request for privacy. 'Ah yes,' said the priest, 'now would you be from the eh ...?' '*Sunday Mirror?*' they responded in unison.

'Ah yes, that will be roight. That'll do just the ticket! Yes that's the one – you'll be alroight on the back row now will you?'

It was not long before there was a very sedate, respectful and quietly reverent row of journalists at the back of the church with their equipment neatly tucked away by their feet under the bench in front. Any serious praying and they probably would have cracked their knee-caps on their aluminium boxes. And the uninvited sat their ground wondering whether the anger of the Lord would be kindled against them. However, they were not there for long. As the church quickly filled up with invited guests, it took more than a little persuasion, and even the local bobby, to remove gently but firmly all those in the back row. While all this was going on at the church, less than half a mile away a small convoy of vehicles was quietly winding its way through Wallasey towards Graham's parents' house in Folly Lane. It was only around the corner from the church and it seemed sensible to use it as first base. It would give them a resting point from Bidston where they could change the girls and get them ready for the christening. Chris and Dave also got ready there which meant that along with Betty and John there were plenty of adults on hand to help with the babies.

Howard Walker continued to snap away and the television cameras rolled as Janet patiently laid out the white cotton dresses, mobcaps and laced socks on a bed upstairs. One take later they were all given their marching orders and the family prepared themselves in privacy.

Finally, Janet tugged at the hems of Jenny's outfit, the last to be straightened out, and she looked at the six gleaming white diamonds that sparkled on the big double bed. 'Right girls!' Janet said, 'I want you all on your best behaviour today. No tears, no crying, just smiles and happy faces! All right?' She gave each of them a tickle and could feel the response in the twelve eyes that were wide open and shining with excitement. The girls could hardly wait to see what this christening was all about; after all their mum and dad had been going on about it every meal time for the last fortnight! With well-practised speed the parents of the happy sixsome got themselves in order. Graham put on his rarely seen but very best two-piece suit and Janet wore a smart blue outfit with a matching hat. One by one the girls were taken to their waiting carrycots in the back of the car, and from the sleepy calm of Folly Lane the family made their way to the happy bedlam of the Church of the English Martyrs.

It was as if the whole of Wallasey had turned out to see them. Nothing could have prepared them for the size of the crowds. It was pure pop star treatment. Because there were so many people Graham could not stop the car outside the main entrance. The only alternative was to drive around to the back of the building and hope to find a safe passage through the back door. Unfortunately, Fleet Street followed, and in the furore of photographers the car jolted forward and planted itself in the corner of the brickwork of the church. The girls displayed their sense of humour for as Janet turned round to make sure they were all right, they were all giggling away as if they found something terribly funny about their dad's driving.

The main reason that they went to the back of the church was the safety of the children. Janet and Graham knew that all the well-wishers from Wallasey only wanted to have a quick look at the babies, but how could they risk exposing such delicacy to this fervent enthusiasm? With so many people it just would not have been fair to the girls to try and walk through such a large gathering. It was probably one of the biggest turnouts Wallasey had seen and a great disappointment to the crowd but Janet and Graham knew what was best, and even though the local paper at the time gave them some flak over the matter, the sacrifice of a pinch of popularity was a small price to pay for peace of mind.

Inside the church everyone waited for the service to begin. There was an added aura given by the arc lights of the television crew, and as the procession made its way up on to the altar a sparkling array of flashes came from the stalls as guest after guest captured the moment for their album.

It was a beautiful service and all the more joyful for Janet and Graham because the aisles were filled with familiar faces. Among them were those that had given so much throughout the times Janet had been in hospital and had so devotedly tended to her and the family before and after the birth. The doctors, the nurses, the health visitors; all the people that they wanted to see were there together on the one day.

Janet and Graham found themselves in the unusual position of being surrounded by their daughters and not having to hold one of them. Hardly moving their heads, every so often Janet and Graham's gaze would sweep along the line of godparents keeping constant surveillance in case any one became uncomfortable. Just as Canon Keogh led the congregation into a chorus of 'All Things Bright and Beautiful' one of Jenny's teeth answered the call. Teething was a common problem at that time and seeing Jenny begin to wriggle, Janet deftly and discreetly brought out from her handbag a tube of teething cream which she passed down the line to where Linda Abdulla's finger was wisely and wonderfully soothing the discomfort!

When the service was over, and the babies were being brought out to the car, the press unfortunately showed the ugly side of its face. The only feelings the photographers showed were for the shots they wanted, and a bank of them had entrenched themselves around the car and on the roof of the nearest building. There were far too many people too close and the photographers would not budge an inch. As Janet was placing Sarah in her carrycot they stupidly surged forward. For a single moment Janet was scared for the safety of her children. Even though there were people around her acting as security guards she felt things had gone too far. 'Stop it!' she shouted out in vain. Those two words were all they needed and they had a quote and a story. It really seemed that they would go to whatever lengths they had to to get an angle on a story and scoop the others. Even if it meant that the story was that Janet was upset by their own actions. After all, the Waltons had sold their story to a rival newspaper so if they could do anything to spoil the story they would.

Despite what some of the papers reported the next day the ceremony was hardly spoiled in any way by those brief moments outside. Once Janet and Graham were safely in the car with the girls and on the way to the reception, the incident was immediately forgotten and they talked only of how beautiful the whole service had been.

Leasowe Castle was the only hotel large enough at that time in the area that Janet and Graham felt could cope with the number of guests they intended to invite. While all the guests gathered in the impressive wood-panelled ballroom at the far end of the building, it was all hands on deck upstairs where the girls were fed and changed. There was no shortage of volunteers to help with their feeds, and before long they were ready to make their entrance.

At the church everyone had to remain in their places and could only see the babies from a distance, so when they entered the ballroom it was the first time most of the people had seen the family together at such close quarters. Janet and Graham were completely taken aback by the flashes of the cameras. With all the media about, it never occurred to them that their friends, relatives and guests would want to take snaps. Once again safety was uppermost in their minds. Fortunately, there was a triangle of food tables surrounding a pillar not far away, and after escaping there, and giving an impromptu photo-call for five smiling minutes, Janet and Graham, together with both sets of grandparents, carried the girls to the stage at the far end of the room where they sat them out of harm's way in their baby-seats on the stage. The girls were set back a bit so people could not come right up to them and they were high up so that they were at eye level, and they sat there, happily gurgling away for ages. Considering there was so much going on, they were marvellous.

The day had been full of emotion, and was the culmination of an extraordinary year. It was hard to believe all that had happened in the last twelve months. This time last year they were beginning to look forward to their holiday in Malta and could never possibly have imagined what lay ahead, and if they had, they would never have believed they would have been able to cope, but cope with it they had done, and now, after everybody had gone home and their newly christened daughters lay peacefully in their cots upstairs, they sipped coffee in the lounge and quietly indulged in opening the presents – six by six.

Eleven

'Jim'll Fix It'

♡ ♡ ♡
♡ ♡
♡

Janet and Graham had already come to terms with the fact that their lives would never be totally their own; fate had seen to that. So whatever privacy they could salvage for themselves and the girls they would grasp hold of and not let anyone take away. Their independence as a family unit was important and the problem of learning by experience was the same for them as it was for all first-time parents. It was critical for them to prove that they could cope on their own without outside help.

During the hours when they were alone, Janet and Graham decided to make every effort, no matter how difficult, to feed the girls their bottles at the same time. Perhaps there was a little bit of wishful thinking applied here for this was by no means a straightforward or easy task. The only practical way of doing this was to place the girls in their cradle seats, which were specifically designed to rest on the floor. Once they were all strapped in, Janet and Graham would each take three bottles and grip two in one hand and one in the other.

The baby that was fortunate enough to have one whole hand to itself, clearly drew the long straw and was able to suckle away cheerfully on the teat of the bottle to its heart's content. That meant that two of the six were fine. Although Janet and Graham did their best to alternate the proceedings, it was still extremely difficult to hold two bottles at the

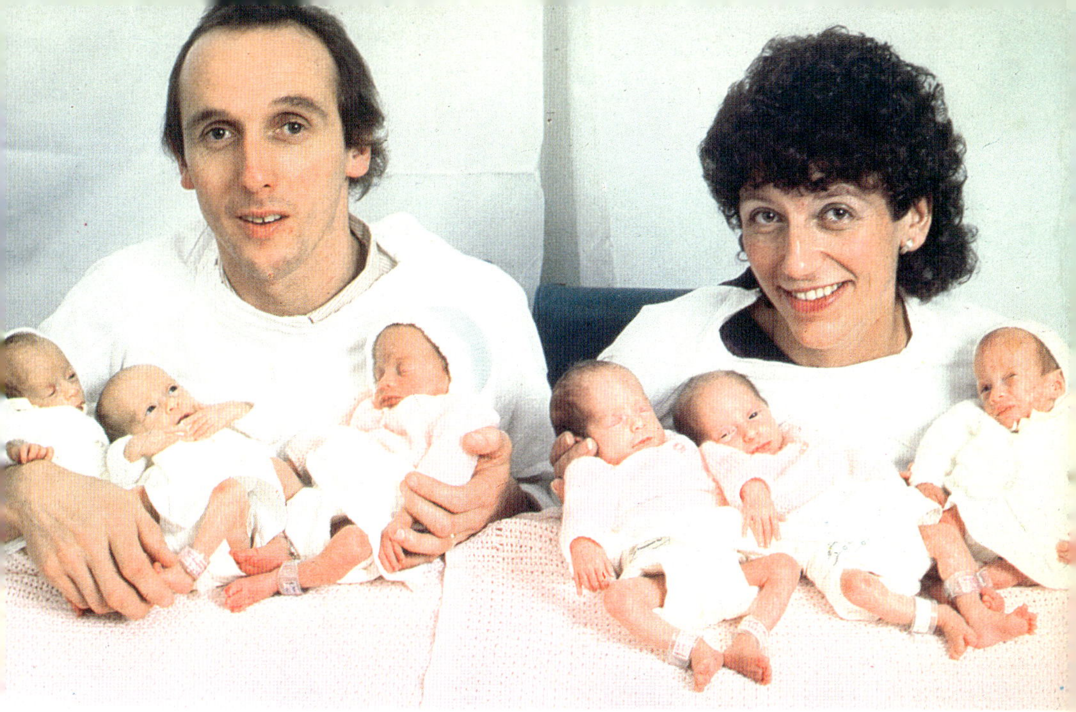

Welcome to the world! The first picture of the girls taken at the maternity ward eighteen days after their birth on 6 December 1983. *Left to right:* Sarah, Ruth, Jenny, Kate, Lucy and Hannah.

On the steps of the verandah at Shugborough Hall, the country home of the Queen's cousin, photographer Patrick Lichfield.

Top: The girls decide to go on guards duty half way through the Lichfield session. *Left to right:* Jenny, Sarah, Lucy, Hannah, Kate and Ruth.

Above: The classic bench shot, taken at the same Lichfield session, that magazines throughout the world published in celebration of the girls' second birthday.

Top: Dungarees and wellies could sometimes be little protection when half a dozen ice-creams were the order of the day. *Left to right:* Ruth, Hannah, Jenny, Sarah, Kate and Lucy.

Above: Happy Families with both sets of grandparents. *Left to right:* Grandad Peter with Ruth, Nanny Nancy with Jenny, Janet with Hannah, Graham with Kate, Nanny Betty with Lucy, and Grandad John with Sarah, September 1984.

Top: Feeding time at Statham Avenue. *Left to right:* Lucy, Kate, Jenny, Hannah, Ruth and Sarah.

Above: About to walk on to the set for the first shot in the making of a television commercial for Vantage Chemists in March 1985.

Top: A well-earned rest during a long walk on the hills near the family home in Wallasey. *Left to right:* (front) Jenny, Lucy, Kate and Ruth; (back) Hannah and Sarah.

Above: 'I see no ships!' Looking out to sea on New Brighton promenade. *Left to right:* Hannah, Lucy, Kate, Ruth, Jenny and Sarah.

Top: At Heathrow Airport en route to Tokyo, July 1987. *Left to right:* (front) Jenny, Hannah, Kate, Lucy, Sarah and Ruth; (back) Sue Thomas, Nanny Nancy, Janet and Graham.

Above: On the set of the popular Japanese television show 'Naruhodo the World' on the day the family was introduced by Fuji to the press. *Left to right:* Graham, Janet, Hannah, Lucy, Jenny, Ruth, Sarah, Kate and Nanny Nancy.

Top: A warm welcome from Mickey Mouse at the entrance to Tokyo Disneyland on the last day of their trip to Japan.

Above: On a visit to London in August 1987 the girls enjoy their favourite delicacy on a hot summer's day alongside the Thames at Hampton Court.

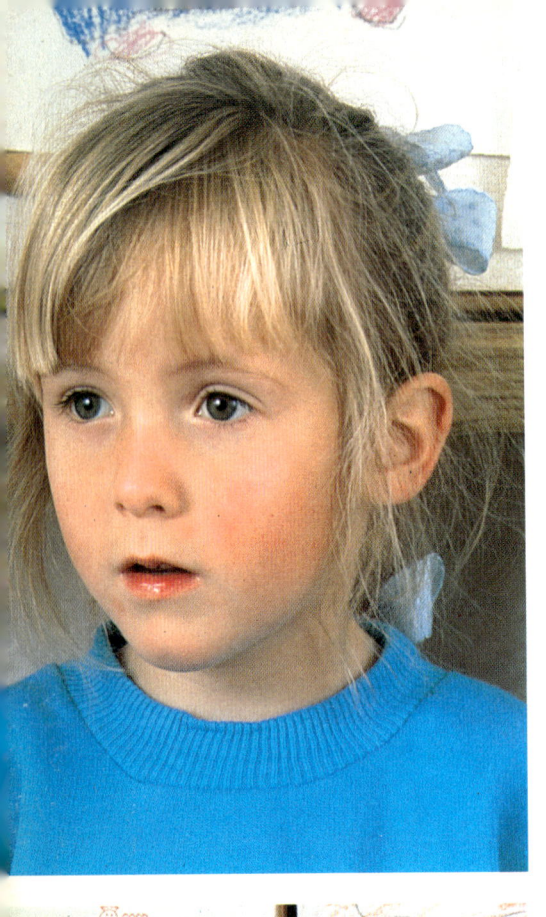
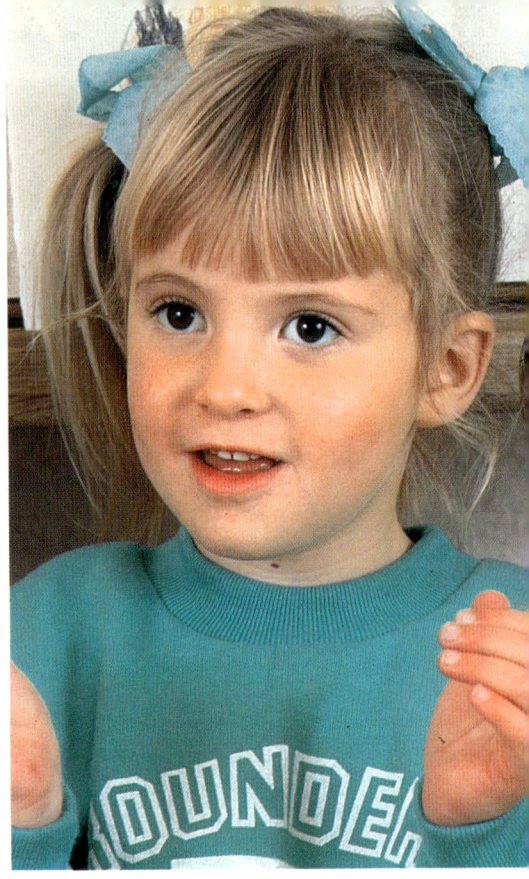
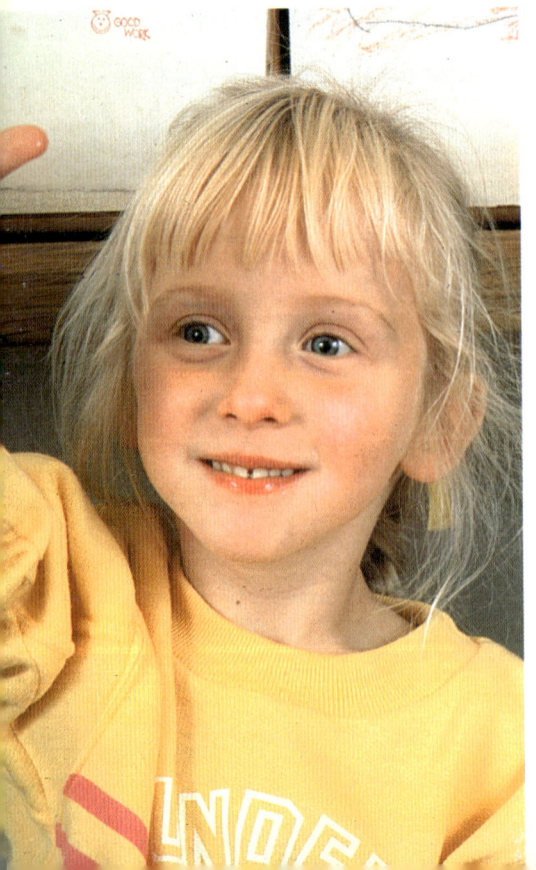

Above left: Kate
Above right: Jenny
Left: Hannah

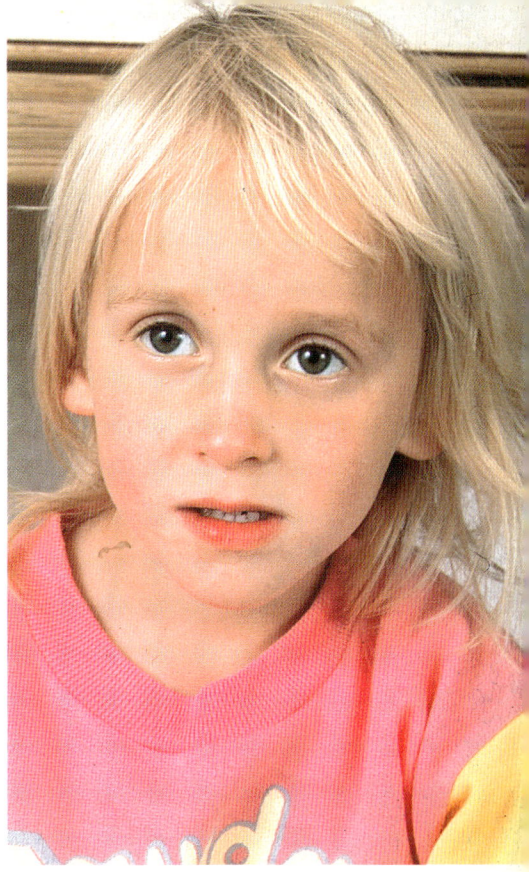

Above left: Sarah
Above right: Lucy
Right: Ruth

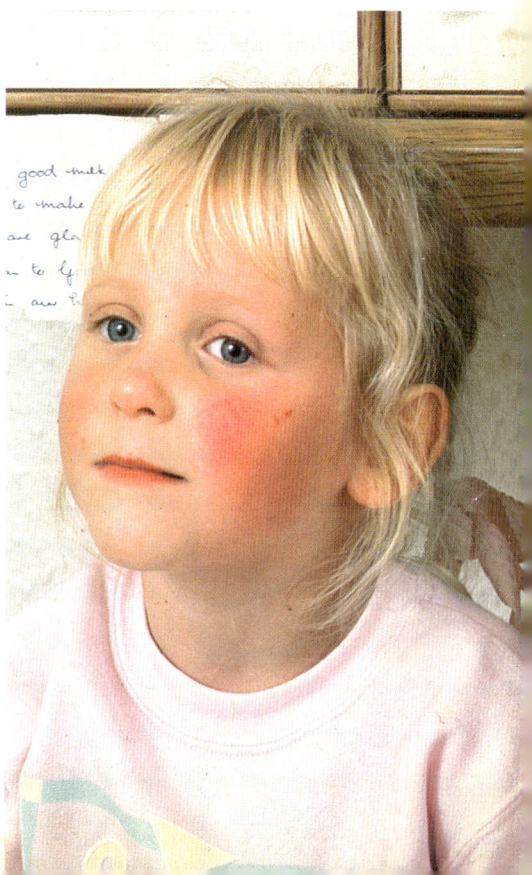

On their fourth birthday Janet made a fancy dress outfit, based on nursery rhymes, for each of the girls.

Above left: Ruth – Little Boy Blue
Above right: Lucy – Wee Willie Winkie
Left: Sarah – Mary had a little lamb

Above left: Hannah – Mary, Mary quite contrary
Above right: Jenny – Little Miss Muffet
Right: Kate – Little Bo Peep

Above: The proud parent

Left: In March 1988 the family was invited to the New Forest to suppo the Rotary Club of Great Britain in their efforts to raise money for thei charity Polio Plus. This shot was taken to help publicise the cause. *Left to right:* Hannah, Kate, Sarah, Ruth, Jenny and Lucy.

Below: Whilst in the area of the Ne Forest, the family visited the famou Motor Museum at Beaulieu. *Left to right:* (front) Graham, Sarah, Jenny and Kate; (back) Ruth, Hannah, Lucy and Janet.

Sometimes shopping can be more like going to the fairground. Not much room for the food!

In November of 1988 the family visited the village at Portmeirion. The girls had tremendous fun playing on the stagecoach. *Left to right:* (front) Ruth, Jenny and Hannah; (back) Kate, Sarah and Lucy.

Top: Practising their dance steps in formation at home. *Left to right:* Hannah, Jenny, Lucy, Kate, Ruth and Sarah.

Above: First term at school. *Left to right:* Hannah, Ruth, Lucy, Kate, Jenny and Sarah.

Six at six! *Left to right:* (front) Jenny, Hannah and Kate; (back) Lucy, Sarah and Ruth.

same time in one hand and attempt to keep the ends of them firmly docked in the mouths of the babies. There were times when this became very frustrating for all and there was much crying out immediately the milk stopped flowing.

As well as having to cope with holding three bottles at once, Janet and Graham also had to be prepared to grab the towels that were laid out in anticipation and to clean mouths and other areas that were not under the protection of one of the thousands of bibs they had in stock. It is true to say that the life expectancy of a bib in the Walton household was not very long. It was another expense that had to be accounted for, and while a single bib is not going to break the bank, multiply it by six over a period of three years and the cost becomes frightening. There were of course, many gifts of them at birthday time and Christmas but, even so, it was a great relief to arrive at the ceremony of the disposal of the last bib.

One thing that become patently clear while going through these early days of feeding was that nothing can be rushed. Janet and Graham desperately wanted to give as much time and attention to each of the girls individually as would a parent of a single child, but this was absolutely impossible. So they were for ever caught up in the predicament of having to do everything as patiently and gently as possible but also with the greatest of speed so that they could attend to the next in line.

How they succeeded in this is a source of wonder to many but succeed they did. There was hardly ever an occasion when the girls did not finish their feeds. Part of the triumph in this area was due to the fact that Janet and Graham were totally organised. Every spare minute was made full use of in preparing for the next item in the daily routine. So, when it came to feed times, the six bottles were all ready and waiting on a tray in the kitchen; these along with the teats having been cleaned and sterilised after the last feed; the bibs and towels were there alongside and the pan and milk were waiting to be heated.

One of the greatest days Graham can remember was when the girls first gripped and held on to a bottle without any help from either Janet or himself. It was a Friday and the family had the house to themselves. No nurses, no friends, no relatives, no visitors. Pure bliss. It had been a long week that had included filming and photographers and what seemed like an endless stream of callers just popping in to see if there was anything they could do to help. Janet and Graham were always very grateful for all the offers of help but on occasion it was obvious that some had just knocked on the door to view the babies, and, whilst it was on the pretext of giving a hand, it sometimes ended up in extra work for Janet who found herself making cups of coffee for the visitor while they made themselves comfortable.

Moments before, Janet and Graham had both been playing with the girls and their various toys. The room was awash with colour. Rattles, building-bricks and plastic rings were being sampled, shaken, scratched and sniffed. Having done all that, the toys were either disdainfully discarded out of boredom, or two girls would use one in a tug-of-war, rocking on their bottoms with their feet firmly pressed together and their fingers intertwined around the toy that both decided was desirable at the same time. This time it was a green rattle that Ruth and Hannah both wanted, and just before the screaming began Janet anticipated the situation and grabbed an identical one and placed it in Hannah's hand.

A new game began and they now began tapping each other on the knee-caps. This was jolly good fun and there were gurgles of laughter whenever their aim was good. Predictably, by the time they got to the third exchange of blows one of them stopped laughing. It was Ruth. She sat and thought about it for a short while, and decided it was no longer funny. This last bonk on the knee from Hannah was a little heavy handed and, quite understandably, Ruth screamed out and let her little lungs speak for themselves. Like a call to arms, this was the signal for all the girls to drop their toys and cry for their bottles.

It was time for action. Together they put the girls in the chairs, and while Janet went into the kitchen to heat up the milk Graham went round the playroom like a whirlwind tidying up. Once done he tried to calm the girls down by telling them all about the special frame he was going to make that would hold six bottles at a time so that either mummy or daddy could feed all the girls on their own. This prospect made them cry louder, and Graham did not think he would ever get round to it anyway.

Lately they had been trying everything to get them to hold on to the bottles without help. Each night Janet and Graham would practice with each of the girls in turn putting their little hands around the bottles and each night the bottles would slip out of their grip. On this occasion it was Kate who was the heroine, and once they had all followed suit and were all able to grip the bottles themselves everything seemed to move a lot quicker. Yet another little piece of pressure had eased off and the feeding times became a lot less hectic. They all had tremendous appetites and any fears of their tiny sizes and prematurity having any long term effects were finally beginning to disappear.

Most of the girls took to solid foods without much fuss. The transition happened before Graham had a chance to build his bottle-feeding apparatus, but the task of feeding by spoon was no easier and he turned his mind to designing a giant fork with six prongs, each with a spoon attached. Meals were all still much more palatable if there was an extra pair of hands about the house to help, and Janet spent nights dreaming of the day when all the girls could hold their own spoons. Spoon holding was a trick that was going to take quite some time for the girls to learn, and Janet and Graham agreed that bottle feeding was, on the whole, a much cleaner and easier exercise than feeding solids.

Of all the girls Lucy missed her bottle the greatest and seemed to want to make a point of her dissatisfaction with the restaurant service at every single meal time. She would look at her bowl of food as if she had not even seen it on the menu, let alone ordered it, and her tiny nostrils would twitch with discontent the moment it approached her mouth. After a while, taking on the task of feeding Lucy at this stage became an act of heroism. The whole thing, of course, could have been an early sign of the mischief that showed in her character later on, but at the time it seemed more prudent for whoever was holding the spoon to wear the bib. At the beginning of each mealtime her lips seemed soldered together. At the same time she would swing her head from side to side avoiding the oncoming attack. It was a straightforward battle of persistence but always, eventually, her mouth would open and as long as Janet, Graham or whoever happened to be feeding Lucy at the time, had their wits about them they would have some success.

The preparation for feeding time was carried out in military fashion with Janet and Graham making sure that everything was ready for the girls before they were brought into the kitchen and carefully, one by one, strapped into the row of highchairs. Any other way would have been disastrous. The last thing you can expect from a nine-month-old baby is patience when hunger sets in and like all babies throughout the world once the girls decided it was time to eat they made sure everyone knew about it right through until they were full up.

More often than not it would be Janet who would prepare the meals while Graham would handle the swilling out and cleaning up at the end. With so many other things to do the simplicity of the fact that the food came packaged and prepared specially for babies was a help but it still had to be mixed, cooked and served. Graham, though, never relished the prospect of the portions of the day devoted to the nourishment of his fold. Like the punished in medieval stocks he suffered the splatter of food on his forehead and elsewhere for an hour at a time. His eardrums would ache and throb to the pounding of plastic cups on the surfaces of the six high chairs. But that was not the noise he disliked the most. There were much simpler sounds that sent shivers up Graham's back. A slurp, a quiet innocuous pop and a rattle.

The slurp and pop came from the ceremony of the opening of the jars of food. Well sealed to guard the freshness within, when pierced to be opened, the jar would pop and make a slurping sound as the air was released and the contents bubbled. Sounds have different meanings to different ears and whilst the babies, if they happened to hear the noise, probably thought it one of the most wonderful sounds of the day, their dad on the other hand associated it with less joyful thoughts. To the girls it may have meant a happy tummy but to Graham the pop and slurp meant that he was going to be covered from head to foot in dinner! Testing the aero-dynamics of various foodstuffs and the effect of gravity on liquids is all good fun for a baby in a high chair but simple experiments of this nature can drive a loving parent round the bend. Multiply it by six and you begin to see the reason why fate should have it that a decorator had been blessed in this way!

The jars of solid food had been supplied by Cow and Gate, one of the principal baby food manufacturers, and incredibly the girls were going through about a hundred jars per week. So much of it was necessary that there was a whole cupboard devoted purely to the storage of these little containers. The jars, four at a time at first and then six as the babies' appetites grew, were placed in a large pan of water and brought to the boil.

How the girls were fed at this stage usually depended on how many adults happened to be in the house at mealtimes. It was either the two-bowl or the three-bowl method that was used. With the nurses long gone and Sue Thomas, the home help, busy doing other things like washing and ironing, Janet and Graham were normally on their own. That meant using the two-bowl method. Enough food for three babies was mixed into each of two red plastic bowls and Janet and Graham went along the line with a spoon in one hand and cloth at the ready in the other. They would patiently wait for an open mouth and deal with it either with their right hand or their left according to which was nearer. Now and again they would catch the falling food and, to avoid hold-ups, point the spoon in the direction of the next one along the line. It tasted just as good and no customer ever complained at that cafe – except, of course Lucy, now and again.

It did not take the girls long to work out a method by which they could remove their own nappies. As is to be expected at this stage in the girls' development, the nights that passed through without anything else being passed by any of the girls were few and far between. Hence each morning the first thing they wanted to do was to rid themselves of anything damp. Quite understandable. So when their parents came to their rooms each morning, the idea of the game was to see who could sling their nappy the farthest. It was all highly amusing for the girls, but not much fun for mum and dad who had to search for these damp offerings. On occasion, it was a case of just following the nose.

It also did not take the girls long to find a way of getting themselves out of the cots. This was something in particular that worried Janet and Graham. It began when the girls were about nine months old and, as might be expected, being the tallest, Jenny was the first to get out.

However long and hard they thought about it there was just nothing they could do to stop this happening. There was no doubt it was dangerous. The distance from the top of the rail-bar to the floor was far greater than any of the girls' height and so at any time they could have hurt themselves by not landing properly. But the only alternative was to strap them in the cots, and that was something that was absolutely out of the question. One by one they all followed Jenny and taught themselves how to escape from the cots. Each morning through one week late in August of 1984 Janet looked in the girls' room only to find one more of them out of her cot and happily playing with the others.

Having cringed a few times on hearing the odd thud on the bedroom floor, and having seen that on each occasion the girls never seemed to be hurt, Janet and Graham's fears lessened but their curiosity as to how they were managing to perform such acrobatics increased. One morning Janet determined to see how it was done, set the alarm for five thirty and waited outside their door until the first girl awoke. It was Lucy. She was in a right mess and was standing up in her cot struggling to remove her disposables as quickly as possible. Like an Olympic shot-putter she hurled the nappy over her head and flung it to the far corner of the bedroom behind the rocking horse.

Janet was watching this performance through a small gap in the door that was slightly ajar. She wanted to go in and it was all she could do to stop herself. She knew that these early moments were ones the girls had been used to having to themselves; they had not been crying out for their parents when they woke up, primarily because they had other things to occupy their little minds like sneaking out of their cots and playing with their toys.

Janet very carefully pushed the door a tiny bit further so that she could get a clearer view. A tap on her backside made her jump slightly and the door was moved a touch more so that Graham could also see the performance. Once Lucy had discarded her nappy she decided to fall back on her bottom and gurgle and sing for a bit. Never one to do things in a quiet way, it was not long before both Sarah and Kate were stirring.

Suddenly Lucy stood up and gripping the rail of the cot began trampolining up and down, bouncing to her heart's content. Each time she reached the top of her jump she alternately called out one of her sisters' names. Jenny was fortunate in that she was a heavier sleeper than the others and so slept blissfully through all Lucy's bugle-calling efforts. The others, however, were not so lucky. And so, satisfied she had gained herself an audience in the form of Sarah and Kate and glancing one last time over towards Jenny, a familiar mischievous glint appeared in her eye and she cocked her left leg up and tried to rest it on the rail. She failed. She tried again, this time bouncing as hard as possible on her right leg.

Janet and Graham both tensed up expecting the worst, and just as they were about to charge into the room to stop her, Lucy was up, over and out of the cot. She had vaulted the side perfectly. Having gripped the bar with her left foot and using it as a lever she had dragged the rest of her body over the top and somehow managed to land on her feet. There was nothing but utter delight expressed on her face. Beaming with her achievement she immediately taunted the others. Then like a little waitress she proceeded eagerly to take orders from Kate and Sarah who requested various toys and playthings to be passed over the rails to them. After watching them for a while there was nothing left for Janet and Graham to do but go back to bed and make the most of that extra half hour in bed, which was becoming more and more precious as each day seemed to get slightly longer as the girls needed slightly less sleep.

The tumble drier in Statham Avenue served a dual purpose in the Walton household. Janet found it invaluable as a rather useful teaching aid. Strapped into their highchairs surrounding the kitchen table there was no escaping lessons, and the girls at the tender age of one and a bit obediently gave mum their full attention as she, in the manner of a magician, conjured up from the depths of the drier various pieces of clothing.

'Right, girls,' Janet would begin. 'Who can tell mummy whaaaaat... THIS is?' The word 'what' would be stretched as far as it would go in order to build up the excitement, and by the time she had got to the end of the question Janet would be holding up one of many vests or pairs of knickers or perhaps a babygro.

The various stages of displaying movement and agility began once the girls were able to master the very basic art of holding themselves up. Each time they were sat up straight they would wobble like a large blancmange and flop to the right or left. At times Graham and Janet felt their vocations in life really should have been shelf-stackers in a supermarket as they spent an inordinate amount of time simply sitting the girls up straight and lining them up next to one another.

Once they were all pretty stable the next task was to get them moving. Every child is going to be different in this respect, and the Waltons proved that six out of every six baby girls will learn to crawl in a different way. Jenny did not require any limbs whatsoever at first and made extraordinary ripples with her belly as, like a little sea-lion, she flopped her way forward. Hannah cocked one leg out to the left and pulled whatever would follow in that direction. Sarah did the same except to the right. Kate, as hard as she tried, could not move forwards and so did the next best thing and let her head follow her feet and went backwards. Ruth, as versatile as ever, decided it was far more sensible to do it upside down and so she began moving by somehow managing to crawl on her back.

That left Lucy. Whatever she tried and whatever she did she just could not budge from the spot on which she sat. The only way forward on her hands and knees was with the aid of a friendly shove on the bottom from mum or dad.

It was not so much a case of when the first steps would be taken as who would be the first. In fact it turned out to be Ruth. It must have taken some courage to let go and waddle unsupported for the first time, and the early display of fearlessness was to become part of Ruth's character as time passed. What she did was to run as fast as her uncertain legs would carry her right across the lounge of her great-grandmother, Nanny Fox. There was a rousing cheer from a full room and Ruth hid her face in her mother's skirt, enjoying all the fuss over her but embarrassed by it all the same.

It seemed weeks and weeks after all the others were walking about the house when Sarah finally decided it was more fun on two legs rather than crawling around on all fours. The passing into waddlehood though was not exactly the smoothest of runs for Sarah.

Without doubt the Darwinian theory of survival of the fittest applied more to this home than most, and the girls had shown their ability to stand up for themselves many times by then. However, it was beginning to look as if Sarah may be falling behind as time went on and she just could not get herself off the floor. It was not that she did not want to or was not trying to take those first few vital steps on her own, it was because every time she stood up one of her sisters, who by this time was showing off more intricate styles of different paces at different speeds, whizzed passed and knocked her over. So she did the sensible thing and safely stayed on her knees.

When she did finally make those first steps, to the delight, joy and relief of her parents, she walked with legs that looked like two little stiff pitiful planks. But she proudly marched around the house like a clockwork tin soldier and never stopped until tiredness set in and she needed to rest before winding herself up to go on parade again.

Janet had received a great many letters from little girls who had absolutely adored seeing the babies on television, and many of them mentioned that they had written to 'Jim'll Fix It'. Hosted by Jimmy Saville it is one of the BBC's most popular programmes and is based on making dreams come true for people of all ages. Everything from meeting the Prime Minister to taking a flight on Concorde has been covered by the show, but at the beginning of 1985 the two most popular requests were to meet the pop star George Michael and to spend a day with the Waltons. So many thousands of letters had been sent to Jimmy about the babies that the programme's producers decided to make the dream come true for two little girls.

Janet and Graham were delighted to agree to take part in the show. It not only meant a trip for them to the studios in London, but a chance to see a show and have a weekend break they both badly needed. Betty and Nancy immediately agreed to take the helm for a couple of days, so the arrangements were made and a date was set.

Before the studio filming took place, the BBC sent a crew up to the house for a day so that they could show the dream coming true in between Janet and Graham's interview with Jimmy Saville. The two lucky girls chosen were ten-year-old Glenda Fish and eleven-year-old Louise Cunliffe. The crew collected the girls on their way to the house, and they all looked forward to enjoying a very special day.

Louise was a very confident little lady. She was practical, talkative and far from shy about getting on with whatever little job Janet gave her to do. Glenda was a little less forward, much quieter and, by the time the filming began, seemed a bit overawed by the cameras and lights. It was as if she could not really believe she was actually there with the six most famous babies in the world, and it was exactly the kind of reaction the director was looking for. Nevertheless she paid as much attention as she could and was never far away from Janet throughout the day. Louise and Glenda helped dress the babies, feed them and play with them as Janet and Graham went through their daily routine.

Part of that routine meant making sure that the babies were taken out in the buggies for some fresh air. The director had desperately wanted a shot of just the two girls walking along pushing the six babies. With three double buggies to contend with it would have proved impossible. Not even Janet and Graham had attempted that particular trick. The fact that they could not push their own babies together safely and sensibly without the help of a third person was just another of the many little frustrations that they had had to accept. The difficulty had neither discouraged nor diverted the determined director, and he called upon the services of Cindico the manufacturers of the buggies to see if their research department could come up with any ideas.

A couple of days before the crew were due to arrive a post office van pulled up outside the house. Graham opened the door to find the postman holding an eight-foot-high spear-like package. 'Could you sign the delivery note please, Mr Walton?'

Graham wondered what on earth the peculiar parcel could be. 'As long as you don't ask me to use that to write with!' He noticed Cindico's name on the delivery note. 'Actually,' Graham continued with a smile on his face, 'since the family has grown so much we've started having the spaghetti delivered in bulk!'

The idea was to use Cindico's elongated pole to bolt all three buggies tightly together so that the two girls could stand in the middle and push all six buggies along the quiet country lane behind the house. But whichever way the director, cameraman and lighting engineers tried, it just would not work.

In the end it was a straightforward strapping of string that served as a solution, and with all three double buggies soundly secured, rigged and roped together, the director set about shooting the sequence. There was a worrying moment when the wheels of the outer two buggies wobbled menacingly as the girls tried gently to push the world's widest perambulator along the road, but finally the cameraman got his shot and the director was able to go home happy.

During the rehearsals in the London studios, Jimmy Saville was about the most relaxed person Graham had ever seen. He was wearing a track-suit, had loosened the laces of his training shoes and, settled comfortably between his lips, was an enormous brown Havanah. The cigar and the track-suit are his hall-marks and he is hardly ever seen in public without either one or the other.

It was as if he was in his own front lounge. Like King Solomon holding court, he relaxed on an extraordinarily large armchair as guests who were to appear on the show went up to meet him or production people sought his advice on camera angles and the order of events. There was no doubt whose show it was and it was remarkable how he directed and managed to influence all that was going on without moving from his seat. He simply never got up! As Graham looked at the other guests around him and at the kids whose dreams had been realised, he could see how Saville's method of working and professionalism immediately settled everybody down.

By unfortunate chance, while playing five-a-side football a few days before going to the studio, Graham cracked a bone in the big toe of his right foot. Having been plastered up and presented with a pair of crutches at the hospital, it had made coping at home with the girls all the more difficult. It had naturally put extra pressure on Janet that week so the prospect of a couple of days away from the bottles, burps and bottoms was looking more and more like an oasis in the desert. She had not, though, bargained for having to carry the suitcase everywhere they went, in the theatre, where tickets had been booked for them, they had seats on the front row of the upper circle which meant negotiating a lot of stairs. The restaurant, in which a table had been reserved for them, just happened to be on the third floor, and there were yet more steps to be reckoned with in the studio.

Graham did not want to go on for the interview with his crutches so during the rehearsal time he practised hopping from his seat to the stage and back again with his hand placed firmly on Janet's shoulder. Satisfied they could manage it without too much difficulty, they went back to their seats and waited for the show to begin. Eventually the film was shown of Glenda and Louise visiting the house, and by the time it ended they were comfortably seated next to Saville with Graham's plaster just out of camera shot. The interview went well and everything would have been perfect had not Janet, having presented the two little girls with 'Jim'll Fix It' medals and said thank you very much to the host, promptly marched off back to her place completely forgetting about her disabled husband on stage. The applause of the audience turned into roars of laughter as Graham's look of disbelief could not escape the lens of the camera. Known for his charitable work with hospitals and having helped out as a porter on more than one occasion, Saville rolled his cigar around in his mouth, held it between his teeth, and, with a smile on his face, volunteered his services in helping Graham back to his seat.

· Twelve ·

An Ill Wind

♡ ♡ ♡
♡ ♡
♡

All babies and children are expected to suffer various illnesses, and the Walton girls were no exception. Chickenpox, German measles, mumps and tonsillitis, each was to pay their respects to the family over the first five years, each leaving their mark and taking their toll. At the tender age of two, German measles came first with Lucy taking the honours and sharing them in no time at all with Ruth and Kate. Jenny and Hannah followed suit in pink polka-dot fashion a few days later and Sarah showed signs within a fortnight.

It was difficult to decide what would be worse, for all the girls to go through an illness at the same time, thereby getting it out of the way in the shortest possible period, or for them to catch each of them one or two at a time. The former would, of course, mean that life would be absolutely dreadful for a couple of weeks, perhaps, but at least it would be coupled with the saving grace that there would be an end in sight. The latter would allow whoever was ill to have the extra attention of Janet or Graham, which is naturally what any parent would want, but it could result in the horrible thought of a house full of spots, sore throats and sickness that lasted for months. The idea of each being ill for eight to ten days at a time and the fearful prospect of measles or mumps being around for maybe sixty days or more was not something to relish.

They decided not to speculate and not to worry until it happened. Then, as with everything else, they would deal with each problem as it came along. By the time the first of the illnesses did arrive on their doorstep the nurses were long gone, and while they could not help thinking that this was a time when they really could do with some extra help they knew that one way or another they would cope and get through. As soon as the first scent of something was sniffed, Janet and Graham, after praying that neither of them would take ill themselves, would send smoke signals to both sets of grandparents to warn of possible requests for an extra pair of helping hands, stock up with provisions, roll up their sleeves and expect the worst.

As it happened, the worst did not come in the form of measles, mumps or any of the expected run-of-the-mill diseases. At the end of the summer of 1984, when the girls were about nine months old, Jenny had been showing enough signs of being under the weather for the doctor to be called. Her temperature seemed a bit too high for the problem just to be a spot of constipation that was diagnosed, so an extra eye was found between Janet and Graham to watch over her.

It was lunchtime a couple of days after the doctor's visit, and Graham was about to prepare the girls' feed. Another meal and another opportunity, he thought, to test who would be more grateful for the food; the girls, the floor-tiles or the wallpaper! The babies with healthy appetites after an extended morning ride in their buggies, were already banging their plastic spoons on their high-chair tables. As Graham first attended to folding and collapsing the buggies and putting them away, and hanging up all the anoraks, Sue Thomas, having finished the morning's ironing, was also in the hallway putting on her coat ready to leave at her usual time of twelve thirty.

As he was about to hang up the last of the girls' coats, he and Sue were jolted by the shrill sound of Janet's voice calling urgently to Graham, and it sent them both racing into the kitchen. Janet was standing by Jenny and, having placed the palm of her hand over Jenny's forehead and detected an incredibly high temperature rise in what must have been a very short time, was already loosening her clothing and trying without success to get a response from her daughter. In a state of semi-consciousness Jenny was reeling to and fro like an exhausted marathon runner. Her puzzled eyes began to roll and her face was ashen white. She swayed from one side of the seat to the other and finally flopped to her left. She was secure from falling any further by the sides of the high chair and its straps which Janet was frantically unfastening.

She laid her limp and pale daughter at the side of the sink and finished loosening her clothes. 'Jenny!' Janet called again and again as she dabbed her head with a damp cloth. 'Jenny!' The baby's eyes could only roll in response. She began shivering and shaking, and at the suggestion of Sue, Janet stripped Jenny and began to splash water over her body. Probably only a minute had passed before Graham called for an ambulance but it was enough for them to realise that this was something they could not handle on their own.

The ambulance men were in the house within five minutes and one of them immediately placed a plastic mouthpiece between the baby's lips to prevent her biting or swallowing her tongue and to keep the airways clear so that she could breathe. Her temperature was still very high and Janet and Graham still could not get any response from her. There was now no sound ... nothing. It was obviously serious, serious enough for them both to want to travel to the local hospital, Arrowe Park, in the ambulance. A new dilemma reared its head as they realised that one of them would have to stay behind to look after the other five who, oblivious to the commotion, were still cheerfully munching on their crisps. Sue saw their concern and insisted on staying with the girls till one of them returned.

When they arrived at the accident and emergency unit, Jenny was hurried into a side room and laid on a bed. Janet and Graham continued to call her name but, although her eyes had stopped rolling, there was still no reaction whatsoever from her. It was so pitiful to see her lying there taking up such a small portion of the table, listless and still. Janet looked at her and saw nine months of life reduce before her eyes to a tiny premature baby once again. The only movement that came from her was a slight detectable quiver of her lips as she seemed to gasp for every shallow breath.

A haunting thought returned to them both as they watched the doctor examine Jenny. It had been heavily impressed upon them, when they were first told of the major multiple pregnancy, that it was unlikely that there would be complete success, and somewhere in the back of their minds whenever any of the girls were ill during the first six months of life was the thought that six babies just cannot all survive. But, so far, they had done. They had beaten all the odds, and had developed into half a dozen of the sweetest and prettiest of babies.

Despite the glazed look in Jenny's eyes, the doctors were confident that she would be all right. 'Jenny has had what we call a febrile convulsion,' he said gently. 'It's not an uncommon occurrence in young children and, while she should be fine, it's best she stays in for a couple of days for us to keep an eye on her. We can arrange for Mum to stay, too, if you like.' There was no hesitation. Janet had no intention of leaving.

It was a long time before Jenny began to come out of the shell that had imprisoned her, and hours and hours seemed to pass before she showed signs of revival. Slowly she moved into a phase where she was a bit dozy but was still not responding. Then her eyes lost that unnatural glazed look, but she still could not focus through her drowsiness. Meanwhile, Graham made his way back home to explain to the others that mummy and Jenny were going to be away for a couple of nights – not that they understood but Graham felt better for telling them. Somehow Sue had managed to feed the other five single handed or at least double handed, and none of the girls seemed to have any complaints about the service!

During the second evening Janet was at the hospital she waited until Jenny was fast asleep and quietly slipped away to dash back home for a change of clothes. She naturally did not want to leave Jenny for very long but as she rushed towards the house she tripped and fell at the kerb. The pain in her ankle was intense but she was able, just about, to walk on it and drive herself back to the hospital. By the time she arrived there, though, she was grateful for the offer of a lift in a wheelchair by a young hospital orderly – even though he did use her sore foot as a lance to prod open the swing doors as he charged down the corridors! His over-enthusiasm to hurry Janet through to the X-ray department made her rather wish she had not hitched a ride after all, and that she had quietly limped back upstairs to her bed next to Jenny's cot.

Fortunately there were no breaks or fractures, but it still seemed that it was she and not Jenny who had reason to have been in hospital as she hobbled out the main entrance with Graham and her daughter the next day. Safely tucked away in his inside pocket Graham had a leaflet explaining all about febrile convulsions so that they would be aware of what to do if it happened again. Once home, Jenny babbled and gurgled her story to her sisters, and thoroughly enjoyed being the centre of attention for a while.

It was not until twelve months had passed, following an attack of German measles on each girl in succession, that the mumps arrived, and Janet and Graham found themselves with a wounded army of little rednecks. The girls were not too miserable about it, though, and the bottle of Calpol, which most of the girls found to be an acceptable aperitif, was rationed and spoon fed to the troops by the medical orderlies Janet and Graham.

The worst thing about this particular plague, however, was its timing. Two weeks before the girls' third birthday Janet's sister Alison was to be married. Not long after the girls were born Janet had thought about the day her sister would marry, and decided then that if it was to happen at a time when the girls were old enough, it just would not be fair to have them all as bridesmaids. Too much attention would no doubt be given to the girls on a day when all the attention should be on the bride. Even so, plans were made for the girls secretly to attend the function after the service. There was to be a certain amount of discretion for fear that if the press knew that there was a possibility the girls may be attending their Aunty's wedding, as bridesmaids or not, it would have been a brilliant picture opportunity for them, and that was something that Janet and Graham definitely did not want.

Although it was planned, therefore, for all the girls to attend the reception, Janet and Graham decided to let Sarah, who was Alison's goddaughter, make a surprise solo appearance at the church. Unfortunately, though, the idea stumbled on the bumps of the mumps, for, as fate should have it, Sarah was the first to suffer with the illness. Even so, early on the Saturday morning Janet dressed Sarah all up in her new white dress that was finished off with the cutest of pink sashes across the front, new socks and new shoes, and then tied her hair back with a new white ribbon. The miserable mumps took a back seat as Janet's voice oozed with excitement. 'You're lucky, aren't you Sarah?' Janet said, putting a bow in the ribbon. 'You can go to Nanny Betty's and we've got to go to the silly old wedding!'

The tone in her mother's voice suddenly spirited a sense of self importance out of Sarah.

'Nanny Betty getting married as well?' There was a hiccuping hesitation between each delivered word.

Janet patiently waited for the whole sentence to come out and delighted in the sparkle on Sarah's pale face. Sarah was pleased with her query.

'No,' Janet chuckled back, 'she's already married to Grandad John; but you'll have a lovely time there won't you?' Sarah simply smiled and nodded in agreement.

Sue Thomas, along with husband Trevor, both now firm friends with Janet and Graham, had been seconded to bring Sarah along with a horseshoe to present to Aunty Ali, so, under the circumstances, it was left for them to decide whether it should be Kate, Ruth, Jenny, Lucy or Hannah who was to be Sarah's understudy. It meant that not even Janet or Graham knew who was going to make the surprise appearance.

The service went beautifully, with Janet, dressed in pink to match the girls' sashes, performing her role to perfection as matron of honour. As she, along with all the relatives and friends, followed the bride and groom out of the church into the brilliant late autumn sunshine, her eyes suddenly filled with tears of pride as she saw Hannah first, then Jenny holding Hannah's hand but shyly walking one pace behind, step ever so cautiously so as not to scrape their shiny new patent shoes, towards them. They were wearing outfits similar to the one Sarah had been dressed in that morning, but there were subtle touches of different coloured ribbons and shoes so that they did not look identical. When Janet looked around her she realised that she was not the only one shedding a tear, and as the girls walked up and gave Alison the horseshoe there was not a dry eye to be seen.

After the photographs were taken at the church, Sue and Trevor drove back to Wallasey with Hannah and Jenny to pick up Kate, Ruth and Lucy. By the time they arrived at Graham's parents' house, where the girls had been waiting, Sarah had long since succumbed to the weariness brought on by the mumps and was soundly asleep in the spare bedroom. She did not hear her sisters skipping and singing their way to the car outside to be chauffeured to the reception.

Although the others escaped the mumps for the wedding, they did not escape for long. Within a week Hannah and Lucy had received the unwanted gift from Sarah, and the other three decided to spread things out a bit by having it on a weekly basis through to the middle of December. Somehow they all managed to feel well for just one week in between all this – but perhaps the mumps took heart and decided not to spoil their third birthday.

'Wheels for the Waltons' was just one of the headlines that appeared in the newspaper when Janet and Graham took delivery of a large estate car loaned to them by Fords. The *Daily Star* used the word 'Bootiful!'

above a picture of the babies in their six carrycots neatly slotted into the back of the car in two rows of three. The space afforded by this vehicle allowed all of the girls to travel in the safest possible manner. In the old family car there was only enough room for two single carrycots, so two of the girls would have to be carried by Janet and two by either Sue Perry, the nursery nurse, or perhaps Nancy or Betty. Skyway, the local dealer, had taken the project of sorting out the family's transport problem very seriously, focusing on space and safety. Fitting a car with seatbelts for the rear seats has become virtually standard procedure for many manufacturers, but fitting seatbelts to strap in six carrycots safely was not exactly an everyday request. Coincidentally, it was garage boss John Walton (no relation) who commissioned draughtsmen and engineers to ensure that the family would be able to travel securely.

Janet and Graham were, therefore, delighted with the car. It opened up all sorts of new horizons and opportunities. So under the by-lines of 'Super babes ride in style' and 'Easy riders', Janet and Graham gratefully took possession, albeit only for six months, of what was also referred to by one paper as 'the world's poshest baby buggy'.

Inside the carrycots were standard straps restraining the delicate contents from wriggling, rattling and rolling. This was all very well for the first couple of months but by the time the summer came along Houdini could have learnt a trick or two from the sightseeing sixsome. The speed with which the children had learnt to shed their shackles shocked Janet and Graham, but it was only natural that they should want to see more of life than the lining of a carrycot, and with so many sisters to 'talk' to it was too much to expect them not to sit up and struggle to unharness not only themselves but each other. Lucy was the worst offender and on more than one occasion Janet, sitting in the passenger seat up front, would look over her shoulder to find Lucy in the wrong carrycot snuggling up to Sarah or gripping Ruth's rattle or Kate's rag doll or caught between Jenny and Hannah's carrycot.

While having the car had all the tremendous benefits of allowing the family to get out and about, whenever they did go somewhere it was a nightmare trying to keep a semblance of safety and order in the back as little heads and bums popped up and down in each cot. It was like travelling in a nursery on wheels. And next to the babies in the carrycots was all the paraphernalia necessary to keep a happy camp.

Preparing to travel was just another routine Janet and Graham had to cope with. It was far from straightforward and usually took as much strategic planning as a polar expedition! There was so much to remember to take each time and it was so easy to forget or mislay things. Wherever they were likely to go it was unlikely there would be appropriate seating arrangements for six babies so invariably the girls' baby seats, which had to be dismantled first, would have to be squeezed somehow into the back of the car and then rebuilt on arrival. Physically making the journey to and from the house with all the equipment, not to mention the children, was in itself exhausting work. And with all that, the odds were six to one that a nappy would have to be changed at the last minute or one of the babies would be sick during the journey. One of the most frequent trips the family made was the one that took them back to Neston where not only Janet's mum and dad but all her family still lived.

Nancy was still working full time as a cook at Yeoman House in Neston. Her experience of feeding en-masse was not wasted, therefore, on her days off, which she mostly devoted to her growing grand-daughters. It was, though, a long journey to her daughter's, and normally either Janet or Graham would give her a lift at the end of the day. Occasionally, though, during that first summer Nancy spent the night at the house in Bidston, either in the spare bedroom or on a camp bed downstairs, and then Janet and Graham would give the babies a treat and the whole family would go for a ride to take Nanny Nancy home.

On the way back to Nancy's one Sunday afternoon, with the car suitably rearranged to accommodate an extra adult, Janet, trying to stop Kate climbing from one cot to another, suggested that they stop off at Nanny Fox's on the way to Nancy's. 'She hasn't seen the girls for ages and she's bound to be at home,' Janet said. 'The girls are due for their next feed soon so we could do it at her house. She'd be made up to help us with the girls' bottles.' She refastened Kate's straps, gave her a tickle and asked her daughter's opinion. 'Would you like to see your Nanny Fox, Kate?' The baby beamed at the personal attention.

'Shall we give your great-grandmother a big surprise girls?' Graham asked, but without waiting for an official count of the population in the car as he turned in the direction of Janet's grandma's home.

When they got to Nanny Fox's, one by one Graham, Janet and Nancy took the girls inside the house, each making two journeys. The last to be carried was Lucy, and as Janet picked her out of her carrycot and turned away from the vehicle she slammed the tailgate shut at the same time. However, no sooner had she done so, she was instantly aware of an echoing click as the central locking system automatically secured all the doors. The keys were still in the car.

Her first thought was that all the girls were out of the car. That was more than a relief. The idea of one of them being trapped sent shivers down Janet's back. However, at first it all seemed a bit of a joke. The girls were inside the house, safe and warm, and all they needed to do was to find a way of breaking in to the car. But it was not that easy. Faced with such a sophisticated locking mechanism Graham soon had to admit defeat, and he went back inside to deliver the bad news.

Ruth was the first to start asking for her milk, and soon her crying was a signal for Lucy and Sarah to join in the chorus. They all knew the tune, and as the other three joined in, the audience of adults knew this was not a show they were going to enjoy. Usually when crying filled the air, Graham's instinct was to draw from his pockets the six-shooting silencers which he would pop into the girls' mouths. He might just as well have drawn blanks as his hands reappeared with only one lonesome-looking dummy – hardly an effective remedy under the circumstances.

Graham and Nanny Fox did their best to comfort the girls and Nancy phoned her brother-in-law Paul, who lived nearby, to give her a lift to the nearby village chemist store to buy some powdered milk, bottles, rusks, dummies and anything else she thought they were going to need in the survival kit. Janet then picked up the phone. 'Good afternoon, Neston Police station, can I help you?'

She moved the phone slightly away from her ear as the deep bellowing baritone boomed through the receiver. It was friendly though and gave Janet a feeling of confidence that she had done the right thing.

'This is Janet Walton speaking ...' She could have left it at that but this was an emergency and she had to pull out all the stops. '... the mother of the sextuplets.' Janet cringed, embarrassed at using that word that she and Graham tried to avoid when talking about their own children.

It was the desk sergeant who had taken the call, and once Janet had explained her dilemma he assured her that the police would be to the rescue very soon to sort out the problem. Within minutes a grey-haired grandfatherly sergeant and a confident young constable arrived and were meticulously mating the locks with an enormous bunch of car keys. While this was going on, Janet was busy mashing up bits of banana and anything that seemed suitable from the fridge for the girls. The girls, though, just would not eat it and demonstrated their distaste for the makeshift diet by turning up the volume.

The noise from the house was getting louder and things were getting out of hand. Forced into a frustrated submission, as one key after another failed to fit, the sergeant admitted defeat and did what any conscientious member of the constabulary would have done under the circumstances. He telephoned the Automobile Association. Graham began to think that the chain of rescuers would get longer and longer until they found a car thief but the arrival of the AA saved the day, and, without revealing how he learnt his skill, the patrolman soon sat triumphantly in the front seat of the car. Meanwhile, the family raced to get everything out of the back of the vehicle and into the house. They were followed closely by the sergeant and his constable, their spirits not discouraged and still willing to help.

Janet, keeping with what had become a tradition of making full use of all available hands when it came to feeding time for her babies, gave each bobby a baby and a bottle. The sergeant, who had obviously had some experience, was feeding Sarah; the constable, looking a little nervous and pale, had custody of Kate; the AA patrolman gladly serviced Jenny; Janet, Graham and Nancy saw to the others, and Nanny Fox saw to the tea.

As Sarah happily suckled away in the safe hands of the sergeant, he looked concerned as he glanced at his colleague. 'Up a bit lad, up a bit!' he advised, demonstrating the way it should be done. When all the crying had stopped and the girls had settled in the baby seats in their great-grandmother's front lounge, Janet and Graham thanked the three uniformed men for all their efforts. As he closed the garden gate, the sergeant turned and gave a broad grin. 'All in the line of duty, Mr and Mrs Walton,' he said, as if it was something he had always wanted to say but had never found the right moment, '. . . all in the line of duty!'

The children who lived on the Ford estate, which bordered the small batch of houses built on Statham Avenue, were frequent callers on Janet and Graham. They often would knock on the door and with bunches of daffodils in their hands would say that they had picked them specially for the girls. Some of the other front gardens in the road were beginning to look suspiciously bare but nobody complained about the divestment, and if the neighbours had seen the faces on the kids who carried the flowers they would have found it hard to disapprove.

A few nights after the first documentary had been transmitted, there was a bold knock on the front door. The last feeds of the day had been given, nappies changed and most of the girls had settled down in their cots contented and without fuss. But the routine of the day was far from over and Janet was as usual scuttling around the house bundling an array of the girls' not-so-best bibs and tuckers and all the other washing into her arms ready for the evening laundry. The washing machine never seemed to stop and its hum was as constant as the click of the kitchen clock.

Graham was in the playroom on his hands and knees tidying up after the girls' hard day's work. Every so often he winced as one of his hands came firmly down on one of the brightly coloured pieces of plastic building blocks. Along one wall, smartly standing to attention like a regiment of the Queen's guard, was a row of half a dozen red latticed laundry baskets that were used to store the toys at night, and just as he was throwing in the last few items he heard an urgent volley of raps on the front door. 'I'll get it!' Graham shouted as he cast a satisfying glance across the cleared carpet.

As he turned the latch and opened the door he was surprised to find nobody there. In the distance he heard the faint sound of laughing and assumed that it was the kids from the estate who had thought better of disturbing them at night and had taken flight. Just as he was about to close the door a little head popped round the corner of the wall. It was a boy aged about ten years old with a round fresh freckled face and tightly cropped spiky blond hair.

'Was that you making all that noise?' The chirpy and friendly tone of Graham's voice encouraged the little boy to shuffle around the corner towards him.

'Yeah!' The boy was wearing a very tatty pair of blue jeans, suspended at half mast from his waist by a pair of braces, and an equally tatty shirt. And on the feet of this little ragamuffin was a shiny pair of black 'bovver' boots.

'Are they your mates, are they?' Graham asked, referring to the noise in the distance.

'Yeah!' The voice now sounded much more sure of itself.

'Cowards, eh?' ...

'Yeah!' The lad's chest expanded as much as his braces would allow, and he smiled at the recognition of his valour.

'Right then,' Graham braced himself as they stood opposite each other. 'What can I do for you then, son?'

The boy looked at Graham straight between the eyes. 'Eh Mister, do them six babies live here?' The words sounded as menacing as the tiny strips of metal on the toes of his boots.

'Yes, that's right.' Graham looked at him and expected the worst.

'What are their names?'

Graham bent down, lowered his head and put his hands on his knees. 'Hannah, Lucy, Ruth, Sarah, Kate and Jenny,' he replied.

A big beaming smile spread the freckles on the boy's face. 'You know what, Mister?'

'What?' asked Graham.

In a quiet voice padded with the shy softness of a spring lamb, the little skinhead said, 'I love them babies!'

It was the kind of thing that reflected the friendliness of the whole neighbourhood. Statham Avenue really had been a great place for them to live over the first two years with the girls. From the wayward actions of a few, the Ford estate had gained a reputation at the time of being a rough area but every time Janet and Graham went for a walk down that way people would pop out of their houses to see the girls, say hello and wish them well. During the time they were living there construction work was being carried out at the nearby Bidston Hall Farm. It was not until after the new wing to the farmhouse was completed that Janet and Graham discovered that the area had been given a new landmark. Carefully carved within the lintel above a window that overlooked the public footpath alongside the farm, the stonemason had created a triangle of six little hearts. There are no words alongside it, and no doubt some will be curious as to its meaning, but the local people will be able to tell of the happy times spent there by the girls from the house round the corner.

· Thirteen ·

Return to Wallasey

♡ ♡ ♡
♡ ♡
♡

Whilst the house in Statham Avenue adequately met all the family's needs, and would have continued doing so for a few more years, a decision was made to make the break after only two years. Janet and Graham had always viewed it as a house rather than a home. Without doubt it was a pretty house and far grander than their little semi in Browning Road, but even that was to hold far deeper memories than Statham Avenue ever would. And the move had been completed in the public eye, something the couple never resented but accepted in a compromising fashion. They were grateful for the deals that were completed on their behalf but were aware of the importance of their privacy, their own lives and their own self-respect.

Janet and Graham often think back to the first day they walked together hand in hand up the wide path of the house in Warren Drive. It was an icy February evening in 1986, and the large front garden looked sad and weary. It was a very imposing building. Four large bay windows were perfectly balanced, two on the ground floor and two above, and on another floor were two smaller windows. It all seemed very grand, and the couple felt like first-time buyers again as they tip-toed up to view the property.

Emotions of that nature were not given a moment to settle. Determination had set in well before they had brushed passed the fourth laurel bush on the right, and, without anything being said, by the time they had passed the cold grey rockery in front of the two bay windows, the decision was made.

To return to Wallasey was something Janet and Graham had dreamt of virtually from the moment the family had left Browning Road. They spent many evenings in Statham Avenue sipping a glass of Liebfraumilch, enjoying the precious silence as the girls slept quietly upstairs, and talking of the time they would find a big old house somewhere back in Wallasey Village. It would be somewhere they would know instinctively was to be their home until the girls grew up. It would have large rooms downstairs with plenty of space for the girls to wander around, and ideally there would be a large pleasant lounge to ensure Janet and Graham some privacy and in which they could entertain their friends. Maybe even a dining room as well; a room that could be used by the girls as a very special treat at Christmas, Easter or birthdays.

They imagined the rooms upstairs would be much larger than those in the Bidston house. The children would be able to move about easily and play in their bedrooms without feeling inhibited; there was, after all, no question of them having their own rooms – that not only would have required a mansion, but, more importantly, it would not have been something that they would have wanted for their children. The girls enjoyed sharing bedrooms, and that was important given that they would have to get used to sharing many things over the next few years. And if the house really was the one they were looking for, it would have a special room for the girls to call their own. Somewhere that was bright and cheerful, full of colour and joy so that they could shout, scream, laugh and cry to their hearts' content, or discontent as the case might be.

And then they would dream about how the garden would be Janet's domain and how Graham would make it a special project to paint and decorate the house from top to bottom, and that there would be a pretty little guest room where perhaps nanny Nancy could stay instead of having to make the long journey back to Neston.

Now and again, however, on those quiet evenings, when thoughts of the future and of the past tripped and journeyed across the hearth with the warmth of the fireplace smouldering peacefully, crackling now and again and mingling with the conversation, the familiar sound of one of the girls would be heard. Then there was quiet. Then again, but a different sound. 'That was definitely a different noise.' Then louder. 'It's Hannah and Lucy.' The noise would grow louder again. 'But that was Ruth, I'm sure ...' That makes three. 'O-Oh ... here comes trouble!' Like a great philharmonic orchestra tuning up, one noise played with another and just as each instrument has its own distinctive sound, thus the girls created their own unique whimpers, cries and shouts. The chain reaction had begun and one by one, conscious that they were now in the throes of a battle for attention and ever increasingly aware that mum and dad could only each deal with one of them at a time, the noises grew. Under these circumstances, a different king of caring, confidence boosting and love was called for. When all hell breaks loose, there is no time for soft whispers of encouragement back to slumber; there is, after all, no danger of anyone else being woken. It is time for determined practicality and keeping control. Like two life boat volunteers, Graham and Janet would run up the staircase reacting to the alarm bells and losing no time. All that was lacking was the sou'westers which, on occasion, would probably have come in quite handy! Then, like two great octopuses performing magic tricks they would resolve one crisis after another; a change of nappy, new sheets, a drink of water or a glass of milk, a hug, a kiss, and listening. Always listening. Perhaps most important of all Janet and Graham knew that they always must listen to the girls.

When they were both back downstairs together in front of the fire again, a drink was necessary. The type of drink was directly related in quality or strength rather than in quantity, to how rough the sea had been upstairs. Mildness and a good straightforward run usually meant abandoning the Liebfraumilch and moving on to tea or coffee. Choppy waters and an uncomfortable voyage gave way to a few further glasses of white wine and a force ten gale meant a hardy scotch for Graham and a large gin and tonic for Janet.

The nights of dreaming then turned into nights of planning. There were formalities to complete, of course, as there is in any house purchase, but the decision had been made; both Janet and Graham knew then as they were shown around from room to room that Warren Drive was exactly what they had been looking for. Whatever lay ahead for them as a family, they would face together as a family. It was not just a house of bricks and mortar, it was a home – a real home where all the joys and heartaches would be shared. And a determination set in to make it as perfect as possible.

All the space they had wished for was there, including a large comfortable room Janet and Graham decided to use as their own lounge. There they would put all their nicer pieces of furniture and ornaments and the girls would treat the room with care and respect.

Upstairs there were five large bedrooms, two at the front with large bay windows, one of which would be the master bedroom, the other for two of the girls. A similar large room with a bay window overlooking the garden at the rear would be ideal for two more of the girls and another bedroom at the rear for the other two. At first the spare bedroom was to be for guests and eventually it became Hannah and Sarah's room.

Opposite the top of the staircase across the landing a door led to yet another staircase, at the top of which were three further rooms. Two of them were small and would be ideal as a storage room and a study. At the front, though, high in the massive roof area lay the crowning glory. Measuring over twenty feet by twenty feet, it would make the perfect playroom for the girls. A room they could call their own.

As time went by and the family settled into their new home, Janet and Graham became used to learning something new about dealing with the girls every day. They soon realised that putting the girls to bed was one of their most difficult tasks unless a well-prepared plan of action was carried out first.

Even though the girls were well into walking there was always a quantity of outstretched arms at the bottom of the stairs and begging faces pleading to be picked up and carried to bed. It is a natural thing for any parent to want to do, but for Janet and Graham it would have taken most of the night to pick up each child, carry her upstairs and tuck her into bed. One of the tricks that Janet and Graham devised, however, had a reasonable amount of success in avoiding this dilemma.

After pyjamas were on and enough playtime had been allowed downstairs, Janet would shout out, 'Right! Will all the girls stand in a line!' Jenny would normally come to attention first dragging Sarah behind her, and then Kate, but Hannah, Lucy and Ruth, with a little bit of mischief in their eyes, would always wait until they were grabbed by either parent and placed into line. Then, raising the pitch of excitement in her voice, Janet would give a cue to the girls to join in a familiar marching song or nursery rhyme. Once they were all singing and lifting their little legs up and down like soldiers marking time, a shrill 'Follow me!' would ring out and one by one the girls would march behind Janet, with Graham following up the rear keeping the stragglers in order.

After three circles of the room, Janet would promptly lead the pack through the door, diagonally across the grey carpeted hall to the bottom of the staircase, and glancing over her shoulder to make sure the ranks had not broken and receiving a wink from Graham, would shout out above the sweet screeching of the choral ensemble, 'O.K. Up the stairs!' When it worked, it was almost pure *Mary Poppins* and before you could whistle they were all in bed fast asleep – not necessarily the right bed, but still, fast asleep.

When it did not work, however, a bit more ingenuity was required. Something perhaps more akin to rugby or American football. Sometimes the girls bunched together just before the moment when bedtime was called, closed ranks as though in a scrum or when American footballers gather around the quarter-back to work out the next game plan, and debated the best strategy for prolonging their time downstairs.

Jenny would hide behind the couch and Sarah would tuck herself in neatly between the folds of the curtains. Hannah might hop about in pain and cry out for a change of elastoplast on an old war wound – it would never do to go to bed with a dirty plaster. Kate always wanted to listen to a particular nursery rhyme tape just one more time. Lucy would hide in the toilet. She would sit there defiantly until having had her name called at least half a dozen times – 'Lucy have you finished yet?' – by either parent, she would anticipate the arrival of one pair of long arms that would secure themselves under her arms and raise her from the throne.

In the middle of the melee, centre stage as it were, Ruth would throw what became to be known as a 'wobbler'. In reality it was a frustrated reaction from tiredness and a fiery determination in her character to get her own way. The performance, though, was never matched by the others. She would lie prostrate in the middle of the room, having thrown herself to the ground like a religious fanatic, and begin to move her limbs. First the right arm, then the left leg, followed by the left arm and right leg. All working in perfect unison, feet stomping and fists thumping the carpet. There was no hiding, delaying tactic or excuse from Ruth. This was a straightforward protest of 'I don't want to go to bed!'

Ruth had to be sorted out first. Graham or Janet would grab her by the legs and, if she was lying on her tummy, would turn her over to ensure eye contact. Held by the ankles, the game would begin.

'You know what time it is, don't you?' Janet would say as she pulled Ruth towards her.

'No!' Ruth would scream back. Giggling would be heard going on in the background from behind the settee and the curtains.

'What time is it?' Janet would persist in a tone she used when telling the girls the fairy story of *Goldilocks and the Three Bears* ('Who's been sleeping in my bed?'). For a second time Ruth would be pulled back and once again she would scramble away as far as the length of her little legs would permit. 'It's ... bedtime!' And as Janet spoke those words she would pull Ruth once again towards her and in one swift movement she would let go of her ankles. Then using her hands like the tentacles of an octopus Janet would place them on Ruth's tummy and a relentless tickling session would begin. The screams of protest would collapse into fits of laughter, squeals of delight and shouts of, 'Again ... again!' and 'More, please more!'

Out from behind the curtains Sarah would come, not wanting to miss out on the fun, and with overpowering curiosity Jenny, too, would concede defeat and come scrambling out on all fours from behind the sofa. Hannah's sore knee was all of a sudden a thing of the past, and in no time Kate was jumping up and down in an effort to get a better view of what all the laughter was about.

Meanwhile, from the toilet, if she had not already been sorted out, and whether or not she had had any success, there would be a forlorn shout from Lucy, 'Mummy ... daddy! There's no toilet paper!' Muffled by the commotion in the front room, her cry at first would fall on deaf ears. Again she would shout, this time louder, and this time she would be heard by dad, who was crossing from the kitchen to the living room to see what all the noise was about. Once she had been sorted out she would dart into the room before Graham had a chance to flush the loo, and by the time he would arrive in the front room Janet would have all six girls lying down in front of her, all on their backs. And with their eyes sparkling like a dozen diamonds, the room would come alive with the sound of 'Me, me, me next!' from one, and 'No, me! me! me!' from another. It did not matter who said what. They all wanted a turn and that was that.

This was probably the most lively xylophone in the world. As Janet's hands moved from tummy to tummy, the girl whose belly was receiving the attention would squeal with laughter as Janet would sing, 'Doh, ray, me, far, so, lah, tee ... doh!'

On seeing that everything was under control Graham would seize the opportunity to go upstairs and get the pyjamas. The big pile of nightclothes would be dumped in the centre of the room, and with the girls generally a little more tired and more amenable to the idea of bed, on hearing either mum or dad call out, 'Who's going to be the first to get into their pyjamas!' a mad scramble would ensue. It would be like a giant pillow fight where the pillows had burst open and instead of being filled with feathers they had been stuffed to the seams with clothing – t-shirts, shoes, socks, knickers, vests all floating about the room. 'Mummy! I can't get my buckle undone!' Sarah would shout full of excitement. 'Help me. Help me! The uvvers are going to winned me!'

'I'm going to win, I'm going to wi ... in! So there!' Ruth would taunt with her head hidden, struggling to escape from the hole in her pyjama top and with one leg in Kate's pyjama trousers.

'No you're not!' Jenny would say quite matter-of-factly. 'I'm going to winned anyway!'

Adding a touch of class to the situation, Hannah would add something refined, like, 'Me knickers are up me bum!' Well things like that do happen to a three-year-old! In any event the winner of the race was, of course, partially determined by Janet and Graham. Those that were good at doing things for themselves, like undoing buttons and buckles, were left to get on with it, while Janet and Graham helped the others. But there were always special moments when, out of the corner of their eye, either Janet or Graham would catch perhaps Ruth or Jenny, without any parental prompting, helping one of their sisters with buttons and things.

Preparing the girls for bed at the end of the day was without doubt, exhausting hard work. It called for all Janet and Graham's imagination to work up the girls' enthusiasm for it. Spirits had to be raised and games had to be invented and played to capture their attention and gain their co-operation. An adult, being a lot bigger and stronger than a child, can easily make the child do as he or she wishes, but this was something that Graham and Janet consciously went out of their way to avoid. Sharing and working together with the girls was the only way to succeed, and so while there was always going to be the inevitable smacked bottom at bedtime, they made special efforts to ensure those episodes were few and far between.

It is curious how for toddlers sores and scratches are so important as items of display once the pain has subsided. Invariably, in the Walton household, no matter who the visitor was at the door, the girls would swiftly whip off shoes and socks to show off tiny marks of redness on the legs or little toes.

On Saturday mornings Graham's mum, Betty, regularly came to visit the girls. Her arrival one day during the summer was, as usual, heralded by shouts and screams of joy as the girls greeted her. Once the welcome was over and most of the girls had dispersed, Jenny slowly but ever so slowly, rolled up the leg of her jeans. She glanced up at her nan each time she exposed a little bit more leg to make sure she had not lost her attention, and then like a jeweller showing off his most precious stone she proudly revealed a little blot of dried-up blood on her knee. The smile of excitement in being able to show such evidence of bravery disappeared for a moment as she reflected on how it had happened, and with a tear in her voice she looked up and said, 'I felled over,' but to underscore the heroics of the event she added, '... but I didn't cry!'

While Betty was sympathising with Jenny, Ruth noted that her sister was getting all the attention. And not only that, for when it came to sores, bruises, bumps and scratches, Ruth was an expert in the field. In short, she was the Princess of Elastoplast.

Betty had not got further than the hall, and was uttering consoling noises to Jenny, when Ruth screamed, 'Look at this!' Not wishing to be rude to Jenny, who had, after all, been the first to gain attention, Betty did not respond to Ruth's request. Big mistake. While Lucy held all the foghorn medals of the household at that time, Ruth was never far behind! Three times louder and three times longer Ruth repeated her call for attention. 'Look ... at ... THIS!' followed immediately by a whining, 'Ohhh ...' and a half whimpered cry, '... look!' by which time Betty realised that it was not wise to ignore Ruth much longer, and she turned her attention from Jenny's knee to two bony elbows that had been placed in front of her eyes that her nose was in danger of being pinched. 'And this ...' Ruth added as Betty deftly dodged the elbows by bobbing her head backwards like a well-trained boxer. Ruth lifted a knee catching Betty square on the chin. 'And this!' Her blonde locks showered her grandmother's face as she swivelled around on her 'good' foot and lifted her heel to show another tiny scar. The plaster had come away ages before, leaving the usual sticky dark area surrounding the sore, and as Ruth completed her turn she managed, on the downswing of her foot, to catch Betty somewhere in the midriff.

Ruth finished off the scenario with a broad smile and the word 'See?' meaning, of course, that now that Betty had been shown these horrendous battle scars she would immediately be able to tell from the manner in which they were displayed that they did not bother their owner one little bit. Ruth did not wait around to be told how brave she was. She knew it already!

Believe it or not there are books devoted solely to potty training! But reading about it and putting it into practice are two very different things. For Janet and Graham, at times it seemed as if these plastic portable conveniences would forever be attached to the girls' behinds. Whenever anyone happened to be visiting the house over this potty period, there always seemed to be an ungainly yellow protrusion in sight.

The plan was to let the pots casually become part of the scenery. Quite a good tip really. The idea was to leave the pots in a corner of the playroom, bedrooms and bathroom and wait until the girls became curious. Well, one piece of plastic is just as interesting as another to a child of two and it was not long before having become bored with one toy that these interesting hats in the corner looked like fun to one, then another, then another, until eventually all six had them on their heads. That was the cue for mum to move in and embark on the next important stages in the metamorphosis from babyhood into childhood. As difficult a time as this is for parents, it is even more so for the child. Graham and Janet were very much aware that it was a massive hurdle for the girls to get over.

Having successfully created an interest in the pots by arousing the girls' curiosity, the question was, what to do next. Making the girls realise that the pots were to be placed on a different part of the anatomy other than the head was not too difficult, although there was the odd occasion later on when a semi-filled pot had to be swiftly removed from a day-dreaming hand just as one of the girls was about to anoint herself. The real hardship lay in getting the girls to do something once they were sitting comfortably. Janet turned to Nancy and Betty for counsel in the matter. They both prescribed the same remedy that they had used on their own offspring, and neither hesitated in recommending a simple course of bribery.

Hannah, when it came to potty time, was like a well-plumbed tap. She took to the seat like a duck to water, and was able to switch on and off as she pleased. This stood her in excellent stead when the bribes were being handed out, and it was not long before Janet began to wonder who was manipulating whom; clearly Hannah had cottoned on to the fact that the performance was well worth the bait. The bait was an enormous tin of delicious chocolate sweets all wrapped in an assortment of coloured cellophane. The rules were made and the girls immediately understood the game. They had already become used to sitting on the pots and it was now just a matter of making proper use of them.

Jenny, Kate, Sarah, Lucy and Ruth looked on in wonder as Hannah tantalised them by slowly and seductively removing the wrapper of her prize for doing the business. They moved their pots in closer and gathered around her like a board of directors around their newly appointed chairman. She knew she was ahead of the others on this occasion and was making the most of her moment of glory. She held court with all the majesty of a queen on her throne and even made the holding of the wrapper a privilege for one lucky sister.

Visitors to the house over the next few weeks were often greeted by the sight of a little girl sitting on a yellow pot munching happily away at a coconut whirl or a strawberry cream. It was a bit like in one end and out the other, but the important thing was that it had the desired effect and it was not long before the Walton girls were dry as a bone and well on their way to nappyless days.

There were, of course, the odd spillages and the carpets took a bit of a battering which was only to be expected. There was more than one occasion when Ruth would spring from her pot delirious with joy and in an excited frenzy would run to tell her mum or dad, only to kick over three other recently filled receptacles on the way. Dragging Janet or Graham by the arm she would squelch her way back into the room, proudly pick up her own pot and with an unsteady hand display the contents.

Sarah and Kate were a little slower to respond to potty training – even though they were always bursting for a sweet. Sarah would frequently tug the hem of Janet's skirt and, with hopeful eyes, look up and show what appeared to be an empty yellow pot in her right hand, saying, 'Did it, did it, look, look, wee-wee!' Sure enough sitting rather lonely in the centre of the bowl was the tiniest drop of something. 'No Sarah. Go and try a little harder.' Janet knew that if she relented and gave her a sweet and covered her up she would only wet herself again within minutes. It was exactly the same for all the girls, and although time and time again Janet and Graham felt awful they both knew that if they were not hard about it they would end up losing the battle.

One afternoon Janet, however, broke her own rules. She had been going about the daily chores, and half way through the afternoon she noticed that Kate must have been trying for what seemed to be hours, just patiently sitting on her pot, reading a Donald Duck book, singing Ba-Ba-Black Sheep and waiting for something to happen. Now and again Kate had got up, taken a walk around the back of her seat, examined it in detail, and frowning had taken up her position once again like a soldier on guard duty.

'How are you getting on Kate? Have you done anything yet?' Janet cheerfully enquired with a voice full of encouragement as she passed her daughter in the hall.

'Fink so,' came Kate's meekly delivered response, suddenly having to contend with her mother's interest and aware there was nothing to show.

'Oh good,' said Janet. 'Let's have a look.'

Janet was standing behind Kate who was by now very much in the doldrums thinking that she was about to disappoint her mum. As Kate rose slowly Janet quick as a flash squeezed a flannel soaked in orange juice into the pot and said in the most excited way she could, 'Oh, Kate. Good girl, Kate. That's very good! I'll just go and get you a sweet.' Kate had no idea how it had happened but her face beamed with pride and joy. She had been so good just sitting there and trying without once complaining that Janet's face also beamed with pride and joy.

· Fourteen ·

Growing Pains

There can be no really safe way to lift more than one child at a time. Most medical books that concentrate on the subject of back pain, lumbago and other related problems will normally go to great lengths to illustrate the best way to lift a heavy weight, but not a child. They will even point out that high among the sufferers are housewives and mothers, and strongly advise that time should be found on several occasions during the working day to relax and do some exercises. But the routine at the Walton household left Janet and Graham little room for such indulgence. From the day the last nurses had left, the pressure was naturally greater, the stress and strain factors were bound to increase and, not surprisingly, eventually something would have to give. What gave was Janet's sciatic nerve.

With the children safely tucked away in bed, Janet had come downstairs to clean and tidy up. Graham was outside putting the trikes, tractors and wheel-barrows back in the shed and generally tidying up the garden area when he thought he heard Janet cry out. He ran inside to find her bent over, holding the small of her back with one hand and the side of her right leg with the other. Janet had suffered back trouble before, but nothing as excruciatingly painful as this. She had just been picking up various odds and ends in the hall when something inside her seemed to give way and she had been too weak to shout out loudly. She knew immediately that this 'something' was more serious than any other back twinge she had suffered before.

Graham tried to guide Janet into the lounge so that she could lie down on the settee. At first she would not move. Tears of pain were rolling down her cheeks and an awareness that any movement could make things worse made her momentarily freeze. As Graham stood in front of her, various thoughts flashed across her mind. How lucky it was that Graham was not playing five-a-side that night. But what about the cakes she was supposed to bake that evening for the Women's Institute fete in two days' time? And then another thought – one that made her go cold and virtually anaesthetised the pain – Graham and the girls needed her there. She knew Graham could cope, but there was far too much to do and hospital was out of the question. With that in mind and with Graham's help, but at the pace of a snail, she slowly but surely made the journey from the hall to the lounge. It took nearly ten minutes.

There had been several occasions when Janet had picked up more than one of the girls at the same time. In the first six months both Janet and Graham had become most adept at dealing with even three girls at a time. Naturally, though, the girls had been putting on weight, and, although Janet did not realise it at the time, the strain of carrying them was taking its toll.

Rest was prescribed and Janet had no choice but to lie in bed for a couple of days. There had been a time when the whole family was stricken with the flu not long after the last nurse had left, and they had given in to their doctor's insistence of bringing her back for a couple of weeks after he told them that they were showing obvious signs of exhaustion. But even then things had not come to a standstill. This time, though, it was a physical impossibility for Janet to do even the most basic chores. So, comforted by Graham's assurances, Janet tried to put the worry of the girls out of her mind and lay quietly until the pain passed. And in the meantime six tiny waitresses took turns helping their dad bring her meals on a tray together with bunches of flowers they had picked from the garden. From then on, though, Janet left the lifting of more than one to the man of the house.

The health of the children, however, because of their prematurity at birth, was something the hospital kept a regular eye on over the first few years. Hannah was the first born, and in the mind of the examining doctor, therefore, she was the first in line to do everything on their annual visit to the special care unit for their assessment. When they stacked the files, Hannah's was always on top.

On the bright February morning when they arrived for their appointment, though, Hannah was surprisingly shy. She was never like this at home or indeed anywhere outside the house, but being a little older now and more aware she did not know what to expect and was therefore probably more reserved. Had she not been the first one in line, she might have felt differently. The ideal person to have gone first would have been Ruth. She had bounded in as if she went there every day or like a well-prepared pupil about to take an important exam. She was obviously looking forward to demonstrating her skills.

The girls also had their eyes tested. At one end of the room the doctor held up a flip chart and asked them to read out the letter displayed. As each card was flipped over the letters got smaller and smaller. By the time the doctor had got to the last letter it was practically illegible; in fact, it was purposefully beyond the range of normal vision. The last letter was an 'H' but as much as Janet strained, squeezed and generally contorted her eyeballs, it still looked just like a dot. There was absolutely no way that she could read what it was. Hand on hip and casually raising one eye towards the card, and in a tone that said isn't it obvious? Ruth quick as a flash shouted, 'H for Hannah!' The doctor and Janet just stood there and laughed.

Another of the tests the girls had to do was to thread beads on to a piece of string. Simple enough, one may think, but when you are a little over four and your fingers are just about getting to know each other it can be quite trying to thread ten of those tiny things with even tinier holes on to what must have felt like a great big thick piece of string by the time the fifth bead had bounced across the office floor and come to rest against the doctor's leather soles.

They also had the pleasure of playing ball with their doctor. This particular test involved catching a ball with cupped hands, and was supposed to analyse the girls' speed of reaction and co-ordination rather than for the doctor to get in some bowling practice during the day. He was obviously a keen sportsman and was used to handling a ball, for by the time he got to Ruth he was casually catching the ball with only one hand. As soon as she saw him catching the ball in such a casual fashion, she immediately did the same, to everybody's amazement, except of course Ruth's.

The hopping they were asked to do was not popular with some of the girls. Sarah had shown herself, along with Kate, in the last few weeks to be braver and braver. They had both been doing things that were out of character and much more forthright. The tests today had therefore not proved as difficult for them as Janet and Graham had expected. Hannah, on the other hand, was reluctant to hop, and when asked to stand on one leg she looked at the doctor with eyes that said, 'What do you think I am – an ostrich?' and she immediately buried her head in the sand-coloured skirt Janet was wearing.

Lucy had put up a good show. Considering she must have felt awful having just come through a particularly bad bout of the 'chickenpops', and was still showing off a number of blotchy medals and battle wounds all over her little body, she put on a very brave show indeed and did most of the tests quite well. She must have been moving along the road back to recovery as she put as much strength and enthusiasm as any of the others into banging on the doctor's door while her sisters were each having a private consultation, and yelling, 'Who is it?' which was not only a good game but also quite a good joke judging by the amount of giggling that was going on.

This was not Jenny's day. She really surprised Janet and Graham by refusing to do anything at all in front of the doctor. Any parent naturally wants their child to whiz through tests of this kind with flying colours. Although these tests are not undergone by every child, they are carried out as a sensible monitoring procedure for children who are born prematurely. Parents know instinctively how their children are developing and whether or not they are doing things they should be, and Janet and Graham were aware that all the girls were fit, healthy and showing signs of normal intelligence. So today Janet and Graham knew that, unlike Hannah, it was not through shyness that Jenny was refusing outright to do anything at all that the doctor asked of her. She did though display an interesting resistance, standing up for herself by saying in quite a grown-up fashion, 'Don't be stupid!' to most of the requests. Of all the girls Jenny was the most mature, and here she was, a sophisticated four-year-old going on five, being asked to hop on one foot and stand on one leg! This to her probably did seem ridiculous. These were, after all, tricks she was doing way back in eighty-five, when she was a sprightly young two-year-old!

Jenny decided that the only way to put an end to this particular pantomime was to dive under the table. This she did with great agility before either her mother or the doctor could stop her, and there ended the appointment. The next name was duly called on the roll-call, and Jenny went outside to her sisters and put on the most perfect display in front of them all of everything she was supposed to have done inside the consulting room, for which she had been awarded a capital 'R' for refusal on the list of options the doctor had for marking the progress that the girls were making. The other two options were pass and fail. Nobody achieved the distinction of the latter. In fact, the doctor had probably taken only a few minutes when the family had first arrived at the hospital to come to the conclusion that all the girls were making brilliant progress and were all perfectly normal happy healthy children.

Nursery school was a testing ground for the years of proper school that lay ahead and, surprisingly perhaps, a full set of Waltons would arrive regularly at the school gates each morning.

One morning, though, not long before the last day of nursery school term, Jenny had been noticeably lagging behind the others. She had overslept and when she finally entered the breakfast room, she was looking a little off-colour. She sat down, however, and along with the family ate all her breakfast. But when it came to the time to get into the car, she coyly held back but still said nothing.

It was clear to Janet, who by now was keeping a careful watch on Jenny, that all was not right but she knew Jenny would say something if she really did not feel up to going to nursery school. Janet could sense that Jenny was being very brave and was determined not to make a fuss about a silly tummy ache – school was more important and there was no way she wanted to miss painting. Janet gave Jenny every opportunity to tell her if anything was wrong but Jenny would not submit and climbed into the car with her sisters.

As always when one of the girls was sick, the others hardly took an interest. As the car moved along the road, Hannah, like a press officer giving out a news release, informed Janet that Jenny had been sick. There was a time when the girls were younger, when this would have caused a great deal of excitement and all the girls would gather around and examine the evidence, but now, like a boring old card trick, it had been seen so many times before that no one was really bothered.

Jenny's bravado had rapidly diminished. The battle was over and the tears hiccupped from Jenny's eyelids and trickled down her pale cheeks. In anticipation, Janet had already placed a towel over Jenny's dress. No objection had been raised at the time, just an understanding eyebrow, and when the time had come, Jenny's aim was good.

Janet pulled up outside the school gates. She momentarily considered the situation. Now what to do, she thought. Five to go in, one to stay in the car? No. Can't leave Jenny on her own in the car. She glanced at her watch and saw the long second hand threatening to make the last jump between one-minute-to and the o'clock. She quickly turned round and gave the orders.

'Right! Everyone stay in your seats! Mummy is going to clean the mess and then open the door for you all to get out!'

'Is Jenny going to school?' Hannah asked.

'No.'

''Cos she's been sick?'

'Yes, that's right luvvy.'

'Mummy!' Lucy was now trying to attract her mother's attention.

'I'll make you a painting, Jenny!' said Sarah thoughtfully.

'Mummy!' Lucy was on the usual second attempt.

'Think I might be sick, too, mummy,' said Ruth with a mischievous glint in her eyes.

'Mummy!' Lucy was now on her third run up.

'No you won't, madam!' said Janet now aware of Lucy's calls for attention but keeping Ruth in line.

'Mu . . . u . . . mmy!' Lucy was now bellowing at her best and beginning to make Janet think what other disaster she was going to be afflicted with that morning.

'Yes Lucy, what is it?'

'The sick's smelly!'

It was a very astute observation for a four-year-old, but fighting off the temptation to laugh at Lucy's statement Janet opened the car door on the pavement side to let all the girls out. Having lined up the five fit females of the force along the school railings, she gently picked up Jenny and held on to her while the others obediently behaved themselves, held each other's hands, and in one group of two and one of three, they followed their mum into school. After a quick explanation to Mrs Gavaghan, the girls' teacher, and before Janet had left, Kate, Sarah, Hannah, Ruth and Lucy were all at their easels ready to paint a 'get-well' picture for Jenny.

Back home, Jenny had snuggled into the settee in the front room and, looking pitifully forlorn and disappointed, settled into staring at the television. She was tired, still feeling sickly and wishing she was with her sisters drawing and painting. Normally all the girls would immediately ask for a video, but today Jenny just was not interested. She was half asleep and Graham, who had set aside the week to finish off painting the outside of the house, left the television quietly murmuring in the background while Jenny drifted into slumber. From a long way away at the other end of the house came the familiar noise of her dad whistling through his teeth as he applied the final coat of maroon gloss to the back door.

Graham looked in on Jenny a couple of times and took her in a cup of tea and a biscuit. There was no adverse reaction and clearly nothing to worry about; it was just a sickly turn and she would probably be as fit as the others by the time they got back with their mum.

Just as Graham was finishing off he looked up to see Jenny standing in the doorway.

'D'you know what dad?'

'What's that Jen?' he replied. 'Feeling all right now?'

'D'you know what?' she persisted, having forgotten all about being ill, missing nursery school and feeling sorry for herself.

'What Jen?' Graham answered gently, encouraging her to continue.

'We ... ell ...' she said slowly, 'we don't get green bananas, we get yellow bananas!' And she proceeded to relate to Graham in the finest detail the story of how bananas end up in all our houses after they have been picked from the trees in South America. 'When they are green,' she continued, 'they have to go into two boats and two lorries before they end up in the shops where mummy can buy them, and it takes all that long time to go yellow and you can eat them, otherwise you get ill!'

Graham could feel his Adam's apple bouncing up and down his throat and could feel his eyes glistening as they opened wide with amazement. It was a growing-up moment; a moment when reflections of the past and all that had happened since the girls were born flashed across his mind and met at some half-way point visions of the future and a realisation that they will all grow eventually into teenagers and then pretty, young independent women. She was not just talking to him fluently on a one-to-one basis, it was more than that. She was the teacher and gave the impression that she felt she had to educate her father on this incredible story she had just seen on television about the banana. It was as if she felt her parents could not possibly be aware of all these facts; after all, the story of the banana is not something you go out of

127

your way to read to your child when it's time for bed!

As new words increased their vocabulary, the girls' wit was getting sharper by the minute. One morning Graham was on his haunches helping Jenny adjust her collar on her dress. Knowing Jenny especially loved to be given compliments, and even more so if it had something to do with prettiness or beauty, Graham, who was looking at her at eye level, said, 'Jenny, I like your beauty spot,' referring to the little brown speckle on the front of her neck. Without hesitation she lowered her collar an inch displaying another one even smaller, but a genuine one just the same, and said, 'I've got two *actually*!' The word 'actually' was almost aching for a Mae West accent, indicating that if you thought that one spot meant beauty then two must mean twice as much.

· Fifteen ·

The Eye of the Public

♡ ♡ ♡
♡ ♡
♡

From the moment the girls were born, commercial minds began to tick away at the endless possibilities of using the family to help promote products. Offers came flooding in from manufacturers of clothing and baby goods, and Janet and Graham soon found themselves having to decide which to accept and which to turn down. In many ways it was a fortunate position to be in; it was obvious that with every normal cost of raising a baby being multiplied by six, the expense involved in bringing up the girls was going to be horrendous. On the other hand, there was more than a little concern about how much effect the exposure of this kind would have on the children.

The pressures involved for any couple faced with the prospect of raising a family are immense. Besides the obvious practical problems that have to be faced, coupled with the emotional strain, menacingly hovering overhead like an ignited match above a thatched cottage roof is the smouldering worry of finance. In the first instance Janet and Graham were grateful, just as all parents of multiple births in the United Kingdom are, to live in a country where a National Health service provides for care both before and after birth. In other countries where no such provision exists and insurance has to be relied upon, not all the costs would necessarily be met. But Janet and Graham were very much aware that help of that nature was only going to pay a short visit, and, in any event, they did not want to have to rely if at all possible on outside help. It would not be long before they would be on their own to face the financial burdens, and so where there seemed sensible opportunities to accumulate money, they carefully chose and took those opportunities, doing so in the long-term interests of the family.

Not long before the girls were born, a number of national newspapers carried a survey that detailed how much it would cost the average family to bring up a child from when it was born to the age of sixteen. The figure they had arrived at was £75,000. For Janet and Graham, multiplying the cost six times gave the rather daunting figure of £450,000. If they had stopped to think about things like this they probably would have found coping far more difficult than it already was, but they simply did not have the time to worry about such speculation. They were far too busy getting on with the job in hand, looking after the babies.

Many papers in the excitement of the moment made much of the 'millions' that the family would be able to earn from the situation. This, of course, was utter nonsense. Had the birth taken place in the United States where people are even more commercially minded, market places are far bigger and companies are more used and willing to pay out far greater sums of money, then maybe Janet and Graham would have had the opportunity to consider such figures. In Britain, however, companies are perhaps not as quick to see such commercial opportunities and tend to take a more reserved and conservative viewpoint, and while there were a couple of offers for advertising the majority of approaches made were on the basis of giving the family discounts or supplying Janet and Graham with a product in return for photographs and promotional work.

Exploitation was inevitable, and more than one company did their best to make the most of the family's instant fame. One car manufacturer had their knuckles rapped by the Advertising Standards Authority after they placed a full-page advert in the edition of the *Sunday Mirror* that carried world exclusive pictures of the babies. The advert pictured one of their vehicles with a baby's bottle, a dummy, a rattle, a teddy bear and even a potty being thrown out of the window, under the very large headline of, 'Well done Mr and Mrs Walton. Now, about getting them home . . .' In small letters underneath the vehicle it boasted that it had plenty of room for six pushchairs, six dozen nappies, six carrycots, six potties, six rattles, six romper suits, six teddies . . . and two tired adults.

It was clever and well timed and gave the impression that there was some sort of relationship between the manufacturer and the Waltons. But Janet and Graham's permission was not obtained and their complaint was upheld. The manufacturer's action was said to be an unjustifiable commercial exploitation of Janet and Graham.

One of the most gratefully received offers of merchandise came from Cindico, a company that specialised in babies' pushchairs but also manufactured other essential baby products. John Fothergill, the company's marketing director, made it clear he wanted nothing specific in return, not even a photo session. He was aware that Cindico would benefit merely from the babies being seen using their product. He visited Janet and Graham at home to assess what their needs would be, and within a couple of days the three double pushchairs arrived and, not long after, the six highchairs and the six babywalkers. Janet and Graham did not have the benefit, unlike most large families, of putting these items away each time one baby grows out of them and saving them for the next arrival. It would have cost a fortune to buy all these items in one go and so, not surprisingly, Janet and Graham were delighted to accept the offer.

When Janet and Graham had moved from Browning Road to the much needed larger house in Bidston, many believed that they had been given the new property by the builder in return for advertising. Although there was an agreement for some promotional work, in reality only a relatively small discount was forthcoming and, like everyone else, Janet and Graham found themselves with a hefty mortgage to pay. There was some welcome relief, though, when babyfood manufacturers Cow and Gate offered Janet and Graham, in return for a picture session, enough feeds for the first twelve months. It was another much needed saving. The most obvious product, nappies, were not the subject of any arrangement and that meant that with six changes per day six times over they had to find money for nearly 2,000 nappies every month.

With Graham having decided to take time off work, the principal source of income for the family came from a series of exclusive interviews, photosessions and television features. The girls had become overnight celebrities and it was up to Janet and Graham to decide how often the girls were to be exposed to the public. After the girls' first birthday Janet and Graham, began to limit the photosessions to special occasions like Mother's Day and Father's Day, but in June of 1985 the Queen's cousin Lord Patrick Lichfield was commissioned to take official photographs of the girls to celebrate their second birthday. The arrangements were made through Roger Eldridge of the London agency Camera Press and the date was set for 6 September giving just enough time for the photographs to be distributed to magazines all over the world for publication on 18 November.

Lord Lichfield was aware of Janet and Graham's difficulties of travelling with the girls to London so he suggested that his stately home, Shugborough Hall, set in the heart of the Staffordshire countryside, would be an ideal location.

The weather was fine the morning of the sixth, and having squashed every last necessity for every eventuality, including Betty, Nancy and Sue Thomas, into the vehicle, and having made an early morning call to the Hall, Janet and Graham set off at a sedate pace hoping that the fifty-mile journey would not be too much for the girls. If nothing else, Graham thought, as he drove the van on to the motorway, the trip would prove that they could at least travel longer distances as a family. Up until then they had felt safer restricting journeys with the babies to local areas, and the furthest they had been was to Janet's mum's house in Neston less than ten miles away.

As the van came up over the hill and within the sight of the welcoming party at Shugborough, Lichfield, showing an uncharacteristic sign of nerves, with his hand shading his eyes from the bright sunlight, was heard by one of his party to say, 'Oh my god, here they come!' He had no idea whether the session would work out or not; famous for photographing slightly more mature beautiful ladies, the prospect of what he had agreed to do was just dawning on him. When he had been the official photographer at the wedding of Prince Charles and Lady Diana Spencer, one of the most difficult shots he had to contend with then had been the group family photograph. The picture was essential as a historical record but there were over fifty people to deal with and he had to get everybody smiling and looking in the right direction at the same time. All of a sudden that did not seem such hard work compared to lining up six little two-year-olds.

'Morning!' Lichfield called out as he played the part of doorman opening up the side of the van. 'Welcome to Shugborough.'

'How do you do?' said Janet. One by one all the girls were unstrapped and taken out, and as the line of little children grew before him so did the difficulty of the task that lay ahead, which did little for his confidence. It was, after all, an extraordinary sight that never ceased to amaze anyone who saw the family for the first time.

While Patrick Lichfield went off to prepare all his equipment for the session, he left Janet, Graham and the girls in the charge of his own children's Nanny, having told her that if she could look after his three children then nine should not pose a problem. The girls found themselves in a wonderland of toys of every description as they used the playroom as a makeshift changing room. It was a nursery having been used for the same purpose for generations. One wall was lined with a colourful array of books and against another a Victorian doll's house stood proudly as a centrepiece. The girls did not know what to play with first. As three of them stretched to reach the reins of a rocking horse the other three picked up dolls that were scattered about the floor. To their amazement a large seagull hovered tantalisingly above them in the centre of the room. Standing on her tiptoes Jenny could just tickle its belly with her fingers, and the spring that served to suspend it from the ceiling caused the seagull to frisk and flap its feathers creating great festivity among the flock of followers below.

There was not much time for play, though, and after an anxious reminder from Lichfield who was concerned about losing the excellent light the morning's sunshine was showering over Shugborough, each of the girls was plucked off the floor by Janet, Graham, Nancy and Betty, put on a knee and dressed in identical pink dresses with white collars and pale-grey trimmings, short white ankle socks and white sandals. Only Kate and Hannah's hair was long enough to put ribbons in but together the girls looked sparkling.

Lichfield had decided to use his rose garden as the setting for the first shot. In the centre a sundial held court over a myriad of different species of rose. The garden's beauty was reflected in years of cultivation and care by generations of gardeners and was the perfect background for the girls' bright outfits. After a few false starts and abundant shouts of 'Oi!' by his Lordship in an inelegant effort to get all the girls' attention, there was enough confidence that there was at least one good shot, out of over forty taken, for everyone to move on to the next location Lichfield had in mind.

At the side of the magnificent house a white marble bench sat peacefully shielded in the shade of a semi-circle of bushes. 'Will the girls sit on the bench on their own?' Lichfield asked, reflecting the picture he already had in his mind.

'They'll probably scream if we leave them there,' answered Janet.

The girls had each stretched their lungs throughout the first session and it might be pushing it a bit to expect them to sit quietly in a line for as long as it took to take the photograph.

'Well if you and Graham sit either side of the girls then let's see what happens.' Lichfield had laid his plan. Since he was shooting against the sun he used two large reflector discs, which resembled two giant white mushrooms sprouting either side of the camera, to give maximum light.

The girls were then plucked like daisies from the lush green lawn and placed in a pink chain on the bench where they wobbled in the gentle breeze as they found their balance. Like bookends, Janet and Graham sat at either side of their line of daughters and the click of the lens shutter began chattering away.

Lichfield needed everyone to be looking in the right direction so he seconded the services of Nancy and Betty who stood behind him and playfully waved their arms about and called to the girls like a couple of circus clowns. Lichfield punctuated their shouts with further trumpet calls of 'Oi!' in between frustrated mutterings of 'Twelve eyes. All I need is twelve eyes!' but he knew it was in the lap of the gods. Jenny was more interested in the stitching on her hemline; Hannah was leaning too far forward with arms stretched out like a sleep walker; Ruth's fingers fiddled with Sarah's dress; Lucy had her hand in her mouth and Kate was examining what was going on behind.

Lichfield's head was down, concentrating on his view finder. Suddenly he saw the opportunity. 'Right, can mum and dad just quietly make an exit for a second?' For a few moments the only noise that could be heard came from the camera and as he carried on snapping, the famous photographer sensed the familiar flavour of success.

With the confidence of having at least a couple of good publishable shots already in the can, the atmosphere became much more relaxed and as the hours filled the morning, rolls upon rolls of film captured the girls' laughter as they spontaneously rose to the occasion. On the steps that led up to the vast windows of one of the Hall's grand rooms, the natural curiosity of one girl triggered the rest to peer through the glass, and Lichfield was quick to seize upon the opportunity for yet another six-pack shot.

When they opened the smart blue folder bearing Lichfield's name on the front and looked at the results of the session, Janet and Graham realised how worthwhile the day had been. It was not just another set of photos, for what they were looking at was something very special, and their feelings were reflected in the response from magazine editors all over the world who gladly published the pictures in recognition of the girls' second birthday.

As part of Janet and Graham's overall plan to protect the children from over exposure, only limited publication of the photographs was permitted in the United Kingdom. While there was a tendency induced by natural parental pride to want to show off their children, it was tempered by the desire for as much privacy as was possible. The thousands of letters Janet and Graham had received since the birth were full of affection and were an indication of how much people enjoyed seeing various films and photographs of the girls but the last thing they wanted was for their daughters to become a kind of public property. Had Janet and Graham been less cautious in their attitude towards publicity, that may easily have been the case.

Even though the girls were not the first set of sextuplets to have been born and to have survived in the world – the Rosenkowitz family in South Africa was the first followed by the Gianninis of Italy – they were the first to be born all of the same sex. It was because of this that the world gave as much attention to the girls as it gave to the famous Dionne quintuplets, born in the little town of Callander in Canada in 1934.

The birth of quins was an extremely rare occurrence at that time, and coupled with the fact that the Dionne babies were identical made it all the more remarkable. They instantly became Canada's most famous citizens and visitors made the journey to their small home town in their millions to catch a glimpse of the children. An industry quickly grew around them, and they were even copyrighted as 'The Quintuplets' and all rights were reserved and thousands of people became involved and dependent on them in one way or another. There was a never-ending stream of commercial contracts and their early lives seemed to be controlled by people other than their parents, who, it must be said, already had their hands full looking after their seven other children!

Apart from the commercial interest, the Dionnes were, more significantly, the subject of endless scientific studies. Professors from the University of Toronto became involved, as did child psychologists, environmentalists, geneticists and a whole host of others. All made extensive examinations of the quins to diagnose distinctions between each child. Every characteristic from blood groups to palm prints were recorded, and an intensive series of tests during periods of play was carried out in an effort to establish the social and personality differences between each of the five and in comparison with other children.

Janet and Graham had received a copy of a book about the Dionnes from a well wisher not long after the girls were born. Having been disturbed by what they read of the studies and tests carried out on the quins, and of the numbers of people who travelled so far to see them, they maintained, over the years, a determined resolve to protect their privacy as much as possible. It did not, however, alter the fact that the costs of raising the girls were extraordinarily high, and so Janet and Graham continued, at least for the time being, to enter into certain commercial agreements.

It was not until after their second birthday that Janet and Graham allowed the girls to be involved in a proper advertising campaign. A company called Vantage was developing a new image for their chain of chemist stores throughout the UK and were looking for ideas for a new campaign that would appeal to families. The milestone of the birthday had been marked by a special feature in *You* magazine, the colour supplement to the *Mail on Sunday*, and the girls took pride of place on the front cover. This, together with the photographs from the session with Lord Lichfield, helped executives from Royds Advertising, which was based in Manchester, and was the largest agency outside London, to convince their clients that associating themselves with the family would be good for the company.

Vantage needed little convincing. They were well aware of how special the family were and how much attention the media had given them since the girls had been born, but they were more concerned about whether or not Janet and Graham would wish to be involved with them. The income the family could earn from an advertising campaign was clearly important and would obviously help to give a certain amount of security to the family but it would not be the critical factor upon which Janet and Graham would base their final decision. Other companies had been turned down before, and it was the understanding, sympathetic and gentle attitude reflected in Vantage's Marketing Manager Alan Turner, and his acknowledgement of Janet and Graham's protective nature towards over exposure and over commercialism, that gave the family the confidence to go ahead and agree terms. The company also made it clear that Janet and Graham's wishes would always come first and that nothing would be done if it was felt that it may be detrimental to the girls, and everything would be done to make things as easy and as comfortable as possible.

The dates for the filming of the television commercial were set for 6 and 7 March 1986, a Thursday and Friday. While it was hoped that the filming could have taken place thirty miles away in Manchester, the facilities simply were not available. It followed that there would have to be a trip to London. That meant a long train journey and a stay in a hotel, each of which would be a first for the girls. They were booked on the Sunday train from Liverpool to Watford, and the more Janet and Graham told the girls about the train journey the more excited they became, although Jenny and Hannah were more interested in the special surprises Janet had promised she would put in their very own travel bags.

Sunday was the quietest day of the week for travelling and so took away a lot of extra pressures that would have come with the crowds of commuters on a working day. Also, a whole carriage was reserved especially for the family to make the journey as easy as possible. As it turned out, this was as much in the interests of other passengers as it was for the family. The girls twittered, cheeped and chirped like a bunch of happy nestlings, and it was clear that had any one else been on the coach they would not have had a minute's peace.

It was important for the girls to keep familiar things around them and so all the baggage, including a suitcase full of the girls' toys, was sent down ahead in the family's van and, to the girls' delight, the vehicle was waiting for them at Watford station to take them to the hotel. One of the drawbacks of the Sunday train was that it added an extra hour on to the journey, stopping time and time again to accommodate the maintenance work that took place on the line while it was not so busy. However, even though a tired symphony of yawns and a cluster of heavy little eyelids showed that the girls were beginning to feel the effects of the trip, they still managed to give a chorus of 'Bumpy, bumpy!' each time the van jumped over the strategically set strips of tarmac that had been laid to remind drivers of the five 5-mph speed limit on the long and winding private road to the hotel.

The Grims Dyke hotel was not as cheerless and gloomy as the name suggests. Set in acres of beautiful grounds the grand Tudor-fronted mansion was once the home of Sir William Schwenck Gilbert the distinguished author and humorist who, together with Sir Arthur Sullivan, created the series of comic operettas enjoyed by millions today the world over. Inside the reception area framed pictures gave a historical record of the house. As Graham went over to sign the register the girls followed and a dozen eyes peered over the edge of the desk to witness the event.

Meanwhile Janet's eyes were firmly fixed on one particular frame. In it was a copy of Gilbert's obituary that appeared in an issue of *The Times* in 1911. Apparently, while out enjoying a walk in his grounds with a couple of lady friends one afternoon, he had decided to show off his prowess and take a dip in the ornamental pond that was the centrepiece of his landscaped gardens. Unfortunately his constitution was not a match for the biting effects of the on-coming winter and he expired amidst the goldfish. It was the familiarity of the date of Sir William's birth that caught Janet's eye. It was 18 November, the girls' birthday.

For privacy and convenience the agency had reserved a whole floor of the hotel for the family. All the rooms were next to each other and extra rooms had been booked to act as dayrooms giving space for the girls to play. The management had done their best to accommodate every visitor and although they had offered an alternative room to one of their long stay guests, who was, apparently, quietly recuperating after one marriage before entering into another, having advised him that with six clamorous two-year-olds running about he was not going to get much peace during the week, he stubbornly dropped anchor and refused to budge. He managed to weather the storm for two days after which he transferred to another room and calmer waters.

On the Monday morning a meeting had been arranged so that the director of the filming and the actor who was going to play the part of a chemist could have a chance to get to know the girls, so that at least there would be some sort of familiarity when they got to the set on the Thursday. The wardrobe lady also came along to double check on all the girls' sizes. She had with her a range of samples clearly purchased from an exclusive children's clothes shop. Mindful of Janet and Graham's decision after the Lichfield session not to dress the girls identically so that they could keep a sense of independence, while pink was the theme colour running through all the outfits, each one was subtly different.

For Lucy there was a pink top with a single wide white hoop on each sleeve and a white collar with pink stripes, pink trousers and socks, and a pair of yellow canvas sandals. The sandals matched well with a peaked yellow cap she had grabbed before any of the others. Sarah wore a sleeveless pink jumpsuit over a white t-shirt with white socks, pink shoes and a white peaked cap. For Ruth there was a pink-and-white polka dot top, pink trousers, white socks and pale-pink canvas sandals. Kate had taken a fancy to a pink jumpsuit that was speckled with cartoon cows, and a pink cardigan with a double white striped border, white socks and pink sandals. Hannah wore a pink jumpsuit with a matching jacket, a yellow belt, pink socks and yellow canvas sandals, and finally Jenny, as a contrast, wore a green, yellow and pink hooped top over a green t-shirt, with socks of the same design as the top, yellow sandals, and a cap the same as Lucy's. Hannah and Kate, whose hair had grown faster than the other four, were to have pink ribbons – along with Ruth who was desperate to have hair as long as her sisters and obviously felt that if she wore ribbons often enough her hair would eventually grow. They stood in a line and together they looked as bright and brilliant as a brand-new box of beads.

Even though the wardrobe lady noted everything down, the girls seemed so similar to her and there were so many different pieces of clothing that keeping track of who was wearing what was clearly going to be a bit of a nightmare. Filming an advert requires as much attention to detail as a television programme or a movie, and clothing continuity, where there would be a great deal of importance in ensuring each of the girls would always be seen in the right clothing, was vital. In this case it was like having to take apart and re-fit a 1,000-piece jig-saw, and seeing that the wardrobe department was struggling a bit Janet, calm and logical as always, quickly scribbled a note of everything to make sure at least two people could complete the puzzle.

Originally both Nancy and Betty were to have come along to give extra pairs of helping hands but Graham's mum had been taken ill and was not able to travel, so the three bedrooms, which had three beds each, were occupied by Janet, Graham and Nancy each taking two girls apiece. The days passed by quickly but it did take a bit of time for the girls to get used to sleeping in strange beds. On the first night when all the goodnights were said and plenty of kisses had been distributed, mingled with hugs that lingered a little longer than usual, Jenny, Kate and Ruth fell asleep pretty quickly, but Hannah, Sarah and Lucy had no intention of being left alone. They made so much noise that from that night on the adults took their twosomes into their respective rooms and pretended to go to sleep on their own beds while they struggled not to giggle as they listened in the darkness to the girls quietly reciting the latest nursery rhyme they had learnt, or whispering their limited vocabularies to each other about what they had done that day, what they would do tomorrow and whether or not the one in the middle was really asleep. When they were sure that slumber had set in they would silently get up, get dressed (if the girls had caught them climbing into bed with their clothes on), and meet in the corridor where two then went off to eat while the other babysat.

On the first day of filming two chauffeur-driven cars waited for everyone outside the large stone-arched entrance of the hotel ready to take the family to Lee International Studios in Wembley. Waiting for them when they arrived was Alan Turner. His face was beaming with the pride of a man who had pulled off a tremendous coup for his company, but his smile also revealed a touch of relief which had just rubbed away the mark of anxiety. If any of the girls had not been well or taken ill, and at two and a half the chances of this were not slim, the whole production would have had to be cancelled. There was not the cushioning luxury of being able to phone an agency for a replacement child, the girls were unique and far from dispensable, and with over fifty professional production people from both the advertising agency and the studio fully committed to working on the project, insurance had come at a high premium.

Alan's Scottish accent was as gentle as highland heather as he warmed to the girls. 'Who's going to hold ma hand then?' he asked in a very unexecutive manner. Lucy shyly shrugged behind her mother's legs but Ruth, remembering him from earlier in the week as a good bet for a sweet and encouraged by Graham asking who was going to be brave, pointed her hand slowly in his direction.

The narrow passageways were filled with the sound of excitement as he led them to where their dressing rooms were situated next to the studio where the set designers, carpenters and production staff had been hard at work over the past few days creating a brand-new chemist shop. As they walked along, Nancy answered the call of 'Carry, carry!' from Hannah, and seeing how comfortable her sister looked sitting on her grandmother's arm Ruth decided it was a good idea and to Alan's delight he found himself giving the same service.

The girls were not the only celebrities working at the studios that day. On the stage set next to the one on which they were to be filming the advert, production was continuing on a film called *The Mission*, which was later to be Britain's entry in the Cannes Film Festival and the winner of a number of Oscars. The dressing rooms were in a row of four and the family were sandwiched in the two middle rooms between the stars of the film. On one side there was Jeremy Irons and on the other was one of Hollywood's biggest names, Robert de Niro.

The rooms were well padded with extra mattresses that had been brought in for the girls to sleep on during the day. Covering two of the walls, in front of dressing tables, were mirrors, each of which, to the girls' fascination, was surrounded by a border of bulbs. Within minutes the room looked like the inside of a pinball machine as the girls ran around the room bouncing in true trampoline fashion on and off the mattresses and repeatedly flicking the light switches on and off. Graham called for order. 'What do you think this is girls, a circus?' The word circus only served to inspire a further series of acrobatics and clowning around. It was like a scene from a Marx Brothers movie. 'Come on, girls,' Graham made a grab for Lucy. 'Stop messing about now. It's time to get ready!' One by one the adults netted the children and began sorting out the correct clothing for each to wear. Janet, who was to be appearing in the ad at all times, was whisked off to the make-up department leaving Graham, Nancy and the wardrobe girls to dress the girls.

Sarah was ready first. She jumped off Graham's knee and made for the door 'Don't go out of the room till we're all ready, Sarah.' Graham had noted the swing fire doors and the last thing he wanted was any trapped fingers. 'And you can't take that with you, love, it'll be all right here till later,' he said referring to the doll under his daughter's arm. The doll was a most peculiar affair. It was more of a face with arms where its ears should have been and multicoloured spindly legs sprouting like a thin beard from its chin. Its pale-blue face sported an orange, beacon-like nose and was surrounded on all sides by a carpet of blue fluff. Beauty, though, is only skin deep and to Sarah her Rainbow Sprite was her best friend and she never went anywhere without it. Her face did not have to drop far for Graham to change his mind and, like a switch, his words turned her pitiful sadness into a bright smile.

By the time Janet returned from the make-up department all the girls were ready except for Hannah and Kate whose ribbons needed tidying up. Doing the girls' hair was a major event every day and always took a long time. Anticipating that they would have to move quickly once they arrived at the studio, Janet had made sure that all six heads were well coiffured before they left the hotel. She quickly clamped Kate between her knees and held her there while her fingers, entwined with rubber bands, knitted their way through Hannah's hair with the skill of a dedicated professional stylist, and gift wrapped the long blonde locks back into two neat bunches.

Although Sarah did her best to do as her father had told her and stay in the dressing room, curiosity got the better of her as she crept quietly into the corridor. At the far end there was a click and another door opened and a figure appeared. All that was visible was the swarthy skin of a dark and mysterious face. It was bordered by long black hair and a severe and sombre black beard of equal length. A robe as black as thunder clouds hung from shoulders to floor where two great toes pointed out of a pair of open sandals in Sarah's direction. She froze for a moment, dropped her doll and then, before the figure moved, scuttled back into the dressing room and hid behind her father who could almost feel her little heart pounding against his leg.

In full missionary costume, Robert De Niro appeared at their door, a smile shining through the harsh exterior melting away any signs of menace. 'Does this belong to anybody?' he enquired in his soft American accent. Graham looked up and Sarah's head popped out from between his legs. Graham took the doll and said, 'thank you,' pointing downwards to Sarah to indicate who was the owner. 'Say "thank you," Sarah.' He was not surprised at getting no response. He tried again. 'Say "Hello" then!' As if the question had been directed at De Niro he immediately responded with the greeting, and then excused himself with a smile and disappeared out of the room before turning his mind to the lines he was about to deliver in the next scene.

As soon as he had gone, Sarah tugged at Graham's trousers and after much word searching told him that the man was wearing a dress and asked her dad why this was the case. 'Well he has to wear those clothes because he is a monk.' 'A monk!' she repeated finding the new addition to her vocabulary quite extraordinary. 'A monk!' confirmed Graham, and Sarah marched round the room stopping to stand face to face with each of her sisters and pass on the information.

The first shot was the most difficult. The director wanted the girls to follow Janet into the shop and he wanted to catch them all on frame for at least one moment before they were to waddle in a proud procession like a litter of little ducklings behind their mum. Easier said than done. Sarah dropped her doll, Hannah ran too quickly, Kate and Lucy went off at right angles, Jenny turned around and walked backwards, after two goes Ruth decided it was silly and stood her ground and the director's face quietly disappeared behind the palms of his hands. It was not until the tenth take that Graham was called in and, with all the girls bracketed between his arms, released them one by one in a straight line and so produced the desired effect.

From then on it was all downhill with the girls each performing a little solo piece by grabbing products off the shelves or giving things to the chemist. Only Kate needed a little extra coaxing from Janet who helped her empty a box of tissues over the shop floor. About half the advert was completed on the first day and it was not until seven o'clock the following evening that, with all the sweets having been distributed and Sarah's doll having been lost and found a dozen times, the director was finally satisfied he had all he needed, and the cameramen, lighting engineers and all the production crew cheered when he finally called a wrap.

As Janet and Graham led their tiny tribe off the set they realised, after doing the usual mental roll call, that they were one short. Obviously enjoying being under the spotlight, Hannah was performing one last act for the cameras. They went back on to the set to find their daughter happily minding her own business sitting on a pot she had discovered on one of the shelves and, rising to the occasion, or in this case sitting to the occasion, she answered nature's call and gave an impromptu demonstration of the finer points of the toilet training Janet and Graham had recently introduced to the girls. It was a moment of light relief for everyone, especially Hannah!

· Sixteen ·

Fame in the Far East

♡ ♡ ♡
♡ ♡
♡

Graham turned his head away from Kate and stared through the small
perspex porthole at the long grass that grew by the side of the runway.
The dew gave rise to a sheen as the sun's rays finally broke through the
miserable Manchester morning mist. His left hand tightened its grip on
the arm of his seat and he could feel the dampness of the sweat of his
palm grease the metal edge. As the engines of the 757 built up to a final
crescendo it seemed to grip every tendon and stretch every sinew in his
body. His eyes closed and he tried to recapture the smell of the scotch
that had given him so much courage the night before.

Just as the plane began to roll forward Kate tugged at his right sleeve.
'Daddy!' There was no response but she did not let go. 'Daddy, can I
open my bag yet?' Janet had packed a travel satchel for each of the girls.
They were full to the brim of 'goodies' to keep them busy on the long
haul that lay ahead. Sweets, crisps, puzzles, more sweets, crayons,
crayoning books and even more sweets packed tightly into six matching
greenish-blue bags with orange borders. It was the first time the girls
had been in an aeroplane and Kate's innocent indifference to the fact
that this multi-ton lump of metal was about to defy all the laws of
gravity had the sudden effect of an electric switch that somehow cut off
the current of fear that was flowing within Graham. His attention turned

144

to his daughter. 'No Kate,' he explained. 'You have to wait until we get on the other plane. This is only a little flight and we'll be in London soon.'

''novver aer'plane?' Kate queried to confirm.

'Yes that's right luv.' Graham was surprised at the steady confidence of his own voice but then realised that he was talking to his $3\frac{1}{2}$-year-old daughter. There had to be confidence. If he showed his children that travelling in a plane was something to fear it could put them off for the rest of their lives. It was just one of the many factors that Janet and Graham had discussed time and again in the last three weeks before accepting the invitation from Fuji Television to visit Japan and appear on one of its most popular television shows, 'Naruhodo the World!'

The invitation was not the first Janet and Graham had received from abroad. Twice before they had politely declined offers from Tokyo, and only six months earlier a Chicago-based toy manufacturer wanted to fly the family to New York for the 1987 American Toy Fair. Besides all the obvious problems of travelling with so many children and Graham's dislike of taking to the air, the girls would have been too young to appreciate any of those trips. Since the offer to go to the United States, though, Janet and Graham had successfully taken the girls by train to both London and Edinburgh and this had given them the confidence to travel longer distances as a family.

The weekend they had spent in Edinburgh was highlighted by a trip to the zoological park where the girls lined up with the crowd and were thrilled by the famous 'Parade of the Penguins'. It had been the topic of conversation around the table for weeks and had made Janet and Graham realise how much of an education travelling could be for their children. The temptation, therefore, to accept this latest invitation was enormous. After all, it may have been their last opportunity to go to such an exciting place, and as Fuji agreed, one by one, to all the points that had been raised to ensure the care and well-being of everyone, the likelihood of the visit actually going ahead, grew and grew.

It was, though, an extraordinarily long journey to make. The family had to be up at five thirty in the morning and, allowing for the fact that Tokyo time was eight hours ahead of London, and the flight time of over eighteen hours, they were not due to arrive at Narita International Airport until one o'clock the following afternoon.

Although Graham felt a little more comfortable after the smooth take off, he tried to hide his uneasiness as he thought about the long journey

145

ahead and whether or not he had done the right thing. The girls were going to be very tired and would be travelling for two of the six days they were due to be away. He unbuckled his seat belt and stood for a brief moment so that he could see the whole family, who had managed to fill the first three rows of the plane. Graham cast his eyes across each of the girls. They were all on their best behaviour and their beaming faces were bursting with excitement. Janet looked up from the book she was reading to Hannah. She had been more worried about Graham than the girls, as far as the flying was concerned. She caught his eye. 'O.K.?' she asked, making no sound only moving her lips. 'Smashing,' he reassured her. 'The kids are brilliant aren't they?' He was referring to how well they had taken to air travel and how good they had been considering they were surrounded by pin-striped businessmen commuting to the capital for a day's work.

The girls were still on a high by the time they had landed and transferred to the new and impressive Terminal 4 at Heathrow Airport. Familiar faces began to appear: Fiona Nunn and Peter Lydon, the producer and director of the latest documentary that was being filmed about the family, Roger Eldridge of Camera Press, who had been with the family for the Lichfield shoot was there with photographer Richard Open. Getting the girls to giggle when photos were being taken was no easier than it is with any group of three-year-olds. For some photographers, begging for the word 'cheese' or even 'sausages' to be shouted out is the usual method, but Richard, who obviously worked on the basis of action speaks louder than words, used the 'falling over the litter bin while walking backwards routine'. His hands flew in every direction to cushion the fall of his equipment and the bruising lasted for more than a few days but the girls were suitably amused and he got the appropriate picture.

Actor Jon Pertwee also came to the airport to see the girls and wish Janet and Graham a safe trip. Jon had made a surprise appearance at the reception after the girls' christening three years earlier, where, in the guise of the character Worzel Gummidge, he had held Lucy and proclaimed himself an 'Honorary Godfather' to all the girls, and had followed the girls' progress ever since.

Even though Janet and Graham had allowed more than one Japanese film crew to visit their home over the years, and they were aware that there had been quite a few magazine articles published in Japan following the girls' progress, it was still difficult for them to imagine that anyone living so far away would know who they were. While they obviously wanted the minimum of fuss over the girls, they were also concerned that Fuji, who after all had paid out so much money on the cost of the trip, should feel that their efforts and initiative in bringing the family over were not a total waste of time.

These thoughts and many more were hovering over Graham's mind as he fought to stay awake during the long dark hours of the flight to the other side of the world. The in-flight movie had seemed a good idea after the satisfying meal, and seeing that the girls had settled down for a sleep and all was quiet, he braced his head with the complimentary earpieces that were one of the perks of Club Class and tuned into the soundtrack of the Clint Eastwood western. It was a fruitless exercise, though, for as much as he tried to force himself to stay awake the travelling had taken its toll, and he drifted in and out of a deep slumber.

Suddenly Graham screwed up his eyes in bewilderment as he woke to the sound of an unfamiliar voice.

'Ladies and gentlemen, this is your pilot speaking. We will very shortly be beginning our descent into Tokyo's Narita International Airport. Our estimated time of arrival is one o'clock in the afternoon local time, and our flight time is approximately one hour ... I'll be speaking to you again when we are on the ground.' That at least sounds encouraging, Graham thought.

The stewardesses moved along the aisles lifting the window blinds and gradually the inside of the plane was flooded with light. Ruth and Sarah slept peacefully with their heads on Janet's lap. Hannah and Lucy, like a pair of blonde book-ends, were propped up on either side of Graham. Kate was stretched out alongside Nancy surrounded by colouring books, and Jenny had made a bed for herself on the three empty seats behind. And then, like flowers that open up in the early morning, one by one the girls woke up and stretched their limbs.

The fame of the family had indeed spread throughout Japan, and their arrival was covered by television news cameras for the early evening reports. As Janet and Graham said 'goodbye' and 'thank you' to the stewardesses they had to squint their eyes as the arc-lights filled the doorway. The very public welcome was not expected and was not easy to bear up to immediately after such a long flight, not to mention the amount of hand luggage to contend with while making sure the children did not wander. Superstar treatment was not something they were either used to or prepared for. However, they were more than grateful for the special help afforded by the British Airways staff. At Heathrow they had been looked after by the Special Operations Manager, Francis de Souza, and he had telexed through to Narita asking for assistance for the family so that they could get through the various controls and baggage collections without too much delay.

Even one man to show them the way would have been appreciated, but they were accompanied by a team of four ground staff with a leader to issue instructions. The leader introduced himself to Graham and told him that everyone should stay close and follow him. He asked Graham to collect everyone's passports which would help speed up their passage through customs. As these were being collected, the 'team' picked up the hand luggage and disappeared, only to reappear not long after in the pickup area of the terminal with four large trollies; the first full of the hand luggage and the other three filled with the thirteen cases – on top of which, to the girls' delight, were two giant cuddly rabbits, one yellow, one pink, next to a big blue furry teddy.

There is something terribly infectious about a smile, especially the ones on friendly faces of Japanese people, and the grinning representative of Fuji who came to the terminal to meet everyone gave the impression that he never left anyone in an unhappy mood. Mr Ishido was smartly dressed in a light-blue summer suit, and despite the shirt collar and tie he did not seem at all affected by the early afternoon heat. He had no difficulty in locating his clients and brought a smile to all the adults' faces when he greeted them with a respectful bow. 'Mr Walton?' he said, having hurried across the terminal towards the only white group of adults that seemed to be outnumbered by children. Graham looked up having just distributed cold drinks all round. 'Yes,' he said, smiling back at the face that was shaped like a full moon. 'That's me!'

'Ah ... very good,' he said, relieved that they had arrived safely. He bowed slowly. 'I am Ishido from Fuji. Welcome to Japan!' Graham bowed back. It seemed like the right thing to do. Still grinning, Mr Ishido continued. 'Please to meet Eeka, assistant ... and Sumi, interpreter.' As each of his colleagues heard their names they broke out into equally happy grins and also bowed. Graham bowed back twice. Janet, Nancy and Sue, who had also come to lend a hand, all bobbed their heads up and down as they were also introduced, thinking their hosts might be insulted if they did not respond. And then, as if they had noticed a slight awkwardness in their guests with this old Japanese custom, Eeka and Sumi quickly broke rank and moved forward with outstretched hands for a traditional western-style handshake.

The journey to the hotel took over two hours, making the total travelling time since they had left Warren Drive at six the previous morning, more than thirty-three hours, including the eight-hour time difference. Even though it had been an enormous journey to undertake the girls had travelled well and were still pretty lively and far from ready for bed. It was the adults who were feeling the effects of the flight more so, but all the tiredness they felt melted as they arrived at the magnificent marbled structure of the Akasaka Prince Hotel. Janet and Graham had been told that it was one of the best hotels in Tokyo but they had never expected such splendour. Its 'V' shape towered forty floors from the ground reflecting blue sky and clouds in its never-ending walls of mirrored glass encased by white marble. There was white marble everywhere and as the automatic glass doors obediently opened, the floors, the walls, the ceilings and staircases all seemed to have been chiselled from a single perfect and polished piece of stone.

As they entered the hotel Jenny tugged at Kate's jacket and whispered something in her ear. She was pointing to the line of Japanese girls who, dressed head to foot in traditional Kimono and accessories, were bowing in harmony with the opening doors. It was their first sighting of authentic Japanese clothing. As all the girls stood in amazement listening to Nancy and Sue explain the outfits, Janet and Graham checked in at reception.

There were more than a couple of points that Janet and Graham needed to discuss having learned a few lessons from travelling with the girls when staying in hotels in London and Edinburgh. The first had been to ensure in advance that the hotel had a children's menu. On one occasion, having been assured that there would be no problem catering to the basic needs of the children, which normally amounted to a simple helping of either sausages or fish fingers and a few chips, a meal had to be abandoned due to an over enthusiastic French chef. And the next night, by popular vote, the family disappeared into the nearby Mac-Donald's where the *table d'hôte* was much more suitable.

One of the difficulties of eating out with the girls at that age was the fact that however Janet and Graham decided to place themselves around the table it was still impossible to feed them all at once. They were only just getting used to knives and forks, and while they could prong a piece of sausage or fish finger, they were not quite ready yet for cutting the food up and pouring out drinks. With all the standing and stretching and mopping up, Janet and Graham knew it would be a long time before they were really going to be able to enjoy a proper meal themselves while sitting at the same table as the girls.

As well as having to take care over the food arrangements, Janet and Graham remembered, after one sleepless night in a London hotel, to double check that any rooms allocated to them were not directly above a dance-room or disco. The most important consideration, though, was to make sure that the three triple rooms that had been booked for Graham, Janet and Nancy were together, so that the sisters would be as close as possible to each other. If that was not the case then there would be major problems. It was, therefore, essential for Janet and Graham to be organised and have everything in one area. Dressing was time consuming since the girls were nowhere near the stage of doing it themselves, and, as well as all that, one by one they had to line up in front of Janet for their hair to be done.

As it turned out, one of the triple rooms was a suite and had a large lounge which made a perfect extra room for the girls as a communal dressing room and a playroom, where all their toys could be stored rather than have them clutter up the hotel bedrooms, and where together they could all watch the Japanese television cartoons.

The television was the first thing to be switched on when they finally settled in to their rooms. A Japanese soap opera appeared and Jenny, Kate and Hannah were fascinated. The unpacking had to be done but before attacking any of the other cases Graham opened the one that contained all the girls' favourite toys. Janet and Graham had packed as many familiar things as possible so that they would not feel too homesick. While their sisters continued to watch the television, Ruth, Lucy and Sarah showed their precious possessions to Sumi, who, in order to get to know everyone better, had stayed with the family after Mr Ishido and Eeka had left to go back to their office.

Sumi obviously loved children and the girls warmed to her immediately. She was determined to learn all the girls' names as quickly as possible and be able to match the right name to the right face. She was not the first person to try and it simply was not an easy task. The girls had become aware of the difficulty strangers were having in getting their names right, and at times their eyes took on a mischievous glint when a new person came into their lives and tried to puzzle it out. They giggled each time Sumi pointed at them and called out a name as she guessed who was who. 'You are ... Sarah!' Sumi said, pointing at Sarah, sure that her guess was correct. 'No!' came the reply. Sumi tried again.

'Ehh . . . Kate!' To Sarah's delight, Sumi was completely taken in. 'No!' Sarah's face feigned offence at the very suggestion, and Lucy squeaked with laughter. The young Japanese student remembered that Sarah, Kate and Jenny had the darker hair and that Lucy, Hannah and Ruth were much blonder, and that Jenny was the tallest of all the girls, so she realised that she was being given the run around but she played along.

She looked at Lucy. 'What is your name?'

Lucy did not hesitate in her reply, 'Ruth!'

That did it! Ruth's eyes slowly peered up from a head that was bowed over a bag of giant lego bricks. She was tired and was not in the mood. 'No it's not. I'm Ruth!' she said in a very matter of fact fashion.

Lucy giggled. This was better than she had expected. Her eyes were sparkling and she glanced from Ruth back to Sumi. 'I'm Ruth!' she reaffirmed to her new Japanese friend.

Ruth blew her top and within seconds Graham was over to find out what was the matter. 'Lucy said I'm Ruth,' Ruth explained between sobs.

'Well that's right, isn't it?' asked Graham slightly puzzled.

'No-o-o!' she protested, 'she said she's Ruth but she's Lucy isn't she anyway?'

Graham understood. 'Oh, *she* said,' he stressed the she in correction, 'she was you? Well that's silly, isn't it?' he comforted her. 'You're tired aren't you, Ruth.' He picked her up and she rubbed her eyes against his shoulder. 'Shall we tell Sumi everybody's name?' Her head moved up and down. 'And then you can go for a sleep, eh?' She was half way there. As he walked across the room he noticed that the other three girls had abandoned the television.

He stared for a moment at the screen where a man sat at a desk with a map behind him. Graham listened to the man for a moment but then he thought how stupid he was trying to understand the news being read in Japanese. He hoisted Ruth up slightly, and just as he began thinking that newscasters look the same the world over whatever the language, the picture changed and he found himself watching himself and his family arriving at the airport. He called to Janet but by the time she got to the room the brief report had finished. 'You know,' Graham said, thinking about what he had just seen, 'somehow I don't think this press conference tomorrow is going to be a small one.'

The press conference had played on Graham's mind ever since he had been told it was one of the fundamental requests of Fuji. All he could think of were the hundreds of hungry faces at the first press conference held at the Maternity Hospital when the girls were born; that was something he never wanted the girls to have to experience. Fuji knew of his concern and, while it would be pointless having the family travel so far to make an appearance on this special edition of 'Naruhodo the World' without publicising the fact, they made it clear that it was not their wish to upset the girls in any way. Finally, after much deliberation and late-night chats with Janet, the press conference was agreed to on the understanding that certain conditions were met. Firstly, the girls would only appear in front of the photographers for five minutes. They would then be looked after by Nancy and Sue while Janet and Graham answered questions, and secondly there would be a limit to how many photographers would be allowed to be present.

It all went very smoothly the next day with little unexpected touches by Fuji helping to make things easier for Janet and Graham. There were cuddly toys waiting at the studio reception for the girls, and where the conference was to take place a desk had been set up for all the family to sit behind while keeping the press at a reasonable distance so as not to intimidate the children. Six place settings had been arranged for the girls, each with a colouring book and crayons. It could not have been better organised.

As soon as the girls sat down they immediately went to work on their new books. They were totally oblivious to the reporters and photographers who had burst into spontaneous applause as they had entered the room. One of the photographers respectfully raised his arm and an interpreter translated the first request. 'Could it be possible for the girls to sit in order of birth please?' Janet glanced along the line thinking that the request was a reasonable one but knowing they were going to have no chance of carrying it out. The girls were already settled and intent on their own scribbling. They were comfortable and any change of place for no particular reason was not going to go down too well. Janet whispered in Ruth's ear to see if she would swap places with Hannah.

In fact it was the only change necessary.

'No!' said Ruth, far too busy to look up.

'No!' said Janet, cheerfully hoping that the Japanese press would be understanding

'No!' said the interpreter.

'Oh!' said the photographer, and thanking Janet for trying he sat down.

Janet could have pushed it with Ruth but she knew it would achieve nothing except a flood of tears.

Graham then introduced his daughters one by one. The whole thing was very civilised. The press were like well-behaved school children looking for gold stars. They had only been allowed in by special invitation so those that were there treated it as a privilege. There was no pushing or shoving for shots. There was no shouting and at the end of each answer all the journalists raised their arms and waited with respect to be called to ask their question by the interpreter.

The girls had worn for the press conference the same outfits they were to appear in on the programme the next day. The whole trip had been in the balance over the matter of what the girls would wear. Fuji, not surprisingly, wanted the girls all to be dressed identically. However, it had been two years since the girls were photographed by Lord Lichfield when Janet and Graham had agreed for all the girls to be dressed the same, and even though the results of that session were fantastic there was still some regret that they had gone against their intention never to dress the girls alike. They were not about to agree for the girls to go on television in Japan or any other part of the world dressed identically.

The more Fuji held their ground over the matter the more Janet and Graham resisted. The trip was the most marvellous opportunity to travel to a place they may never again have the chance to visit, yet they were prepared to forego it had Fuji not been prepared to compromise. An agreement was reached at the last moment. The outfits Janet finally decided on for the girls were pinafores. Whilst the pinafores were to be all the same, keeping Fuji happy, each girl was to wear a different coloured t-shirt underneath with matching socks, keeping Janet and Graham happy. The dresses had vertical stripes of pale pink, green and yellow; Kate wore a green t-shirt and socks, Jenny wore white, Sarah a deep sunshine yellow, Hannah a pale primrose yellow, Lucy a cherry red and Ruth wore pink.

Although the programme was not going to be live transmission, there was still a studio audience to face, but any concern that Janet and Graham may have had for the girls had been dispelled the day before when they had not been at all upset by all the reporters, flashing lights and photographers.

Every Tuesday evening over 30 million Japanese people tuned their television sets into Fuji Network's most successful programme and favourite quiz show of the nation, 'Naruhodo the World'. Contestants were asked obscure questions about amazing events and curiosities all over the world, and the ones that answered best and accumulated the most points progressed through to become eventual winners. The particular show on which the Waltons were appearing marked its sixth anniversary, and to celebrate the producers wanted everything on the show to relate to the number six and for the family to be the show's special guests.

The journey from the Akasaka Prince to Fuji Television took about half an hour and the early evening rush-hour traffic became congested as the coach manoeuvred its way along the narrow streets that surrounded the studios. It was raining heavily, and most of the girls were busy tracing with their fingers the raindrops as they raced down to the sills. Hannah was more interested in twining and twisting her fingers around Sumi's thick long black hair, and as she did so she was repeating what the student was saying. 'O.K. again, Hannah,' Sumi said, wondering how long her concentration would last. 'Ichi . . .'

'Ichi!' Hannah shouted out for everyone on the coach to hear.

'Not so loud, Hannah!' Graham had been looking at Jenny who had curled up during the journey, and, although she had not said anything she was beginning to look a little off colour.

'Ni.' Sumi placed her forefinger across her lips after she had whispered the second new word.

'Ni,' Hannah whispered back, and she continued to echo Sumi as the student-turned-teacher counted through the Japanese numbers until she reached six, 'Ichi . . . ni . . . san .. . shi . . . go . . . roku.'

When they arrived Graham carried Jenny off the coach. At first she would not say what was bothering her but after a bit of coaxing it was clear she was feeling the piercing pain of a throbbing earache. As Janet tended to the others along with Nancy, Sue and Sumi, Graham cradled Jenny in his arms until sleep suppressed the suffering. He looked at his watch. There was a good hour before they were due to go into the studio for their part of the recording but it began to look doubtful that Jenny would be able to go with her sisters. The Japanese nation would no doubt be a bit confused when the programme was transmitted, and the producer would probably pull his hair out, but if one of the girls was not well enough to do something, then there was no way it could be done. However, at the last minute, once she had fully woken from her nap, Jenny brightened up quite a bit, at least enough to convince Janet and Graham that she would be all right, and she bravely nodded her head when Graham asked her if she wanted to 'go to the place where they had their pictures taken yesterday.'

As they all passed under the bright red light which warned that the studio was 'on-air' the girls all turned to each other mimicking the adults around them, and, putting a finger to their lips, told each other to shush. Immediately behind the doors through which they were to make their surprise appearance, a small play area full of toys had been cordoned off for the girls quietly to play in before they made their entrance. This was not a clever idea because when the time came to go on, the toys had to be left behind, and while the girls did not make any noise it was a little like giving someone a new car but no ignition key to start the motor. They were not too happy. Janet and Graham had to work hard and fast with excited whispers of what was to come and before long the girls were on their tiptoes and eager to see what lay on the other side of the doors.

They could hear the voice of one of the presenters and as it built up to what was obviously going to be a cue, the doors opened and Janet and Graham took up position on the studio floor alongside the presenters. Jenny clung to Graham's left side still feeling a little groggy but comforted by her father's cheek against her own. As the surprised and delighted audience showed their amazement, admiration and appreciation and reacted with whoops of applause, Lucy, like a field mouse on a sheaf of corn, shot up Janet's left leg and scrambled into the security of her mum's arm and remained there as Janet and Graham answered a few questions through an interpreter.

The interview only lasted a couple of minutes and for the rest of the programme the girls played in a specially constructed playhouse full of toys that the producer kept a camera and an eye on as the show progressed. Sarah connected herself up to a bright red telephone, and Ruth, much to the amusement of the audience, continuously wound up a clockwork barking dog that seemed to want to make its presence most felt whenever the studio had gone quiet as a contestant struggled to answer a question. The others befriended all sorts of cuddly animals, including a giant panda and an even larger Snoopy dog, both of which, not surprisingly, later found themselves on the plane back to England with the girls.

With such limited time available, great care had to be taken in deciding what to do during the last couple of days. Fuji had invited the family to visit a special exhibition of the wonders of their latest television technology called The Dream Factory. It did not sound as if it was something that would hold much interest for the girls. If they had been a couple of years older it may have been more suitable, but not wanting to insult their hosts' kind hospitality, Janet and Graham agreed that at least some of the family would go along. Jenny, though, was still feeling under the weather after her sudden attack of earache, and Ruth and Kate, when the girls were asked who wanted to go, were far more interested in playing with the new toys they had been given at the studios the night before; so Janet and Nancy went along with Hannah, Lucy and Sarah.

The happy expression on the face of the exhibitions' official photographer slowly turned to one of dismay as he realised that the only pale-skinned blonde girls who were coming off the coach were the ones standing in front of him. He scratched his head and counted three of his left fingers with his right index finger again and again. He popped his head in the doorway of the coach and then went around the other side. Still no luck. After a quick 'ohayo' (good morning) to Sumi, he then looked terribly disappointed when she explained that he would not have the photo opportunity of all six girls. Remembering the ancient Japanese tradition of respect – and the even older one that half a set of sextuplets for a picture is better than none at all – he altered his composure, adjusted his exposure and uttered what were probably the only two words of English he knew, 'Aah ... sorry.'

It began to seem a bit of a shame that all the girls could not have come, as Hannah, Lucy and Sarah put on paper hats, proudly showed off the special name-tag badges that had been made for them and held tightly to a balloon and a bag full of 'goodies'. It was, though, a particularly hot day and after a while of walking amidst the crowds of people the girls were tired. By the time they reached the television multi-screen dome where 1,000 sets had been fixed to the roof like tiles and enormous images passed over the crowd, first Lucy, then Sarah and finally Hannah all had had enough of walking and had to be picked up and carried. They were guided from one special effects show to another and, after about the hundredth 'Aaah ... sorry!' that heralded yet another flash from the photographer's camera, it was obvious that this was not the best of places to bring the girls. The photographer, however, must have kept his job because the next day a number of Japanese Sunday papers carried stories and pictures of the girls' visit.

The documentary film crew, led by producer Fiona Nunn, had been desperately searching around for suitable outdoor location shots. They had travelled 8,000 miles, added thousands of pounds to the budget, and found themselves surrounded by nothing but high-rise office blocks and department stores, not dissimilar to what they had left behind in London. The decision to follow the family out to Tokyo had only been made the day before the family were due to travel, and by the Friday they were getting nervous. If they did not get the shots they needed on the Saturday afternoon it was going to be a wasted trip for them.

'We need something Japanese,' Fiona moaned, her heart sinking in a well of despondency as they sat in the American restaurant of the Akasaka Prince Hotel watching the girls happily munch away on a meal of Japanese burgers and chips drowned in a pool of Japanese tomato sauce, accompanied by Japanese Coca-cola.

'Well, you've come to the right place!' Graham said smiling as he sliced Sarah's chunk of beef into manageable pieces.

'Something traditional,' she went on. 'We need something that shows you've actually been here.'

Mr Ishido suddenly spoke up. The English contingency watched his face intently as he talked, even though no-one understood a word. As had become the way, all eyes, when everyone was sure he had finished, switched over to Sumi.

'Mr Ishido,' she said as he nodded a smile of acknowledgement, 'he say very good place for pictures is Asakuso. It has many market place, temple and, how you say, is good with tourist.' She smiled as she always did when she reached the end of her translation. Mr Ishido, happy to be of service, gave an even bigger smile.

'You mean commercialised?' Graham asked.

'Aaah ... yes,' she agreed, 'commerciarised.'

'Commerciarised!' echoed Mr Ishido, still smiling and nodding.

Asakuso was indeed a very good place for pictures. It was the heart of the old downtown area of Tokyo and was filled with the cobwebs of Japanese antiquity. It was full of tourists too and plenty of souvenir shops to cater for them. They travelled there by tourist boat up the Sumida River, which particularly thrilled the girls. Not that the sightseeing was much to behold as the boat seemed to pass through a distinctly dense industrial area with ugly dull grey buildings bordering both riverbanks. The view did not matter to the girls. They were happy just to be going on the boat. The bright summer colours of the girls' outfits, and their smiles as they passed packets of popcorn around to other children on the boat, were a marked contrast to the background scenes.

When the boat docked, everyone followed Mr Ishido. Ruth took up position of 'lookout' having insisted on being carried on Graham's shoulders, and Janet, Nancy and Sue held the other girls' hands tightly as they crossed a couple of busy roads. 'There!' the lookout called, sighting something obviously important, and at the same time grasping hold of Graham's hair to use as a hand brake. He grimaced remembering his pact with Janet that morning that neither of them would shout at the girls that day as they had been so good all week. 'What, Ruth?' Graham asked coming to an abrupt halt. 'There!' she repeated as if the very word said it all. He looked up and followed the line of her finger which was absolutely rigid and pointing directly at a toy shop.

It was the best shop the girls had ever been in; an Aladdin's cave of multi-coloured battery-operated treasures. Like half a dozen clockwork soldiers that had just been wound up they paraded around the room excitedly inspecting every corner. Every wall was lined from floor to ceiling with everything from wooden banjos to dolls in cradles, and on display there were acrobatic monkeys, one-'bear'-bands (as opposed to the one-man variety), and a barking St Bernard dog that went for a short walk after every three yelps. It was similar to the one Ruth had been playing with at the studio and on seeing it again the girls had made up their mind, and Graham and Janet were subjected to the familiar tune from the 'Ia wanta' opera!

The frown on a shopkeeper's face is the same the world over when without any warning he or she is asked for six of the same thing. The Japanese features may have been different but the look in the eye was the same as Janet and Graham had seen on so many British faces that did not want to lose such healthy business but just did not have the goods. The proprietor of this emporium, however, had a number of outlets in the immediate area and was able to guarantee a full quota if they could come back a little later.

With the cameras now rolling, they walked through the crowded market place towards the focal point for all the tourists, the Kannon

Temple, which Sumi explained was said to have been built in the seventh century and dedicated to the 'Goddess of Mercy'. Graham thought about how much the barking dogs had bitten into his pocket, and wondered if the lady might be able to help! The main walkway that led there was a colourful lane called 'Nakamise' which was lined on either side with hundreds of small souvenir shops and stalls. The extra adults on hand were a blessing, and Janet and Graham felt a little more confident than they usually did when shopping. Most times they were too busy just watching over the girls and worrying about one of them going missing.

At the end of the lane they were shadowed by the magnificent temple. Layer after layer seemed to rise from the ground as one roof-top mushroomed into another, and as well as the centre piece were some smaller equally traditional Japanese structures. Suddenly the film crew had more 'tradition' than they knew what to do with but they got the shots they wanted, and the girls got their new pets, and, as the sun went down on the land where it traditionally rises, everyone went back to the hotel happy.

Tokyo Disneyland lies on an isthmus on the northern shores of Tokyo Bay at the mouth of the Arakawa River. About ten kilometres from the centre of Tokyo, it is situated half way between the capital and Narita International Airport. Its convenient position meant that it would be possible to stop off there on the way to catch the plane, but there would only be enough time if all the bags were packed and Janet and Graham had checked out of the hotel with the girls early on the Monday morning. They knew it would be the highlight of the trip for the girls and it was worth the extra effort in getting ready.

At the end of the expressway that had been specially built to cater for the 90,000 visitors per day, was the largest car park they had ever seen. Thousands of vehicles were neatly lined up, guided into position by the Disney attendants, and with their coach having been slotted into the nearest possible space, they got out and made their way to the main entrance.

Before being taken on a guided tour, as was the custom with all special guests, the family were taken to Disney's reception where VIPs were introduced to the star, Mickey Mouse. The room they found themselves in was designed to resemble the inside of a plantation home of a well-to-do Confederate in the time of the American Civil War. The walls were adorned with gilt-framed paintings of what appeared to be various scenes of the southern States, and at one end of the room, two ornate pillars bordered an open fireplace. A set of beautifully carved and matching high-backed chairs surrounded a large coffee table. The girls sat on the upholstered seats patiently gulping on glasses of orange juice. Every so often one of them came up for air and let out a gasp of satisfaction like a dry-mouthed cowboy after his first whiskey at the saloon.

A kind of sombre reverent mood momentarily engulfed everyone in the room, and awkwardness was about to set in as the girls began to get restless wondering when they were going to see Mickey and Donald and Goofy and all the other characters that had adorned their bedroom and playroom walls ever since they could remember. 'It's like waiting for an audience with the Pope!' Graham said summing up the seemingly solemn situation perfectly. Then suddenly he was there – a six-foot tail-coated, red-trousered, white-gloved mouse.

Sarah jumped, so did her glass. Lucy shot off her seat and buried her face in her mother's skirts, and while Jenny, Kate and Hannah wriggled and giggled, hardly believing what they were seeing, Ruth nonchalantly picked up her glass and took another sip of her drink pretending she was not in the least bit bothered, but her little chest could be seen feverishly pounding in excitement.

Once all her sisters had shaken Mickey's gloved paw, Lucy peered from behind Janet, and like drawing back a curtain she cast aside her cover and marched forward to join the fun. Then following their new leader the girls paraded outside for an impromptu photo session. Within minutes a crowd of curious orientals surrounded the photographers and watched with delight as the family posed with Mickey for the Tokyo Disneyland press. The longer they stood there the faster the crowds grew. Some were pointing at the girls and jabbering away in Japanese, obviously recognising them from the newspapers, magazines and television which had recently given the family so much coverage. They were naturally curious to take a close look at this beautiful bunch of blonde sisters who had travelled so far to be guests in their country. They seemed, though, to respect the family's privacy, and the girls were touched only by their warm smiles.

The first port of call was the Mickey Mouse 'Spectacular', a show that included all the characters and all the famous songs from the Disney movies. The family were swept along a river of shiny black hair as they flowed with the crowds into the theatre. Queues were clearly something that the Disney people knew how to handle and it was not long before the girls' ears were filled with familiar sounds as the orchestra played an introductory medley of favourite tunes. When the show started they could hardly contain themselves.

'There's Minnie!' Hannah tried to whisper as she pointed to the stage, but it was no use, the whole thing was just too exciting.

Janet had almost to gag Sarah as she yelled out, 'Goofy, Goofy, Goofy! I like you Goofy!' She turned to Jenny, 'Goofy's my friend.'

'And mine!' Jenny added not wishing to be left out of the 'right' social circles.

Then the singing started. 'Jan,' said Graham winning her attention having just heard something he hadn't expected, 'how do you say "Oh, boy" in Japanese?'

Janet gave him a strange look, 'I don't know,' she replied.

'Well, Mickey Mouse does! Listen to him!' Graham and Janet looked at each other and burst out laughing. It was so easy to forget where you were when surrounded by one of the most popular entertainments of Western civilisation and it seemed silly for Mickey to squeak and Donald Duck to quack away in Japanese. 'He's hard enough to understand at the best of times!' said Graham.

The girls were like Jack-in-the-boxes, jumping up and down off their seats as soon as each new character arrived on the stage. Then the spotlights centred on the band, and to the girls' surprise all the musicians turned out to be bears of all shapes and sizes, and as each one did a solo, all the others disappeared into the darkness. On either side of the stage in the 'Royal' boxes, there were more bears appearing and disappearing like cuckoos out of a Swiss clock. Holding tight to her packet of popcorn, Ruth watched intently. Every so often when something particularly important happened she left her seat, and as she stood with her eyes steadfastly fixed to the stage, her arm, like a piston in slow motion rhythmically carried a handful of popcorn to her mouth.

At the end of the show once again Disney's management illustrated the art of crowd control. A row of exit doors automatically opened on the left-hand side of the auditorium, and everybody obediently herded themselves in that direction. As the last remaining few exited, a sharp rap rang out from the far side of the now empty theatre and a similar series of doors opened. A fresh audience in a state of great excitement and anticipation hurried in to find the best places. Janet and Graham were very impressed with the clever seating arrangement which is so designed that nobody's view is ever obstructed.

'Finished?' Jenny enquired, totally satisfied with the entertainment.

'I don't know.' Janet replied honestly. 'We'll have to wait and see, won't we?' Jenny was delighted that her mum should be just as excited as she was, and indeed it is hard for the adults not to be affected by the magic. Janet was aware they had not seen all the characters but the show had been so good the last thing she expected was to be ushered immediately into a second theatre. Here the girls were treated to scenes from *Snow White and the Seven Dwarfs, Pinocchio, Jungle Book* and all the other famous films.

For the adults, listening to all the characters sing in Japanese only made it more entertaining; for the girls it made no difference. Even though the only two words everyone could understand were 'Hi' and 'Ho' it was still clear that it was off to work and nowhere else that the dwarfs went. Those two words, however, were more than enough and as they left the theatre, Sarah, Kate and Hannah happily hi-ho'ed their way with the rest of the group directly towards the nearest burger, chips and coke stand.

The girls were having a wonderful time. Once again, Janet and Graham were relieved that there were other hands and eyes about to help watch over the girls as they wandered along the wide walkways watching out for the vintage cars, the fire engine and the horse-drawn trolley which were being used to carry visitors around. Ahead of them was the centrepiece of the whole of Disneyland – the fantasy castle, a replica of the one seen in Sleeping Beauty. It was so pretty, more like a piece of sculpture than a building, and its towers and spires could be seen from nearly everywhere.

Unfortunately, there was far too much to be taken in by the six excited sets of sparkling eyes during their short visit as they moved from one feature to the next trying to see as much as possible. Hannah and Sarah, by now firm friends with Sumi led her by the hand from one place to another; Janet, Nancy and Sue Thomas had their arms stretched by Lucy, Jenny and Kate respectively while Ruth once again took up her position as look-out on her dad's shoulders and benefited from resting her legs as well as gaining a better view.

Wherever they went there was another Disney character, ready to give a hug or stand and pose for photographers. Meeting Mickey Mouse at the beginning had broken the ice for the girls so there was no shyness or holding back when it came to saying 'hello' to all the others. Eventually, though, time sadly ran out, and with half a dozen helium balloons tied securely to half a dozen happy little hands, the VIPs made their way back to the waiting coach and completed their journey to the airport.

· Seventeen ·

Schooldays and Holidays

♡ ♡ ♡
♡ ♡
♡

When the girls started attending school, there was a whole new routine for all the family to get used to. After the first three years of sleepless nights, and having become accustomed to making the most of every extra minute they could lay their heads on the pillow, Janet especially was not looking forward to a six-thirty start.

However, the first day at school went like clockwork. Hand in hand wearing their new uniform, the girls walked up to the gates of St George's Primary School in Wallasey. Although Janet and Graham both had a lump in their throat, there was not a lot of time for feeling emotional. It was the most significant event since the girls' christening, and the press had taken up position both at the house and at the entrance to the school. Going to school on the first day is daunting at the least for any child, but to have to face a bank of thirty photographers and a film crew as well could not have eased any trepidation they may have felt. But there were no tears, the girls all behaved impeccably and Janet and Graham were doubly proud. Amidst all the fuss neither Janet nor Graham noticed that quietly standing on the other side of the road with a tear in his eye was Grandad John who had walked up to the school from his nearby home.

The summer of 1988 was not going to be remembered for a heatwave.

July had seen the greatest amount of rainfall for decades and consequently the girls had to amuse themselves indoors most of the time. Had the girls been able to spend more time outside they may well have used up a lot more energy and have been ready to sleep a lot earlier. Night after night, though, they had been popping in and out of bed and jumping around like squirrels, and night after night Janet and Graham could hear first one, then another set of stomping footsteps. A fine balance between strictness and tolerance was called for and eventually each night they would all fall soundly asleep.

During the first week of school, though, all the girls were in bed and asleep by eight o'clock. It was as if school had some sort of magical spell over the girls. Perhaps it was a mixture of excitement and anticipation combined with the longer school hours that was making the girls feel more tired than they did at nursery school. They were now away from the house from nine o'clock in the morning to three-thirty in the afternoon. But whatever it was, Janet and Graham were delighted.

Having to get up earlier, pay attention all day to a new teacher and make a whole lot of new friends was pretty tiring work. It did not take long for something to be said by one of the girls that made Janet realise how the longer hours of the first few days were taking their toll and were clearly something the girls were going to have to get used to.

On the third morning Janet selected at random Sarah and Hannah to be first to be dressed in their school uniforms.

'You'll be able to watch *Mary Poppins* on the television much longer than the others,' Janet whispered in their ears. So they followed mum up the stairs to the bathroom.

'Mum,' said Sarah, who had taken off her nightie and was standing in the middle of the room in her vest and knickers.

'Just a minute luvvy,' Janet responded as she got a towel out of the airing cupboard. She turned to look at her two daughters. Hannah was well into the sink splashing soapy water over her face and Sarah was waiting her turn.

'What is it, Sarah?' Janet asked.

Sarah shrugged her little shoulders and said, 'Mummy, but I'm just too tired to brush my teeth!'

Before Janet had a chance to say anything, Hannah said, 'It's O.K., I'll do it for you!'

The girls were full of stories at the end of each day and the kitchen table was the place where one by one the girls would tell about something they did or something that had happened at school. Janet was careful not to tell any of them to shut up, knowing how upset or disappointed they might be, but at times the noise factor could rise to such a level that unless there was decorum around the table nobody would be heard by anyone. Naturally, like any five-year-old child, all they wanted to do was to tell their mum all about school but they could never have the luxury of a one-to-one chat. It was hard enough for Janet and Graham to listen when they were together, and if either were on their own it was impossible. The only solution was for the girls to understand that they must give each other a chance to speak on their own. And so one by one they took the platform. It was then that they saw the advantages of this; they had a ready made audience so that if any of them told a funny story the reception they got from the crowd was brilliant.

'Who did you eat your sandwiches with today?' Graham asked them one tea time during the first couple of weeks at school. He was curious to see if they had made any new friends.

Taking the floor and receiving a respectful silence from her sisters, Hannah said very slowly with a serious tone, 'Well . . . I sat by somebody who wasn't a Walton!' It was one of those things that could only be said in their house and both parents wanted to burst out laughing. They held back though because they both realised that Hannah had said something that was not supposed to be funny as far as she was concerned. None of the other girls laughed, which was always a good guideline for Janet and Graham to gauge whether or not to hold back the smiles. It was just a wonderful indication of how a child's mind works, and although it was a perfectly proper thing to say, an adult would not have the innocence to put it so beautifully.

After a couple of weeks Janet and Graham felt confident enough for only one of them to take the girls to school in the morning. This normally meant that there was no time for chatting on the way, but one morning as Janet approached the school gates, carefully keeping her eyes on all the girls as she used her arms as staffs to herd the girls through the entrance, a lady with a child a little older than the girls came up to her and said to her daughter, 'Thank Mrs Walton for helping you with your homework last night!'

Janet looked at her quizzically. 'I'm sorry?' she answered in a tone that begged an explanation.

'Well,' she began, as Janet moved her arms to gather in her flock, 'my little one was having a bit of problem with multiplication tables last night. She was having difficulty with six times four. So I told her to imagine Mrs Walton making sandwiches for her six little girls and if they had four sandwiches each to try to work out how many sandwiches you have to make.'

Janet smiled as three fingers of her left hand regripped the back of Lucy's hood to stop her wandering. She looked at the daughter and asked, 'Well, did you get it right?' The little girl's face dropped and she sheepishly admitted her failure. 'Never mind,' Janet said sympathetically, 'it's not very easy, is it? Don't tell anyone,' her voice had dropped to a whisper and the girl caught a glint in Janet's eye, 'I get the sandwiches wrong sometimes as well!'

A few days after when Graham was walking along the road with the girls having just called for them at school, he was made to look down as Jenny tugged at the hem of his jacket. 'What is the matter Jenny?' Jenny repeated what she had been saying for the last few minutes as Graham had tried unsuccessfully to listen to all his daughters at the same time.

'Look!' she was now stressing and stretching the word to a maximum. When finally she was sure of his almost undivided attention, which she knew was the best she was going to get at that moment, she said, 'It's the twins, and they're not in our class. They're in the other.' Her voice was full of excitement and wonder at seeing this phenomenon of birth.

The word 'sextuplets' was by now familiar to the girls. Janet and Graham had often told them about how special it was when a lady has more than one baby at the same time, and told them the story of how when mummy had six babies all at the same time it was so *very* special that everyone was very happy and it was in all the papers and that was why everybody smiled and waved at them. At the tea table that night Graham and Janet decided to see whether or not the word sextuplets held any significance for the girls now they were at school and to try and relate it to the twins Jenny had pointed out.

'When a lady,' Janet began slowly, 'has two babies at the same time, the babies are called twins.' Seeing she had their full attention she continued. 'Four babies are called quadruplets and five babies are called quintuplets.'

'But when a lady has six babies, like mummy,' Graham continued, 'the babies are called sextuplets. Remember how we told you the story?' They all nodded. 'So what do you think it's called when a lady has three babies at the same time?' asked Graham. They expected Jenny, who had pointed out the twins to Graham earlier, to be first off the mark with the answer, but she was beaten to it by Kate.

'Twiglets?' she suggested as she chewed on her sausage. Seeing their parents' smiles, Hannah, Sarah, Lucy and Ruth all nodded their approval of what seemed a suitable title until Jenny put the record straight.

The Walton girls were no less excited or curious as any other child at the school whenever they saw the twins. Their fascination lay in the fact that there was simply 'more than one', and it made no difference exactly *how* many more.

One of the routines in the house first thing in the morning was for the girls to collect fresh socks from a basket Janet regularly placed in the middle of the landing. For the first couple of weeks all the girls had been going to school wearing matching socks. Janet had prepared herself by buying plenty of sets of half-dozen packs. The patterns and colours of each set would vary but the intention was that there would be a set for each day. With sixty short socks to scrub each week, however, it was not surprising that by the time half-term arrived it was regarded as a bit of an achievement if they did not all end up in class wearing odd socks!

One morning Janet, concerned about the time, came running up the stairs to find the sock basket surrounded by the girls. Bottoms were resting on bare feet and heads were buried as they bent over to find the socks they fancied wearing that day. Each girl by this time had her own favourite ones and as usual there were squabbles and a tug-of-war over certain pairs. Those that were unpopular were indifferently tossed over shoulders, and it was in a shower of socks that Janet arrived. They were, after all, nearly five, and sorting out the socks was something they had decided they could do without the benefit of mum's guidance. Janet had that look on her face of 'I wonder if all mothers have these problems' as the socks fell around her like confetti.

'Right girls!' Janet's voice rang out marking an end to the proceedings. 'That's enough messing around – it's time for school and you're all going to be late! Now, everybody stand by the radiator over there.' There was a pause in the pandemonium as they obediently scuttled to attention. Janet made a quick inspection of her little soldiers' uniforms. Kate and Jenny already had their socks on and they were matching. One third success, Janet thought, counting her blessings. Lucy and Ruth twiddled their naked toes bursting to laugh at the slapstick sock situation. Not much success there, Janet thought and grabbed a couple of pairs from the basket. She threw them to her daughters with a single-word instruction, 'On!' accompanied by a look that was going to stand for no mischief.

'Mummy,' Sarah said sheepishly, 'Hannah said I can't wear these socks.' Her voice echoed with disappointment and her chin was almost touching her toes as she spoke pointing to the blue-and-white polka-dots which were half on at half mast.

'But we can't have the same socks ...' Hannah explained as if the reason was obvious, '... 'cos then the ovvers in school will think we are twins!' She was quite serious about her point of view. Janet gave both Hannah and Sarah a hug and said, 'It doesn't matter if they think you are twins anyway, does it?'

When purchasing the girls' school uniform, socks were just about the smallest of the costs that Janet and Graham were faced with. Even a dozen white blouses were not enough to ensure the girls looked fresh for class every day, and there had to be extra supplies in case of emergencies. They had to buy pleated skirts, six grey pinafore dresses, six grey cardigans, six pairs of shoes and, together with ties, coats, pumps and all the other little accessories, the bill was more than £400. Once again it was the fact that everything had to be purchased at the same time that did not help the family coffers. The last thing that Janet and Graham needed was for anything to go missing, so they also bought hundreds of name tags and recruited the services of close friend Pauline Cook to help with the mammoth task of sewing them on to every item. Pauline's daughter Jenny was the same age as the girls and had often been taken on board by Janet and Graham for a day out, and this caused a few bewildered looks as people were left scratching their heads counting and recounting the number of children.

In order to give the girls the opportunity of making their own indi-vidual friends, Janet and Graham had decided to make use of the fact that St George's had plenty of first-year classes and split the girls up into three groups of two. Kate and Ruth were together in one class, Hannah and Jenny in another and Sarah and Lucy in a third, which made for a lively tea table every evening as all the girls had different stories to tell. It had its disadvantages, though. Janet and Graham soon had to explain why some of the girls came home with paintings, drawings and things they had made at school and others didn't. If one particular teacher on a certain day had decided things should be displayed on the classroom wall and another decided that the children could take their work home, Janet and Graham were forever faced with puzzled looks and quivering lips. Also, Janet soon began to feel like a social secretary as she tried to keep track of all the invitations they were receiving to go to other children's parties. Although there were times when they were all asked together, being split up in class meant that there were many occasions when invites only came for two.

A couple of weeks before the girls' fifth birthday Graham arrived home from work a little later than usual. Janet had already prepared the girls' tea and they were arriving from all directions to get to the table. Jenny had been upstairs and was crossing the hall with her back to Graham. He caught sight of her as he turned to close the hall door, and as he walked in, Jenny said, 'Hi, dad!' She never turned around and carried on to the breakfast room. It suddenly dawned on him how grown up she was; the hesitation in the delivery of her words had disappeared to be replaced by a more confident tone. Not only was Jenny taller than her sisters but also most of her classmates. The five years flashed before him and for one brief moment he felt the full force of the changing wind that finally blows away all traces of babyhood.

For Janet and Graham it was important to listen carefully to every girl's point of view and to show that every opinion counted. There was definitely no room for favouritism. Every day held something new waiting to be discovered by their curiosity, and the world for the girls was like a great lake as they fished out new meanings and interpretations. They had progressed, after all, from an early interest in basic things like snails, squirrels and switches to video recorders and telephones.

Janet had observed another notable change in the girls. She was about to play referee one afternoon just after they had taken off their coats having arrived back from school, and as she turned she overheard Jenny ask 'What's the problem?' in an adult 'I've had enough of this' sort of way.

Sarah cried out to Jenny just as she might to Janet, 'Ruth won't let me have it!' referring to a colouring book her sister was carefully hugging under one arm and pinning firmly down on the table with her crayon-laden right hand. Ruth, concentrating on not crossing the lines of the drawing she was meticulously filling in, braced herself in anticipation of the usual sisterly shove.

Since they had developed the patience to draw with such delicate care and attention and took much time in ensuring they never coloured a coat sleeve the same as a hand, or a clown's head in the same colour as his hair, nothing seemed to create more anguish on their little faces than a mark in the wrong place. It was bad enough when by a slip of their own hand the crayon jerked across the page spoiling a masterpiece, let alone being interrupted by a sister. Elbow room was always a rare commodity and a sudden jolt by one of the ten other arms or legs or ten other hands or feet usually led to mayhem. A veritable battle would commence, resulting in a thousand pieces of colouring book floating around the room.

'Well here's 'nother one anyway, Sarah,' Jenny proclaimed showing an identical colouring book to her sister.

'But I want that one 'cos it's mine,' Sarah continued to protest. Janet made sure she was out of Sarah's sight as she listened to Jenny do a pretty good impression of her.

'But it doesn't matter anyway, does it Sarah? See ...' Jenny said putting a carbon copy of the drawing Ruth was colouring in about two inches from her sister's nose, '... it's 'sactly same!'

The school term seemed to go very quickly, though, and another milestone was reached as the girls sent out invitations of their own and celebrated their fifth birthday. By the time the last month of the year arrived the conversation around the family table had turned to tinsel, trees and Father Christmas.

The girls went to bed straight away and slept soundly on the night of the first Wednesday in December 1988. It surprised Janet and Graham who thought that the excitement of having just spent the evening in the 'special' lounge helping their mum and dad put up the Christmas tree would keep them awake for hours. They expected the usual excuses of 'I want a glass of water' or 'My tummy hurts,' as a ploy to come downstairs to have another peek at the tree. It would have been understandable, though, as this year it was rather special. Graham had bought a much bigger one than in previous years and the girls' eyes had been glued to it from the moment he unwrapped it and placed it in the corner of the room.

As they sat together toasting the beginning of Yuletide, pleased with the night's work and admiring the decorations, they chatted about how well the girls had managed to tie the various bits and pieces to the tree. They had all come home from school the day before with pretend presents and gift boxes, all beautifully wrapped in bright shiny paper, and suddenly Graham had an idea. 'Why don't we let them have their own tree as well as this one. We could put the old one up in the television

171

room. I know it's a bit rickety but what do you think?'

'Good idea,' Janet said, nodding her head in approval. 'I've got another fairy somewhere upstairs and they can hang up all the boxes they've made and decorate it all by themselves. They'd be absolutely made up! And they've got their own cards from their school friends.' It was such a good idea that she could hardly wait to see their faces when they found out. 'Let's wake them up a bit earlier in the morning and they can do it before they go to school.' Graham agreed and before he went to bed he set up the old tree in the television room which, after all, was as much a special room for the girls as the main lounge was for them.

In the morning Janet asked Jenny to organise the girls in a line ready for a secret surprise. Rubbing the sleep from their eyes they listened as Janet told them about the other tree and how, if they ate all their breakfast and got dressed in their school uniforms quickly, they could decorate it all by themselves. Usually getting sorted out in the mornings was a laborious process, with moans of 'I can't do my buttons,' or 'I can't find my shoes', and other things which they could do if they really tried. Choosing a cereal was usually the most time-consuming part and breakfast could last for ages.

That morning, however, Janet and Graham had never seen them move so fast. Breakfast was whizzed down without any fuss and they were all back upstairs, dressed, washed and ready to go to work on the tree by ten past eight, half an hour before they were normally ready for school. Leaving the girls to it, Janet and Graham cleared away the breakfast dishes and slipped up to their bedroom to sort themselves out.

Twenty minutes later, like a flourish of trumpets the girls fanfared their way up the stairs all singing the same tune. 'Mummy and Daaaddy! ... Mummy and Daaaddy! Come and see our special surprise Christmas tree.' Janet and Graham's bedroom door was blitzed with dozens of little knuckles all knocking with equal excitement. The door opened and Hannah could hardly contain herself. 'Everybody hold hands with everybody!' she screamed out in her typical organising fashion.

'Everybody hold hands!' Sarah repeated, grabbing Kate's palm.

'I'm holding Daddy's hand, I'm holding Daddy's hand!' Ruth boasted as she skipped alongside Lucy who had been first to grab Janet's fingers.

'Come on girls,' Jenny said, 'down the stairs in a line ... a straight line!' she added, mimicking her mum. Janet and Graham had never seen them so thrilled.

With fingers and palms entwined, the whole family carefully weaved their way down to the hall and across to the closed door of the dayroom. Outside the door Janet and Graham were pushed into position next to each other and were ordered to hold hands and close their eyes for the surprise. 'How many times have we done this to the girls?' Janet thought, as her eyes transmitted the sentiment to Graham.

'What's the surprise girls?' Graham asked, creating even more excitement in the girls.

'You have to wait and see, silly!' Jenny said as if it were obvious that he had to be patient.

'Close your eyes,' Lucy shouted, stressing the word 'eyes'. Her face was a sight to see as she knotted her eyebrows pretending to be cross but she could not hide her sparkling eyes and an enormous smile.

When the six were squarely satisfied that their mum and dad were not looking they opened the door to unveil the results of their communal efforts. The tree in the corner radiated a flood of glorious colour. The metallic greens, reds and blues of the boxes the girls had made and tied to the tree shimmered in the early morning light that filtered through the big bay window. Like a tramp in a tuxedo the old tree burst with pride as it showed off its glittering new tinsel suit of clothes while the girls danced around it with shouts of 'Surprise!' repeated over and over again.

'We did decorate it itself!' Sarah's excitement was playing havoc with her grammar.

'It's beautiful!' Janet said, genuinely delighted with the result of the girls' work. A few of the boxes were precariously balanced and the tree was obviously leaning to the right, but otherwise it looked splendid.

'It's a bit crook-eyed,' said Hannah, clearly reading her mother's mind.

'But who cares?' added Jenny, using one of Janet's stock phrases when something did not really matter. And in the most adult fashion the little five-year-old shrugged her shoulders and showed the palms of her hands. It was too much for Graham. Already beaming with joy at what was before him, he was sparked into fits of laughter by Jenny's comments. They had such a brilliant way of putting things.

He sat on the couch with Ruth still clinging to his hand, and like the music of the Pied Piper, his laughter seemed to cast a spell on the others and one by one they were drawn towards him. Kate sat on one knee, Hannah on another; Sarah took hold of his free hand and Jenny stood in front between his legs. Meanwhile, Lucy had clambered up on to the back of the couch. She cocked one leg up over Graham's left shoulder and, having made Janet wince as she marginally missed Hannah's head, she swung her right leg over his other shoulder, and secured her ascent by placing her little hands over his eyes. Lucy was now level with the fairy that adorned the top of the tree opposite. 'Mummy, look at our other Christmas tree!' she shouted, referring to the shape that she and her sisters had formed as they all wobbled about their fatherly foundation.

'Oh yes,' Janet joined in to the girls' delight, 'are you the fairy, Lucy?'

'Yes but I'm a school fairy 'cos I've got me uniform on!'

Janet looked at her watch. It was ten to nine. 'Right girls,' she said, lifting Lucy off Graham, 'get your coats on and hurry up or you'll be late for school.' She knew they were running a little late and searched for something to encourage the girls to move out of the house and into the car without delay. 'Listen girls, when you come home tonight we can start to put up all the Christmas cards. Is that a good idea?' They all cheered their approval and went off to school with Graham, leaving Janet to finish writing the four hundred cards she was sending out that year.

Janet's Christmas card list had steadily grown each year since the girls were born. Every time they were in the press or on the television more letters would arrive from strangers, all of them written with kindness and wishing the family well. Few probably expected a reply but everyone got one. Many of them wrote, 'I know how busy you must be, so please don't worry about replying, but I just wanted to say ...' but Janet wrote anyway. Some wrote poetry, some sent pictures and drawings, others wrote to tell Janet about their own pregnancies. She had been so brave and calm to such an extraordinary degree throughout her own experience and had shown together with Graham such a sensible attitude towards coping and bringing up the girls, that many people simply wanted to express their gratitude for the strength, hope and confidence they had gained from following Janet and Graham's story.

It was a mixture of her makeup and her gratitude for her good fortune that drove Janet tirelessly to sit up until two or three o'clock in the morning on more than one occasion scribbling notelets and cards to those who had taken the trouble to write. Even during those first few months after the birth Janet never quite settled until all the hundreds of letters and cards were answered.

· Eighteen ·

Reflections

♡ ♡ ♡
♡ ♡
♡

Late on Christmas Eve with the girls fast asleep and Graham wrapping some last-minute presents, tidying up the tree so that it would look its best for the next day and making sure the six big red stockings that hung from the mantelpiece were all filled with exactly the same things, Janet was quietly scribbling away, answering yet more letters that had arrived over the past few days. She put her pen down on the bureau and glanced at her watch. It was nearly midnight. In the room above, Jenny and Kate were fast asleep. She wondered if they would be dreaming about all the Christmas surprises that waited for them the next morning. As she glanced over the letters, a thousand memories came flooding back. The girls had seemed to grow up so quickly, especially in the last few months since they had started going to school. She thought about Jenny and how determined she had always been to be so good, and never to do anything wrong. Because of her size, everyone had recognised her first over the years, and whenever anyone had said, 'Oh, I know Jenny, she's the big one!' it was as if people were trying to make out that she was a big sister. It was something that Janet knew was an embarrassment to Jenny and she had always been quick to respond in her daughter's defence by saying pointedly, 'She's very tall, isn't she?'

Jenny had assumed many motherly tendencies over the years. If one

176

of the girls was crying over losing something Jenny would immediately go and look for it. Janet thought about all the times Jenny had shared things to keep the peace. Even if they all received the same items, invariably one of them would be mislaid somewhere in the house or garden and Jenny, even before Janet had to ask, would offer to share hers – that is, of course, if Jenny was not the offender.

Only a few weeks beforehand, when Graham had gone off to work and there was the usual rush to get all the girls ready for school, Janet had piled them all into the car and just as they were pulling out on to the road Sarah piped up, 'Oh, I've forgotten my handkerchief!' Janet looked at the forlorn little face through the rear-view mirror. She was upset with Sarah simply because she knew she had made extra sure the girls had everything they needed by going through the usual checklist. The game had been played before and it was good fun making mum run back into the house, especially when there is an audience to share the joke. Janet had to show them who was the boss so the response was a curt 'Well it's just hard luck!' She checked the reaction in the mirror. Sarah's face had reddened and dropped despairingly. She could not believe her bad luck. Only yesterday, Lucy had tried the same thing and had been applauded by giggles and guffaws from the girls. There was silence for a couple of seconds and then, instead of the expected snuffles, Janet heard Jenny in a very gentle, understanding and caring voice, say, 'Well it's all right Sarah, you can share mine!'

It was precisely that kind of protective sisterly attention that Jenny gave, especially towards Sarah, that could make Janet and Graham feel awful. Graham had had the same treatment when he had spoken sharply to Sarah at a time when she was feeling under the weather. A little voice spoke out as if it was his conscience flicking the back of his ear. 'Why are you shouting at Sarah when she's not well?' Jenny had asked reprimanding him as if to remind him of his duty.

Janet's thoughts turned to Kate. She had become a bit of a worrier since school had started. So often, last thing at night, as Janet or Graham sat by her bed to give her a kiss, she had asked whether or not the bits and pieces she needed for school the next day were ready for her to take. Her milk money, her box of letters and words she had learnt that night, her sandwiches and her tie. And then, once she had completed her own list of concerns, she would ask about Ruth, who was in the same class, and whether she had learnt her letters and had everything ready.

Like Jenny, Kate was always going out of her way to try and please her mum and dad. She loved being praised. Janet and Graham knew how important it was to Kate to receive that kind of acknowledgement, and so had always done their best to give her the love and attention she needed when she had done something right, especiallly when she knew she had performed well. It was no different to that which they gave to all the girls but Kate seemed to thrive on it, and Janet smiled as she thought of how Kate's face glows with pleasure, her eyes sparkle and the light seems to just shine out of her. It was so rewarding. Graham would say it was almost worth praising her for nothing just to see her face.

Sarah and Hannah were in the bedroom alongside Kate and Jenny's at the rear of the house. Janet had been up their room a little earlier and had gently carried Hannah back into her own bed. Her long blonde locks of hair had spread on her pillow as Janet tucked her in and gave her a kiss. Janet thought of those big bright eyes that frequently did Hannah's talking for her. Janet and Graham could often tell by the way Hannah raised her eyebrows that she understood what they were saying to her. One of her strengths lay in her wit which was accompanied by a twinkle in her eye whenever she found something funny to say.

Janet remembered the day that Graham had taken the stabilisers off the girls' bikes for the first time. It was yet another of those occasions when it was simply impossible to be able to give all the girls the attention they needed. While Jenny was able to ride her bike almost immediately without the aid of the extra little wheels, the others needed an adult hand on the handle bars to keep them steady. It meant that Graham or Janet would have to walk with one bike at a time and, of course, the moment they abandoned one daughter for another, screams of frustration filled the air. But amidst all the cries and moans, Hannah, having tried to start up on her own and having fallen off for the umpteenth time on to the grass, had sat quietly in the middle of the lawn with a resigned look on her forlorn face, as if to say she realised that her mum and dad only had two hands and she knew they could not possibly push all of the sisters all of the time. There was no crying; she seemed just to accept it.

Janet had also noticed that Hannah still liked to store and hoard things away. Her bed had always been the most cluttered with toys and dolls, and for ages she had gone everywhere with a little brown satchel full of 'personal possessions'. Her birthday presents were still lined up by her bed and Janet wondered where Hannah was going to find the space for her Christmas presents the next day.

Sarah had been the last to settle down as usual, coming down the stairs only three times that night. She was always playful and full of fun but Janet frowned as she thought of how Sarah had found it particularly perplexing when she tried to tell either Janet or Graham something and all her sisters were pulling at their parents' faces and craving for attention at the same time. Amidst all the chattering her voice could be heard straining above the others. 'Listen!' she would say. 'Listen!' Like all the girls, she needed that eye-to-eye contact which is so important between a child and parent. She would get annoyed and her little fingers would pull at Janet or Graham's chin, and all her frustrations would come out as she would say, 'I want to tell *you*!' stressing the 'you' at the end. Janet thought about how Sarah and all the girls did not realise, of course, that it was equally frustrating for Graham and herself. It was so easy to treat them *en-bloc* and yet Janet and Graham knew how important it was to avoid that as much as possible.

Janet recalled how in the early days Ruth's fearlessness was a sharp contrast to Lucy's shyness. Ruth did not seem frightened of anything. The usual parental warnings that the others took heed of at times did not mean a thing to Ruth. Janet remembered when they had only just moved into Warren Drive and Graham had got the shock of his life when Ruth popped her head over the sill of their bedroom window – from outside – as he was applying a final coat of gloss to the woodwork. He had left the ladder on the outside of the house at the front thinking that the girls were safely in the back garden. He did not panic, though, or try to make a grab for her. He kept his cool and said, 'Hello, Ruth. Just stay there a minute and I'll come and get you.' He walked slowly out of the bedroom until out of sight, then ran faster than he had ever done before or since downstairs and outside to where Ruth was holding on at the top of the ladder thirty feet in the air without a care in the world. With his daughter safely back on the ground and a gentle lecture delivered both to the little girl and to himself, the ladder was taken down and put away with relief and a promise that that was at least one thing that would *never* happen again.

For as long as Janet could remember, Ruth had always shown a determination to do things 'by my own'. Clothes, socks, shoes, whatever needed buttoning or fastening she was always the first to want to do it for herself. Independence was a challenge to her and on the occasions when she discovered that her fingers were not quite ready to cope with some new demand of everyday life, the determination would turn to frustration and the tantrums of the 'terrible twos' were displayed. It did not matter if anyone else was watching her, that she had an audience of sisters, she simply did not care. But as quickly as she took off, she would settle down again, somewhat satisfied that she had made her point. However, the independence and fortitude she was showing was something they welcomed as a sign that she would no doubt be able to look after herself in the future.

Throughout the first few weeks of play school, when the girls were two, Lucy always felt better with an extra hug and kiss from Janet when she left them with 'Aunty' Brenda and 'Aunty' Pat for the morning. Even later, Lucy's hand always kept the tightest grip as the girls moved on to nursery school. She had always been so sensitive and loved to spend hours on Janet's knee having her back endlessly tickled. But as time went by she had developed her own kind of determination; determination to be heard with a voice that bellowed above the others; determined to be noticed with her giggling and mischievous ways; determined to be seen as she showed off her agility. Janet thought back to the very first few days after the girls were born and how she heard Richard Cooke on the radio telling the world that 'baby number two was giving cause for concern', and she wondered, as she often did, whether that was one of the reasons why Lucy had needed so much security in the early years. Perhaps it was this determination and strong will that had something to do with her survival.

Her thoughts were interrupted by a gentle peck on the cheek. 'Merry Christmas, luv.' Graham could see Janet was miles away and, glancing at the picture of the girls on the bureau, guessed what she had been thinking about. 'They're smashing, aren't they?' Janet nodded. 'Remember the first Christmas with the girls?' Graham continued, 'when they were all in the little cots at the special care unit?' Janet could see them all lined up with the tiny Christmas socks stuck to the end of each cot and a matching teddy bear for each of them sitting on a shelf above. So much had happened since then. So many emotions. All the doubts and fears of coping, all the determination before and after the birth that all would be well, and, above everything all the joys and happiness that the children had brought them. Tomorrow would be a wonderful day.

As Janet was preparing the tea one afternoon after school, she noticed her daughters were playing a new game. Pleased that they were showing both variety and inventiveness, she said, 'That looks a good game girls. What are you doing?'

Jenny, who was leading the way and giving out the instructions to her sisters, gave a little tut as if to say she was far too busy to be disturbed, but turning to her mum she said, with as much authority as she could muster, 'We're playing school, of course!' Kate and Sarah giggled. 'Stop that laughing in the class or you might have to stand in the corner!' Jenny regained her sisters' full attention and sent her mother out of the class.

As Janet quickly set the six plates, knives, forks and spoons for the girls, she heard Jenny announce that it was playtime. The 'teacher's' voice was lost in a shower of 'I want to be' as some of the girls pretended to be their best friends in class and other children in the school. The girls, Janet thought, were in a brilliant mood. It was Monday of the second week of the second term and they had settled down so well. The winter holiday with Christmas coming right in the middle had been all too short and it seemed that she and Graham had not had them at home long enough.

The girls had been on such a high for so long. The excitement of Christmas had started as it always did as soon as their birthday celebrations had finished, and by the end of it all they were as weary as the year's end. On New Year's day the girls had had no idea what Graham and Janet had been talking about when they tried to explain to their daughters how they should wish each other 'Happy New Year', but still they shouted the greeting to each other dozens of times all day long. By the end of the first week of the new term, though, the discipline and formality of the blackboard and wooden desk had resulted in tired eyes and an early night, but refuelled by the weekend and the freshness of a new week with their new friends at school, the girls were once again bouncing, bounding and bumping around the house.

The hall had become the school playground and the girls were acting out the daily scene. It was Lucy's and Hannah's voice she heard the clearest as she turned to go back into the kitchen.

'Are you the Waltons? Are you the Waltons?' they excitedly asked each other. It was obviously a question they had been asked hundreds of times by lots of other children at school, and it is clearly a question that they will be asked for a long time to come.